THE EARL'S ENTANGLEMENT

BORDER SERIES BOOK FIVE

CECELIA MECCA

ALTIORA
PRESS

*To Bill, David, Alanna, Matthew and the best
sister-in-law in the world*

CHAPTER ONE

lave Castle, Northumbria, 1273
"I neither want nor need a wife."

Garrick Helmsley crumpled the missive in his hand and tossed it unceremoniously into the fire. He walked to the small window that overlooked the North Sea and opened its wooden shutters.

"Her messenger waits below for a reply," Sir Conrad said.

The iron bars did little to detract from the view, which he'd sorely missed during the years he'd spent in battle. The great chamber, a private room behind the hall and just up a set of stairs, had always been one of his favorite rooms in his ancestral home, which was why he'd led Conrad here for their private conference. Though more sparsely furnished than most, with a table for dining and a hearth in the corner, it was the view that brought him here. The steep decline beneath him was scattered with flowers and plants stubbornly refusing to allow the surrounding rocks or the salty gales off the North Sea to stifle their growth.

A wife.

"Garrick?"

His friend was persistent, but he could be more so. "Remind me why you're here?"

Having come to Clave as a boy to foster with Garrick's father, he'd never really left. Conrad navigated the room, coming to a stop beside him. "Clave is much better-looking than Brookhurst. Besides, when I return, my parents are likely to marry me off to some poor, unsuspecting gentlewoman."

Conrad laughed at his own jest, but Garrick was not inclined to laugh along with him.

"Then you should hurry back to Brookhurst at once to remind your parents of how irritable you are," Garrick said. "Maybe they'll reconsider."

"Tell that to the buxom maidservant in my bed. She found my presence quite charming last eve."

Though the hour was early, Garrick had no doubt his friend was telling the truth. Well, he wouldn't remind Conrad that the girl had only turned her attentions his way *after* Garrick rejected them.

"Tell her yourself," Garrick said.

"Gladly, but your mother's messenger awaits in the hall for an answer. Since I have to pass through there on my way back ..."

"Leave it be, Conrad. Mable is attending to the messenger." Clave's steward, as always, was extremely efficient.

Conrad rolled his eyes. "The poor man will be finished breaking his fast shortly. He claims to have traveled through the night, and your mother's instructions were quite clear." Conrad adopted a tone Garrick supposed was to mimic his mother's voice. "'Deliver that message, my dear boy, and make it quick. The earl's daughter will not be delayed. Tell my son—'"

"Enough!" Normally amused by his friend's antics, Garrick couldn't abide them at the moment. "I woke you for counsel, not for a poor imitation of my mother. Who, I'll have you remember—"

"Recently lost her husband. I know, Garrick." His tone softened. "Your father was a good man."

"The best," he amended.

"And died how he'd have wanted. In battle, fighting alongside his son."

The two men fell silent. Unfortunately, Conrad's silence didn't last.

"You pulled me from a soft feather bed for my opinion?" Conrad asked, eyebrows raised.

"I just said as much." He began to pace the chamber, crossing the room in long strides only to turn around and retrace his steps.

"Marry her."

Garrick's fists clenched. He continued his pacing until Conrad stuck out an arm to stop him. He knew that look. His friend had finally dropped the jovial facade. He was ready to offer serious advice.

Though different in many ways, in temperament *and* looks— Garrick was dark and tall, Conrad his lighter counterpart—both men loved the borderlands and would do anything to protect them. And they shared an appreciation for women. On that, they were similar. Which was one of the reasons for Garrick's hesitation now.

"The thought of an acquiescent noblewoman trained since birth to be docile and proper." He shuddered. "Give me a bathhouse in Acre and—"

"This"—Conrad indicated their surroundings—"is not the Holy Land. It is your inheritance. And an earl needs a bride."

Garrick refused to accept the finality of his words.

"A bride, perhaps. But certainly not a Scottish one. Nor one I haven't met."

He hated Conrad's shrug.

"I asked for your counsel, and you joyfully condemn me to life with a foreigner."

Garrick had already known before sending for Conrad. He had known the moment the messenger handed him the missive. His mother had hinted at this, and now that his father was dead, the only way to secure his Scottish inheritance was to take a bride —one whose power was greater than his uncle's.

Conrad had simply confirmed the life sentence he'd expected. Now that he'd returned, it was his duty to Clave Castle, to his mother, to the earldom, to bring home a suitable bride.

"Having a bride does not preclude enjoying comely women in your bed," his friend said, clapping him on the back as if his words offered anything by way of comfort.

Garrick stared out the window for another long moment. Just a few months earlier, he'd stood next to his father contemplating a very different view. The Crusades had been tearing apart families for years, and now the bloody battle had woven its way into his life in the worst way possible. "I'll not dishonor my wife that way."

"Well then, old friend, why are we standing here? You have a wife to claim. And a mother to console. And if you're to be married soon, Clave's village is waiting. I will stay here, but you should take James with you."

James, the young knight who had been sent years ago to foster with Garrick's father, much like Conrad, hadn't left. James's father had betrayed the crown by betraying Montfort in his rebellion against King Henry, Edward's father. The knight had lost his inheritance, as many had because of the uprising, but Garrick did not hold the son responsible for his father's transgressions.

"I do believe Clave can manage without you," Garrick said.

"But can The Golden Fox? Which reminds me, do you think it wants patrons this early? Being that you're to be married soon."

"I did not say I was marrying the Scottish woman."

Conrad pulled him toward the door. "You didn't need to."

"Sara, would you please speak to him?"

Emma looked from her beloved sister-in-law, the Countess of Kenshire, to her stubborn brother. He was arranging his wife's pillows, as usual, fixing them into just the right position. If only Bryce and Neill could see the former border reiver fussing over his wife as such . . .

Emma looked down and smiled at the littlest Waryn in her arms, his face round and perfect.

"Geoffrey, I agree with your sister. There are plenty of men who could escort her."

Emma could have kissed Sara. But Geoffrey still didn't seem to be convinced.

"If she were traveling in England, I'd agree. But across the border? Nay, not without me. Or one of the boys."

It was that very attitude that made Geoffrey so exasperating. He thought her very much a "girl" even though she'd been a lady for some time now. Nor would her brothers enjoy hearing themselves called "boys."

"Well, neither of the *boys* are here, and you can't leave Sara and the new babe, nor would I want you to do so. Which means I'll not be able to see Clara when she needs me most."

The twitch in Geoffrey's jaw told her he was becoming impatient.

Good.

"Emma."

Oh, that tone. It made her feel like a child all over again.

"You can see Clara in the spring, before the babe arrives. Why you need to go off to Scotland in the middle of winter—"

"Shh," she said, rocking Hayden, whose eyes had just popped open. "We'll speak on this later." He would not relent at this moment, so prolonging the argument would not further her case. The best strategy was to talk with Sara. "Didn't Peter say you were needed in the solar?"

The steward had interrupted their conversation twice in the lord and lady's private chambers—a privilege afforded only to a servant of his position.

Her brother leaned down to kiss his wife on the cheek. Her

smile reminded Emma of one of the reasons she adored the countess so much. For some unfathomable reason, Sara loved her brother mightily.

He then kissed Hayden, winked at her, and left the bedchamber.

Brute.

"Emma . . ." Sara chided.

"I didn't mean to say that aloud." Sara was looking at her with that combination of *I understand he can be overly protective* and *be nice, he's your brother and he loves you.*

"I just don't understand him. We have a large enough retinue of men to take all of Northumbria. Not, of course, that we would do such a thing. He trusts *none* of them on a few days' journey north?"

Even so, Emma was finding it difficult to stay angry. Every time she looked down at her new nephew, she wanted to kiss him a hundred times. He slept peacefully in her arms, and Emma's eyes welled with tears at the thought of leaving him. Though he was just a few weeks old, she loved her new nephew beyond reason.

"I'm sorry, Sara. This is my argument with Geoffrey, not yours."

Sara swung her legs around, startling Emma.

"What are you doing? Geoffrey—"

"You are not the only one exasperated with your well-meaning brother."

The birthing had been difficult, and although the countess did not credit the midwife's admonishment to stay abed until she "healed properly," Geoffrey did. Each time Sara attempted to move about, he seemed to sense it and swooped in like a mother bird to tuck her back into bed.

"I do adore Adele, but some of her methods are . . ."

The women looked at each other and smiled. They'd discussed this before, and neither of them was sure who had suffered more during Hayden's birth: Sara or Adele. The midwife had prayed so hard and so often to St. Margaret that it was a wonder the saint herself didn't make an appearance just to shush the old woman. When the babe's head finally appeared, Adele broke down in tears of relief, convinced the combination of her prayers and rose oil had made it so.

Granted, the old woman had delivered Lady Sara herself many years earlier and loved the countess like her own, but Emma would have expected a midwife with so many years of experience to be more accustomed to difficult births. Luckily Sara had done so as well and knew she would be just fine.

Sara reached for her son. "Can you please tell Faye I'd like to dress?"

Emma reluctantly handed Hayden to his mother.

"If I have to stare at this canopy any longer . . . I'm quite ready to join the living once again," Sara said.

If her sister-in-law was representative of the dead, they were a comely group indeed. Though Sara's cheeks were still a bit rounded from pregnancy, Emma could not envision a lovelier sight. Her sparkling eyes and smile spoke of good health and high spirits. It pleased her to no end that some said they looked like twins. Emma had grown up with three brothers, and it was still a dizzying pleasure to have Sara, who had come to feel like another sister.

"As for visiting Clara . . ." Sara rocked Hayden as she had done earlier. "I do believe with the right companions the journey will be perfectly safe. Let me speak to your brother."

"Sara, nay, 'tis my problem—"

"Which makes it mine as well. Clara would be overjoyed to see you, and your brother is simply being stubborn. I will speak to him."

"Thank you." In truth, it was what she'd hoped for, and she couldn't help but smile. No one was more tenacious than Sara when she wanted something.

"You'd best ask Adele to begin knitting the blanket now."

Adele, despite her crooked fingers, was skilled at more than just birthing babes. The blanket in which Hayden was now peacefully bundled was one of many she'd made for the new heir to Kenshire.

"You believe he will allow it?" Emma asked.

"I've not known you to want for something without getting it. And as for me"—she smiled—"I have some influence over him as well."

Between the two of them, Emma had no doubt her poor brother would relent before long.

CHAPTER TWO

"*Y*ou are insufferable!"

"And you, my dear sister, are going to get yourself killed. How you can so easily dismiss dangers after what you've been through . . ."

Geoffrey stopped, likely realizing he'd nearly spoken of the one thing they never discussed.

Their parents' death.

"Clara will be there in the spring. And I will enjoy telling your children someday about the time your brother kept you alive."

"Kept me . . ." She could kick him. "Ugh. You are impossible."

Two days had passed, and neither she nor Sara had yet convinced Geoffrey of the merits of her plan to visit her dear friend. Tired of arguing with Geoffrey, though not ready to resign herself to Kenshire Castle for the remainder of the winter, she stormed out of the solar and made her way through the many corridors, some indoor and others between buildings, back to her bedchamber.

Most young ladies of two and twenty were already married. They ran estates, though most not as large as Kenshire, and tended to their people. Emma's brother did not permit her to ride

9

further than their admittedly expansive property without an escort. Of course, any attempt to convince Geoffrey of the unfairness of her predicament landed on deaf ears. She'd just laid out her argument for him again, for what seemed the hundredth time, and he'd given her the same predictable response.

"Then accept one of the many suitors clamoring for your hand in marriage."

She had rolled her eyes and attempted to change the subject.

"I'm not asking for a husband," she'd said. Only one of those 'many suitors' was even the slightest bit compatible. The rest were bores who'd like nothing better than to control her. She'd seen both of her elder brothers marry for love and planned to have no less for herself. But that was an argument for another day. "I'm asking that you trust me. Treat me as a woman and not a girl."

There. She'd said it.

But her grand announcement had not quite made the impact she'd expected and hoped it would. Emma really did love her eldest brother. He'd sacrificed his own safety and comfort to help provide for them after their parents were killed. Forced to join a band of border reivers, Geoffrey had learned quickly that there was never complete security along the border. Though Emma knew it was the reason for his protectiveness, knowing why he acted in such a way did not much comfort her.

A timid knock on the door was followed by the entrance of her lady's maid, Edith, the daughter of Kenshire's marshal. Edith's pert nose had a natural upward tilt to it, and though the other servants teased her for it, she wasn't at all fussed. Her pretty face and blond hair made her favored by the boys, and Emma spent as much time fretting over Edith's future as she did her own. Though her maid didn't offer herself freely, she had, on occasion, been known to share intimacies best reserved for a husband. She did like to act older than one and nine. And though Emma hated to sound like Geoffrey, she often urged her friend to choose a husband before she got herself into trouble.

"What in the devil?"

She'd not asked for a bath to be drawn, but Edith was followed by an army of servants with a tub and several buckets of hot water. In truth, Emma had *wanted* a bath, for she'd ridden her beloved horse Nella far and fast this morning to exorcise some of her anger toward her brother.

"My father told me ye rode hard, my lady."

Eddard. Of course.

Emma threw her arms around her startled maid. "You are the finest lady's maid in all of Northumbria."

Edith disengaged herself and got to work, but Emma noticed her slight grin as she pulled away.

"Not in all of England?" Edith nodded to the corner of her chamber, where the tub had been placed in its usual position, and the other servants began to fill it with their wooden buckets of hot water. Emma loved baths nearly as much as she loved riding Nella.

"In all of the world," she clarified.

Emma noticed a pin in Edith's cap as she bent down to place the lemon-scented soap next to the tub.

"What a beautiful pin. I don't believe I've seen—"

Edith's hand went to the ivory sticking out of her hair, its cream color pale against her sunshine-colored locks.

"I heard ye spoke with his lordship."

For some reason, Edith didn't want her to know about the pin. So be it. She'd tell her when she was ready.

"Again," the maid corrected.

Emma watched as additional buckets were brought into the chamber.

"He refuses to allow the trip. And though I'll never willingly admit it to him, it appears my visit will have to wait until spring."

Edith arranged, and re-arranged, the soap and drying cloths. She liked to keep her hands busy, even if there was nothing to be done. Much like her father. The marshal seldom sat still and even more rarely took an extended break, even if ordered to do so.

"Why do ye need to visit now before the babe is even born? Wouldn't ye rather meet the babe?"

Her brother had asked her the same question, but Clara's fear of childbirth wasn't for her to share. Her friend was so strong and brave. She'd survived the loss of her ancestral home and the murder of her father by escaping and posing as a boy, a squire, at times completely on her own. But Clara, who seemed so fearless, had once confessed to an almost "irrational fear of childbirth," though perhaps it wasn't so irrational given that her own mother had died that way. While she was overjoyed by the idea of impending motherhood, she would no doubt appreciate a visit now more than later.

Emma just wanted to give her comfort. Tell her of the many wonderful births Sara had witnessed while helping Adele deliver babies. Long ago, back when Clara was staying at Kenshire, she'd made a promise to her friend. She'd pledged to look out for Clara's interests, now and always, although it seemed as if a missive would have to suffice for now.

She turned to give Edith her back. "When I am lady of my own—"

"Oh dear," Edith interrupted as she unlaced her ties. "My father asked me for assistance after I finish helping you prepare for the evening meal."

"And what, pray tell, does that have to do with me being the master of my own domain?"

"Just that it will be dark before long, my lady. And no disrespect, but when you begin such musings . . ."

Though she trailed off, Emma knew what Edith had intended to say. "You've heard it all before."

"Many, many, many . . ."

"Okay," Emma said, stepping from her gown. "But 'tis true. I'll no longer—"

"Have a brother telling you what to do. Ye'll have a husband for that instead."

Emma made a sound that elicited a giggle from her friend. "The precise reason I don't have one yet."

At least it was one of them.

Although Geoffrey could be a mite protective at times, Emma was well aware that she had as much freedom at Kenshire as she was like to have anywhere. And she really did adore the castle and its grounds. It had not quite been two years since she'd moved from her aunt and uncle's modest manor to one of the greatest castles in all of England. At first, she'd been intimidated by its size and grandeur. But now, this was home. And if the worst she had to endure was an overabundance of love from the man she was lucky to call brother, so be it.

Still, that didn't mean she intended to give up just yet.

She smiled as she stepped into the steaming hot bath. She really should stop goading Geoffrey, but it was just so much fun. And she had a surprise ready for him this evening.

Garrick rode ahead of his men, with whom he'd begun to reacquaint himself over the past few weeks. Three years had passed since he'd sailed to Tunis with Edward after King Louis had failed to capture the city. Boys had become men. Clave had thrived under his mother's leadership for the past few months until she returned to their holding in Scotland. Though his home was much as he'd left it, Garrick was not the same man he'd been. Years of training for battle and playing at war in tournaments had hardly prepared him for the carnage of war.

He shook his head to rid himself of the images. *The war is over. You're here riding through Northumbria, and it's cold enough to freeze a pigeon's nest.* Though the cold winter day did little to slow their pace, it certainly made for a more uncomfortable journey. Garrick had become accustomed to the mild winters in Acre. At heart, though, he was still a Northumbrian, and the climate was no deterrent to reaching their destination.

"My lord," one of the men called to him.

He turned, light just beginning to fade from the sky.

"I'm told we are to stop already?" James asked. The knight had a keen intellect, and the worry in his voice was reason enough to pause. As Garrick slowed, the eight men behind them did so as well. He'd not have taken so many retainers but for Clave's marshal, who'd reminded him, as if he'd needed reminding, he was now an earl.

"Aye. Is something amiss?"

James squinted in the direction of Kenshire Castle. They were not far from Clave's closest neighbor now, but they were not yet close enough to see evidence of it. On a clear day, perhaps they might have been able to see the castle from this distance, but a heavy fog lay across the ground, masking everything but their immediate surroundings.

"'Tis said the Lady Sara is unwell after the birth of her first child. Perhaps we should continue and stop at Kenshire on our return?"

Garrick glanced back at the men waiting patiently behind him. It would appear James had also raised his concern to them. These last weeks in England, Garrick had been so engrossed by the implications of his new position—the heaviness of his father's death—that he'd not kept abreast of the latest gossip, which circulated Clave like a hound having spotted his prey.

Was Lady Sara unwell?

The last he'd seen of her, she was not a countess but the only child of one of the greatest men in Northumbria. Richard Caiser and his father had been staunch allies and friends of Clave. Garrick had fond memories of Sara, having been raised in such close proximity. Even so, they had both been glad when their fathers' talk of a marriage alliance had been rejected by the king.

The news of Sir Richard's death and Lady Sara's subsequent difficulties, and marriage, *had* reached his ears, however, and he regretted that he had not been in England to help protect her. He would offer his condolences—and apologies—immediately.

"Nay, James. Though your concern is appreciated, it is unnecessary. If Lady Sara is unwell, our visit is timelier than I thought."

James nodded as he steadied his mount, who'd become restless beneath him.

"I told the men as much, but we wanted you to be aware." The knight looked at Garrick as if he had more to say.

"What is it, James?"

And then he realized. James was treating him with the deference due to an earl. Garrick had not yet become accustomed to either the title or the changes that went along with it.

"How long have you served Clave?"

James raised his sparsely bearded chin. "Ten years, my lord."

"And how long have you known me then?" Garrick calmed his own mount as he moved closer to the young man.

James looked as if he feared giving the wrong answer.

"Seven years, my lord."

"Seven years."

The men became anxious behind them. Garrick could see them begin to stir, their horses pawing eagerly at the ground. All were impatient for the fire-warmed hall of Kenshire Castle and the hospitality they were sure to find there. But this was as important discussion as any and could not wait.

"Tell me of the Garrick Helmsley you've come to know, save the last three years that I've been away?"

Again, James drew his brows together, but he did not hesitate to answer this time.

"I know Garrick Helmsley to be strong and loyal. A man who would fight and die for the men and women in his service. A man who loves his mother." Garrick made a face at the flood of treacle-like comments, and James, taking the hint, did add his overlord's faults then. "And the ladies. Some would say overmuch."

At that last statement, James appeared as if he would lose his last meal. But when Garrick nodded encouragement, he continued.

"A man whom all are terrified to fight, but with whom none are terrified to speak."

Finally, a look of awareness crept across his features. Garrick could only hope it was a lesson he'd not be forced to teach over and over again. He couldn't abide to be treated the part of a lord, especially not when it came to that.

"I am that same man. No more. No less. Do you understand?"

"Aye, my lord."

"Now tell the others we ride to Kenshire. And if you ever hesitate to speak to me or give me news you don't believe I will like because I am now the Earl of Clave"—Garrick tried his best to keep a straight face—"I will kill you myself."

James did not flinch when he replied, "And I will be glad to die for you, Lord Clave."

Garrick waited until James passed along the missive before he began moving once again. First to Kenshire, and then to Scotland. And, unfortunately, to his future wife.

CHAPTER THREE

*E*mma stepped out of the tub and used the drying cloth before dressing for supper. Though it was normally a light repast, at times with food remaining from the larger dinner-time meal at noon, tonight was to be an exception. After much fretting over Sara, her brother had finally agreed that she, not he, was best suited to determine the state of her wellness. She would be joining them for the evening meal for the first time since Hayden was born. And Cook could not resist any temptation to create a celebratory meal.

"My lady, let me help with that."

She hadn't heard Edith enter the room, but she gladly accepted her maid's assistance. It would have been a chore to put on the deep green velvet gown trimmed with ermine without her. Edith loved to pile her long black locks atop her head, but Emma preferred to wear her hair loose. Today Emma won the battle.

"Hurry," she said as she slipped the leather shoes on her feet.

"You are early, my lady. Why—"

"Nella felt a bit warm to me this morn. Eddard says there is nothing to fret over, but I want to check on her before the evening meal."

"My father did mention it. But he didn't appear overly worried." She paused for a moment and then exclaimed, "Oh my . . ."

Thinking it was about her palfrey, Emma startled. "What? What is it?"

Edith wiped her hands on the front of her tunic. "You are quite beautiful, my lady. Pardon me for saying—"

"You scared me so," Emma said, heaving out an unladylike sigh. "I look the same as I do each day." She would much prefer to discuss another topic. "Edith, I wonder. Did Reginald give you that pin?"

Edith shrugged. "Mayhap he did."

Emma moved toward her maid and lifted her chin so the younger girl had no choice but to look at her. "So you told him how you feel?"

Geoffrey's squire had just celebrated a name day, and at eight and ten, he was beginning to take a more serious interest in courtship. Although gossip rarely reached her ears, Emma had been inquiring on Edith's behalf. For an outspoken, sometimes bawdy young lady, she was quite reticent when it came to Reginald. Only Emma knew her secret: Edith secretly pined for Geoffrey's squire. The young man had grown strong and handsome, but her maid liked most the qualities he shared with her brother. Kindness. Loyalty.

"You know as well as I do the boy is as stubborn as his master. Even if his parents want him to wed another—"

"I will tell him," Edith said, but her words were as dismissive as Emma's had been about her dress. She was far from convinced.

"Go," Edith pressed. "My father will still be there if you hurry."

Her maid clearly did not want to discuss Reginald, so Emma didn't push her. Yet. Instead, she winked and picked up the folds of her gown, hurrying out into the corridor. Only when she was a good distance from the room did she belatedly realize she'd forgotten her cloak. Well, no matter. She would be outside but a short time.

Emma reminded herself to slow down. She could hear Aunt Lettie's voice. *Always running somewhere. You'll hurry through life if you're not careful.*

Lettie had become her surrogate mother after her parents were killed in the raid on Bristol Manor, and she often reminded herself to listen to the woman's teachings. Though Aunt Lettie and Uncle Simon lived simply, they shared an irresistible, contagious passion for life that was not diminished by their home's perilous location near the border. They'd just come for a visit, as they'd done often, and it was her uncle's love of horses that brought her to the stable now.

Exiting the main keep, Emma stopped to look up as bits of snow fell on her nose. Light had just begun to fade from the sky, giving the entire courtyard a peaceful glow, as if the daytime were being gently ushered away by nightfall.

For a long moment, she simply took in the beauty of the scene around her, but a deep breath of the cold air made her cough. Perhaps she could enjoy the new-fallen snow another time. Right now she had to ensure Nella's condition had not worsened. This morning she'd been eating just fine, and as Eddard had reminded her, keeping a close eye on the palfrey's appetite was the surest way to determine if there was a problem.

Kenshire's stables housed as many horses, Sara liked to say, as Emma could reasonably care for. Their passion for the majestic animals was something they shared. Indeed, Sara even helped with the birthings from time to time, a highly unusual activity for a countess.

"Eddard?" she called out as she approached the stables.

Edith had mentioned he was nearly finished for the night, and indeed, when she entered the building, it appeared empty. The familiar and distinctive smell of hay assaulted her nose. Emma peered into each stall, but there was no sign of either the marshal or any stablehands. At least one typically remained and slept in the hayloft, especially if one of the horses was ill.

The emptiness of the space seemed markedly unusual.

She made her way to Nella's current stall at the back and found her trusted palfrey lying down, her forelegs tucked beneath her. The horse was merely resting, so Emma reached out to feel her. The fever felt no worse, but she was still unnaturally hot. Nella moved her head toward Emma's hand, her black coat in stark contrast to the brown-yellow hay upon which she lay. Emma couldn't tell if she were simply content or if her sickness was progressing.

But one thing was for sure. She didn't want Emma to leave just yet.

Garrick had ridden ahead of his men, impatient to arrive and wanting to send advance warning of their small retinue's impending arrival. Admitted easily enough by guards who knew him well even after his absences, he assured them he could find his way without an escort.

Even after all of this time, Kenshire's splendor still left him in awe. Unlike Clave, which had been deliberately designed to pack as many buildings and rooms as possible onto the island, Kenshire sprawled out like a cat who had just finished a hearty meal, intimidating enemies and welcoming friends all at once. One of the only features the two estates had in common was their location next to the open waters of the North Sea.

He remembered vividly the first time his father had taken him here.

"If you're impressed by the castle, my boy, you'll be even more so by the earl."

Indeed, he had been impressed by both—and by Lady Sara,

though not in the way a man was bewitched by the lass he'd like to marry.

Garrick remembered the day he and Sara had learned of the attempted betrothal, years after the king had rejected it, in this very courtyard. It had been a blustery winter day very much like this one. He and the future countess had just come back from a hunt, Sara as skilled with a bow as any man. His father overheard the compliment he gave her and rode up alongside them.

"A fine woman, Lady Sara, and you would have made an even finer wife."

Garrick and Sara laughed the entire day, imagining a marriage that would have been preposterous to them.

She was the only woman he'd ever truly felt connected to in a way that had nothing to do with carnal pleasures. He could talk to her as if she were a sister, and when he noticed the extra attention paid to her by one of Richard's retainers, Garrick encouraged the match. Sir William was both honorable and kind, but Sara regarded him much as she did Garrick, more of a brother than a potential husband. The look of devastation on William's face when he was ordered away by Sara's father was one Garrick would never forget.

It was the look of a man in love, an affliction Garrick himself had always hoped to avoid, and he had thus far been lucky in the endeavor. Now, though, as he prepared to enter into a loveless marriage, he regretted that he'd never met a lady he would willingly take to wife.

A light snow began to fall, intruding upon his thoughts. With any luck, the storm would not bring enough accumulation to hamper their travels in the morn. He looked up, but the sky was too dark to determine anything more than that they'd arrived at Kenshire just in time.

The evening meal must be upon them. The courtyard, normally bustling with activity, even in the winter months, was mostly empty but for a lone servant who hardly looked his way.

Since visitors to Kenshire were common, Garrick was not surprised at the lack of attention, but when he reached the stables and dismounted to open the heavy, arched door, he *was* surprised to find it empty. He held his horse's reins in his black glove, pulling them more tightly around his fingers.

Kenshire's marshal and head stablehand were never far from their charges. Could something have happened to Eddard in his absence? He walked inside and stopped when he spied a flash of green on the floor of the furthermost stall, the one normally reserved for sick horses.

Bayard protested next to him, so Garrick pulled him fully inside, closing the door against the cold. He had just finished tying his reins to the stone hitching post when the source of the green garment emerged and called out a greeting.

Holy hell.

CHAPTER FOUR

"*E*ddard?" Emma stood and began to pick pieces of hay from her gown. Velvet. She should have thought better of sitting beside Nella, but it was hard to regret it. She'd do anything to make her comfortable. Anxious to speak with Eddard about the mare's condition, she bolted from the stall.

And froze.

Not Eddard, but a stranger.

A handsome, intimidating, and . . . goodness me . . . a very handsome stranger.

Words stuck in her throat as he stared back at her.

It was his eyes she noticed first.

The room was dark, and she couldn't see their color from this distance, but the intensity of their gaze sent a shiver down her spine. His dark hair had a distinct wave to it, even a bit of a curl in places, making his otherwise foreboding countenance just a bit more approachable, but his jaw was shadowed by a few days' growth, which almost nullified the effect.

The stranger-knight was easily the most attractive man she'd ever had the good fortune to look upon. That is, he would be if he deigned to smile. At the moment, he did not seem inclined to do so.

"You are not Eddard," she said.

"Nay, I am not." Well, of course he wasn't.

Nella snorted behind her. Did she sense it too? When he spoke, the ground itself seemed to move beneath them. His voice was low and deep.

"Who are you?"

His lack of a response may have been due to the impertinence of her question. But there was no one here to introduce them, and he was the visitor, not she.

By all that was holy, this man was . . . intense.

"Where is the marshal?"

So he refused to give his name. Very well. She would do the same. "I'm not sure. 'Tis odd that neither he nor the stablehands are here."

Though visitors to Kenshire were not unusual, the late hour of his arrival was somewhat strange. Before she could think it over, she found herself saying, "What are you doing here?"

Even for her, the question came out all wrong. She'd been accused of being direct before. Mayhap too much so. Her words had been outright rude this time, but he could at least offer a name.

"I'm here to visit Lady Sara."

She was about to respond when he began to stride toward her, growing larger and larger as he neared. Emma wanted to back away, but she'd not show fear.

Not now. Not ever.

"I assume you're here for the same purpose?" he asked.

"To visit?" Ah, yes. "Aye, I am here to visit Lady Sara as well." In a way it was true—only her visit had lasted years.

He stood close enough now that if she reached out a hand, Emma could touch him. Her hand rose an inch or two unbidden before she convinced it to return to her side.

"Garrick," he said. And that was all.

So not a knight? She peered around him to look at his horse again. The massive destrier was undoubtedly a knight's horse. But the familiar greeting, much too familiar since it must be clear she was a lady, proclaimed him something else. Mayhap a merchant?

But then what of the horse?

"I rode ahead of my companions," he said.

Oh, but that voice . . .

"Emma," she blurted.

"Lady Emma," he corrected.

In all of her life, Emma could not once remember a time she'd offered her given name to a stranger so easily.

There was just something about him. She'd first felt it when he'd started to move toward her, and the strange sensation had not left her since. It was as if she were being pulled to him.

"Either," she said, knowing the implications of such a statement. Not caring.

He raised his brows and she shivered again.

The stranger glanced down as if to say, *No cloak?*

She had indeed begun to regret not bringing a cloak with her, but then she'd not intended to stay in the stable for more than a few minutes . . . and the cold was not the reason for her body's uncontrollable shaking.

His gloved hand moved to the clasp at his throat, and a moment later, he swung the heavy material away from his body and began to wrap it around her.

Emma gasped.

"Sir Garrick," she accused, the admonishment in her voice very real.

Her instincts had been correct. Though she didn't recognize the crest on his surcoat, the man's dress proclaimed him a knight at least, more likely a lord of some sort. The overbearing, suppressive sort, most likely.

"Aye," he said, as he moved even closer and finished wrapping his cloak around her shoulders. When he leaned toward her, Emma couldn't help but notice his scent. Musky and clean, it was entirely too pleasant. She swallowed as he turned his attention to the clasp.

Though he'd had no trouble removing it, the clasp was evidently harder to fasten with gloves. He pulled the edges of the black fur-lined cloak together with one hand, and held the other hand out to her.

She looked down at it in bafflement and then back up into his eyes. Blue, they were dark blue.

They stood much too close to be proper—so close it addled her wits. Sir Garrick nodded toward his hand, and she looked down again, realizing he wanted her to remove his glove so he could fasten the cloak.

Of course.

Emma freed his hand. Like everything else about him, it was large and strong, though the impression was fleeting—it quickly moved toward her throat to finish the job of securing his cloak firmly about her shoulders.

When he stepped back, Emma simply stared at him for a long moment, unsure what to say. *Thank you* seemed appropriate, but the words would not escape from her mouth.

"Warmer?"

She nodded, remembering the glove. She reached out to hand it to him, and when he took it, his finger brushed against her thumb ever so slightly.

Emma was not sure what was happening to her or why she'd given a stranger leave to call her by her given name. Or why, though she was no longer as cold, her hands continued to tremble.

He'd waited across the field from angry Saracens who were prepared to lop off his head. He'd sat across from the future King of England, a man whose temper was legendary, and dared to disagree with him, unsure if he'd pay the ultimate price for his lack of deference.

But Garrick had never before stood immobile as an awareness of another human being crept into his very soul. When Emma —*Lady* Emma, he corrected himself—had emerged from that stall, he'd thought two things at once, evident from her posture and expression.

This was a woman who, despite her station, was neither biddable nor docile.

And he wanted her.

He wanted this raven-haired beauty with an intensity that should have sent him running from the stable immediately. *You are nearly betrothed to another woman.* Yet here he stood, taunting his own instincts, moving much closer to her than was wise. Conrad would roar in laughter if he ever came to know how completely Garrick's usual instincts for how to woo a beautiful woman had left him. For several minutes, he'd been completely tongue-tied, and when he finally introduced himself, he'd unaccountably shared his given name.

Why did I withhold my title?

She was small but well-endowed. He shouldn't have noticed such a thing, but she'd lacked any kind of coat to keep her warm against the winter chill. He certainly shouldn't have noticed her lips were made to be kissed.

When he moved in closer to wrap the cloak about her, Garrick was drawn in by her gaze. Those ice-blue eyes stood out in stark contrast to hair so black it shone. But it wasn't the color of her eyes he noticed as he wrapped his cloak around her. It was the strange intensity of the moment, as if it were somehow significant.

Garrick wanted her, whoever she was, which was exactly why he took a step back after securing the cloak.

"Aye, thank you," she said, the words seeming to come from

deep within her throat, the simple thanks penetrating the icy chill he'd worn since leaving Clave.

The door to the stables creaked open behind him.

"My lord? My lady?"

The invisible net that had been cast around them was lifted as a stableboy ran toward them.

Garrick turned, watching as the boy stopped next to Bayard and took a step back. Not that he blamed him. The warhorse was massive, his head as wide as a tree trunk. He'd been bred for the kind of fighting he'd left behind in the Holy Land.

"He senses your fear," Garrick told him.

"I'm not afraid," the boy replied. He ruined the effect by taking another step back. "I just ne'er saw a beast so . . ."

Pulling his woolen cloak tighter around his shoulders, the boy cocked his head and looked at the long scar that traveled the length of Bayard's neck. With a bow to the woman who'd so stunned him earlier, Garrick made his way toward his mount.

"There are others," he said. "They should be arriving at any time."

"The marshal sends his apologies, sir. 'Tis a groom's naming day, and he gathered us all together to celebrate. We didn't expect travelers so late. Not"—he rushed to continue—"that it is too late, of course. I'm glad to care for him and his companions."

Garrick couldn't decide what was making the boy more nervous, him or Bayard, but at least the lad had explained Eddard's absence. The marshal cared for the boys who worked for him as if they were family.

Voices outside the stable announced the arrival of the other men. Garrick looked out through the open door to see they traveled with escorts from Kenshire. While his arrival had gone largely unnoticed thanks to his familiarity with the guards, his men had not been afforded such a boon. He turned back to take a final glance at Lady Emma. She nodded in parting, a quick, regal bow of the head.

Leaving Bayard to the boy who'd finally gained enough confidence to approach the enormous steed, Garrick joined his men as they dismounted and made their way across the expansive courtyard, now deserted for mealtime, toward Kenshire's keep.

One night.

If she joined them for the meal, he'd have to endure the proximity of the woman for just one night. He was here to pay respects to Lady Sara, not to seduce one of her guests. Tomorrow, he'd best rise early and leave Kenshire, attempting to forget he'd ever met the undeniably exquisite Lady Emma.

CHAPTER FIVE

"Garrick, I'm pleased for you to meet my husband, Sir Geoffrey Waryn."

Geoffrey was now the Earl of Kenshire, a position of equal ranking, so he and Sir Geoffrey nodded their heads in greeting. They stood just inside the entrance to the great hall.

"My apologies for not greeting you properly—"

"Nay, my lady. It is I who should apologize for arriving so late and just before the evening meal."

Garrick watched as Sir Geoffrey gazed at his wife. Was he worthy of the good reputation that had reached Garrick's ears? He was at least relieved to see a look of fierce love and admiration in the man's eyes.

Knights and retainers moved past them and into the hall, but Sara seemed reluctant to do so just yet. She moved off to the side, and he and her husband followed.

"I'd prefer to speak with you before our conversation can be overheard," she said.

Garrick inclined his head to direct three of his men, who moved past them and into the rapidly filling hall. With darkness came the need for candles, which lit both the passageway where they now stood and the great room, which he'd always thought of as one of the grandest in all of England.

"Gladly, my lady, as I wish to do the same."

Having moved away from the entrance, Sara took his hands in hers, surprising both him and, Garrick suspected, her husband.

"'Tis so good to see you, my friend."

He squeezed her hands. "And you, Sara." He glanced at Geoffrey, but the man did not appear disturbed by their familiarity. Another mark in his favor. "My deepest condolences for the loss of your father. I've never had the pleasure of knowing a better man."

"And I'm sorry to have to say the same. It seems this past year has not been kind to either one of us."

They were silent for a moment, and then Garrick squeezed her hands once more before letting them go. "I came not only to offer my condolences, but to apologize for not having been here to help you. When I heard what happened—that bastard Randolf . . ."

"Garrick never did like Randolf," Sara explained to her husband.

"Good," Geoffrey said, looking at Garrick. An understanding passed between them—both men would lay down their lives to protect Sara.

"I'm glad you were here," Garrick said to the new earl, nodding at him.

"As am I."

When the earl looked at his wife again, Garrick relaxed.

Yes, there was to be no doubt—her husband loved her.

"I'm grateful for your visit," Sara said, "but apologies are not necessary, Garrick. You were across an entire ocean fighting for Edward. There was nothing you could have done."

"Fighting to right his father's follies," he said, hoping his voice did not betray him as a traitor. Although Sara knew he respected the man's position, she likely remembered he had no love for Edward's policies—and approved even less of his father's. But this was neither the time nor the place for talk of politics.

Sara's husband looked around them as if searching for one of the king's spies.

"My husband can be overly suspicious," she said by way of explanation.

Garrick followed his glance.

"Oh dear," Sara said. "And I thought I'd have an ally when you arrived. It seems I'm to be overrun by the good intentions of over-protective men."

"Sir Geoffrey—"

"Geoffrey." He stuck his hand out to him, and Garrick shook it firmly. Aye, he liked this man with the same raven-black hair as . . .

"Oh!"

They all turned as the very woman who'd entered his thoughts nearly ran into him. She halted, breathing heavily as if she'd been running.

"I thought I was late," she said, staring at him.

She looked exactly as she had in the stables, though with less hay clinging to her velvet gown, and her effect on him was undiminished.

"Emma." Sara moved toward the vision—the woman—and placed a hand on her back.

"Meet a very dear friend of mine. Sir Garrick Helmsley, the sixth Earl of Clave. Oh, and you are now a Scottish earl as well, are you not?"

Garrick hardly heard the words. The woman's gaze pulled him toward her, compelling him not to look away, and he was easily swayed.

"Aye," he managed to reply. Years of training and decorum saved him.

Garrick took her hand in his own, relishing in how small and dainty and warm it felt, as Sara finished. "This is my sister-in-law, Lady Emma Waryn."

He was just about to place a brief kiss on her hand when Sara's words penetrated the fog in his mind.

Sister-in-law.

He kissed her hand and released it, not able to let the contact linger. Forcing a neutral expression, he looked at her brother, who eyed them both with the intensity he'd expect of a man protecting his sister.

"I'm pleased to make your acquaintance," he said, looking back to Sara. Anywhere but at Emma.

"And I yours," she said prettily, as if she had not nearly plowed into him a moment before.

"Linkirk, am I correct?" Sara pressed, naming his father's earldom in Scotland. He was surprised Sara remembered. He'd spent much more time in England, though his mother, who had inherited the title and property that passed to his father upon marriage, traveled there often. She considered it more of a home than Clave.

"You have a good memory, my lady."

"Garrick's father was the Earl of Linkirk, which makes our guest a powerful man indeed. On both sides of the border."

He said nothing. It was true, after all, and it was also the reason for his current predicament.

"Linkirk," Geoffrey said. "My family is now related to their neighbors and Clan Kerr."

"I've heard as much," Garrick said, trying not to look at Emma. "I'm quite interested to learn more about the circumstances around that union."

He knew Clan Kerr well. As Geoffrey said, his land in Linkirk bordered one of their holdings. But he remembered the Kerr chief as a private man, much like his father. Not one prone to readily accept allies. That he had willingly done so with their southern neighbors was a surprising revelation. Though not as surprising as the fact that the former enemies were now relatives, Bristol back under the control of the Waryn family.

"Then come inside while we tell it."

He must have sufficiently redirected his attention away from Emma. For if Geoffrey had any notion of the thoughts he was having about his sister, he would not be so welcoming.

One night. That was all. He'd retire early from dinner. Leave early in the morn. He could conceal his thoughts—his attraction—for just a few hours.

With any luck, the two would not be seated together.

Why did he have to be seated directly to her left?

If either Geoffrey or Sara had any inclination of the thoughts flitting through her innocent mind, surely they would have seated him elsewhere on the dais. What poor timing for them to adhere to convention.

An earl. Twice over, from the sound of it.

The revelation made him less attractive, though that wasn't saying much. Everything about him still made her thoughts—and her knees—as shaky as Cook's pudding. But when she'd thought him a simple knight, or a minor lord at most, he'd beckoned to her more than any other man ever had, made her want to abandon all of the reasons she'd ever given her brother for rejecting her suitors. But an earl was exactly what she did *not* want, although her traitorous body did not seem to understand as much.

Emma's gaze continued to unwittingly turn toward him. Her hands refused to remain still. Her heartbeat persisted in pounding in her ears.

He is an earl, she reminded herself.

Very likely as pompous and pretentious as the majority of the powerful men in his position. Her brother excluded, of course.

He had happened into the title, and his disposition was more that of a border reiver than a man of the realm. Even if, by the grace of God, the stranger had managed to remain as humble as Sara despite his station, he had undoubtedly become accustomed to controlling the people around him. She'd met nary a lord who didn't. Which meant he was perfectly incompatible with her. No need to look his way. No need to be nervous. He was just a man, like any other, passing through Kenshire. Soon he would be gone.

Gone.

"Is he sick?" Garrick asked.

Emma had eaten an entire course without making a fool of herself. But she wasn't so sure she could continue the deception, especially if he insisted on talking to her.

She'd give it "one hell of a try" as Catrina would say.

"My brother?" she asked as she reached for the goblet of wine in front of her.

She strained her neck forward to glance at her older brother, who was whispering something to Sara.

She took a sip, concentrating on the smooth taste of the red velvet vintage slipping down her throat. Think of the wine. Emma very much loved—

"Your horse."

"Wine." God's teeth, what was she saying?

She looked at him then. Wouldn't it be rude not to? He appeared quite confused, and rightly so.

"My brother enjoys wine," she said, trying to make sense of her prattling words.

"As do I." He proved the truth of his words by reaching for his own goblet.

"Aye, she is sick," she said, finally remembering to answer his question. "Eddard is not worried because she continues to eat, but she is not acting quite herself."

"Nella," he said. "What other symptoms does she have?"

Why did her horse's name seem like such an intimate thing for him to say?

Oh yes, symptoms.

"She is warm. And was lying down earlier when you . . ."

Sara and Geoffrey did not appear to be paying them any mind, but on the off chance that they were listening, she didn't want them to know they'd met prior to their introduction outside the hall. So she stopped talking.

Garrick raised his brows and whispered, "So very scandalously gave you my cloak?"

Though he said it in a teasing tone, his words were quiet enough for her ears only, ensuring their rather improper meeting would remain a secret.

"I didn't think to be there so long," she answered. "Otherwise I would have brought my own cloak."

He took another sip, this one much deeper, his eyes on her as his lips covered the rim of the goblet. She swallowed.

"I will check on her after the meal," he said.

"You will?"

His expression was so neutral, Emma couldn't tell what the man was thinking. She'd often wondered whether great lords were given some sort of special training to conjure such unreadable expressions. But when she'd asked Sara about it, her sister-in-law had simply laughed.

"I have an affinity for horses," he said. "An interest in them that placed me too often in the stables growing up, if you listen to my mother tell the tale."

An affinity for horses.

So many thoughts and feelings bubbled up in Emma at that moment. She'd grown up wanting nothing more than to be with her horses. To ride them. To simply be in their company. Being with Nella gave her more pleasure than being with just about anyone. For some reason, though, Emma kept her thoughts to herself. She didn't want him to know all of that. Something told her it would only make this, whatever it was, more difficult.

"Thank you, my lord."

He inclined his head just slightly, properly acknowledging her thanks.

"So, Garrick," Sara said. "You mentioned passing through Kenshire. Where do you go next?"

Emma concentrated on the pattern of flowers etched into her goblet. She'd never noticed how pretty it was, the stems of the roses entwining—

"To Scotland, my lady."

"Linkirk?"

"Aye, my mother is there. After she received word of my father's death in Acre, she thought it a necessary trip."

"I see."

"Will there be trouble?" Sara had clearly detected a layer of meaning beneath his words that had eluded Emma.

She chanced a glance at Garrick, wishing immediately she hadn't. He was looking at her; his eyes, mesmerizing, made it difficult for her to focus. Her eyes darted back to the glass. *So these flowers . . .*

"I go to ensure there is none."

"You know Kenshire is behind you. Always."

Garrick lifted his drink in salute. "As Clave is for Kenshire."

Emma knew very little about Clave beyond that it was partially in the sea, only accessible by foot during low tide. She could not recall anything else of their southern neighbors, but if the earl was an ally, why had he not assisted Sara in her claim to Kenshire after her father's death? Dozens of questions crowded her tongue, none of which she could afford to ask lest she reveal her interest in the earl.

"Wait!" Sara exclaimed.

"No, Sara . . ." Geoffrey said next to her, somehow knowing what she was about to say. Emma did not. Her thoughts were still swirling around Clave and Kenshire and her sister-in-law's early struggle to retain her title.

"Linkirk is not far from Dunmure Tower, is that correct?" Sara asked smartly.

Emma looked from her sister-in-law to her brother, and then to Garrick. Linkirk. Near Dunmure?

"Aye, it lies directly south of Dunmure, my lady."

"Sara . . ." Geoffrey's tone was a warning, one she did not heed.

"What wonderful news, Garrick! You see, Emma's dear friend Clara, Alex Kerr's wife, is with child."

Oh no . . .

"And Emma has been desperate to get to her. You see, they've grown quite close. But my husband—" She turned to look at Geoffrey. "He does not want to leave the babe."

If Emma guessed correctly, Sara's glance was sharp. But likely no sharper than the expression Geoffrey was leveling at her in return.

"Babe?" Garrick asked.

"Sara and Geoffrey have a baby boy," Emma said, so proud to call herself an aunt. "Hayden."

Garrick raised his cup again. "Congratulations, my lady. My lord. That is wonderful news indeed."

They all drank to the young heir's health, but the wine no longer felt comforting to Emma. For she knew what Sara intended to ask of Garrick. And though she desperately wanted to visit her friend, the thought of being escorted there by the earl was . . . disconcerting. The effect he had on her was completely out of her control.

"He trusts no one to accompany her there, save himself," Sara continued. "But if you are passing through . . . Of course, Emma could find no safer escort than yourself, Lord Clave."

She'd used his title intentionally. For there was no way Geoffrey could argue Emma would not be safe in the company of an earl, let alone an old friend of Sara's, and his retinue.

Emma finally gave in to temptation and glanced at Garrick. What would he say? What *could* he say? Sara had left him little choice.

His face, as impassive as ever, gave no indication of his thoughts. Instead, he raised his goblet for a third time, inclined his head just slightly, and said, "I would be honored to escort Lady Emma to Dunmure, my lady."

Emma whipped her head back to Sara and Geoffrey. Her sister-in-law beamed. Her brother scowled. She didn't know who she felt more inclined to agree with. But it didn't really matter. Sara had asked. He'd accepted. She'd appear a fool to shy away from the arrangement after her weeks of begging and cajoling her brother.

And then, as if Sara could hear her thoughts, she said, "Wonderful. Then 'tis settled."

Emma raised her own goblet this time. "To Scotland." She downed its contents in one great big gulp.

CHAPTER SIX

*G*arrick, mounted and waiting for Lady Emma to join them, tried to still his horse. He and Bayard had been together for long enough that Bayard could sense his moods, and there was no doubt that he was ill at ease—all the more so after his conversation with Sir Geoffrey earlier that morning.

"My wife has high praise for you, Clave."

Geoffrey had pulled him aside in front of Kenshire's main keep as the party began to assemble. The blustery January wind promised to make their second day of travel a cold one.

"As do I for Lady Sara," he said. "But you don't know me. And therefore don't trust me."

Garrick was never one for subtleties, a trait that had gotten him into trouble more than once.

It seemed he had that in common with Sir Geoffrey.

"I don't like it," the man immediately replied.

They both knew what "it" was, and Garrick did not blame the man. Whether or not Geoffrey sensed his attraction to Emma hardly mattered. He was escorting an unmarried woman, a most beautiful unmarried woman by any man's standards, for three, perhaps four, days. Even if Sara and her husband had not heard about his reputation with the ladies, the earl would do well to be cautious.

But Garrick did not bed virgins, and Geoffrey's sister certainly would not be the first, although he doubted the man would appreciate hearing as much. There was, however, something he might say to comfort him.

"I travel to Scotland to become a husband."

Those words, spoken aloud in a definitive manner, took all of the bluster from Sir Geoffrey's speech. Though it apparently did not warrant any gentler treatment, for the affable man he'd met the evening before seemed to have disappeared overnight.

"You didn't mention it last eve," Geoffrey said.

There was no denying the truth. He tried not to think on the arrangement, much less make his unwanted future wife a topic of conversation.

"Nevertheless . . ." Garrick had stared down Saracen soldiers who'd possessed less angst than this man.

"Very good," Geoffrey finally said, reaching his hand out in front of him.

Garrick took it, knowing the silent pact they made and happily agreeing to it. Escorting Lady Emma was a favor he owed Sara, and he would ensure the lady arrived safely at Dunmure. Unharmed, untouched. No matter how much it killed him.

He shook Geoffrey's hand, their eyes locking one final time in understanding.

"You'll stay at The Wild Boar?"

Garrick nodded. "I'd previously planned on Kenston House as well—"

"Emma will not—"

"But will not stay there with your sister in attendance. It is obviously not appropriate for a lady."

"So the abbey, then?" Geoffrey asked.

"Aye and, if necessary, on Clan Scott land."

Although Geoffrey didn't appear pleased by this piece of news, neither did he object to the possibility.

Garrick pushed the conversation from his mind. His men grew impatient, but when Emma arrived a few minutes later, all turned to look at her.

Lady Emma was a difficult woman not to notice.

"I will," she was saying to Lady Sara as she planted a kiss on each of her sister-in-law's cheeks. "It will be but a few weeks."

She turned then and glanced at him. The preparations, his men . . . everything ceased but the simple smile of a lady whom he'd sworn to protect. She mounted another horse, Nella not being well enough for the journey, with the help of a groom, as did the maidservant who'd be accompanying her on the journey. The girl was a young chaperone, but a chaperone nonetheless. Part of him was grateful she'd have one.

When Sara approached him, Garrick shook himself from his reverie and dismounted.

"That was quite unnecessary," she said, her tone as regal as one would expect of a countess.

He lifted her gloved hand to his own, his lips connecting briefly with the cold leather. "As you will, my lady."

He turned from her, but Sara stayed him with a gentle touch to his shoulder.

"Geoffrey told me of your purpose for this trip," she said quietly.

He shrugged. There was not much more to say. Sara herself had almost entered a marriage of convenience to maintain her position. She knew as well as he did that such things were sometimes necessary for men and women in their social class.

"When you return Emma, you'll tell me more?"

He did not want to ask for her aid when he had not been available to help her in her time of need. The reasons for this betrothal . . . the possibility of trouble in Linkirk . . . they were his problems.

"Of course." And although it did not need to be said, he added, "She will be safe with me."

"I know she will be, Garrick."

With that, Sara joined her husband, who'd taken up a position by the door, his scowl still in place, and Garrick mounted his horse. After ensuring all were ready, he nodded one last time to Sara and urged Bayard forward. Two men fell behind to guard the women, and Garrick's party made their way across the outer courtyard, through the gatehouse, and down the slope that would take them north, away from Kenshire.

Garrick's plan was simple. He would remain in the lead, limit his interaction with the ladies, and focus on the only thing that mattered—getting them to Scotland without incident. He just hoped the lady's maid was as comfortable on horseback as her mistress.

"What do you mean she can't continue?"

They'd stopped for the night at one of the most well-established inns along the border. The Wild Boar had been known for its neutrality as long as Garrick could remember. Arguments between Scots and English were not tolerated within its doors. It was as safe a place as any to stop for the evening. Modest but clean and comfortable.

Emma, whom Garrick had successfully avoided all day, had cornered him at the entrance to the stables.

"Look," Emma said, pointing at her maid, who was indeed walking in a pained manner that implied she'd never ridden a horse before.

They stepped aside to allow one of Garrick's men past them. Night had just begun to fall, and Garrick was ready for a fire, a hot meal, and a cold mug of ale. Raised in Northumbria or not, the weather had taken its toll on him after a long day of travel.

"Can we discuss this inside?"

He hadn't intended for his voice to sound so harsh. But if it scared Lady Emma away from him, he could justify the tone.

"I suppose," she said, her lack of movement at odds with her words.

They stepped forward at the same time, Garrick bumping into her shoulder. She rubbed it, and he restrained himself from asking if she was hurt. Were she another woman he fancied, and were he not nearly betrothed, Garrick would have used it as an opportunity to touch her arm, offer words of comfort. Every instinct told him to soften his tone. To smile at her in hopes she'd return the gesture.

Instead, he moved forward again, forcing her to trail after him. It would be best if he seemed indifferent, if she thought him rude.

The innkeeper found him as soon as he stepped inside.

"So you are in charge of this rabble, then?"

Magge would earn a pretty coin for the evening courtesy of this "rabble."

"I am, Mistress Magge," he said.

"Lord Clave!" Her face split into a huge grin. Ah, so she hadn't recognized him at first sight.

"Do I look so different, then?"

The plump, aging woman, her apron as clean as the king's drying cloth, grabbed his cheek and squeezed it. His father had always thought the woman impertinent, though Garrick rather enjoyed her straightforward, if not bawdy, manner.

"Just a bit older is all. Get these men food and drink immediately," she said to a nearby serving wench, the girl no older than Emma's young maid. "Who's that yer hiding, my lord?" She peered around him.

Garrick turned just as Emma removed her fur-rimmed hood. She allowed the dark material to slide through her gloved fingers, revealing a mass of black tresses that pooled around her in waves of silk. Perhaps he just imagined it, but all conversation seemed to cease around him. More than one head turned in her direction. It was as if she became the center of every space she entered, simply by virtue of being herself.

"A private dining room, if you please?"

He had not intended to ask for such a luxury, but neither was Garrick accustomed to traveling with someone like Emma. Of course she would attract attention in the inn's bustling great room.

"Of course, my lord," Magge said. Normally, she would have laden the words with innuendo, unable to restrain herself, but something about Emma must have given her pause.

"Lady Emma and her maid will dine in private," he said.

"Dine?" The maid appeared from behind him, her cheeks red. "Oh, Emma, please don't make me sit. I'll miss the evening meal, every meal for the rest of my life, if you'll allow me to lie down for a spell. My lady, I—"

"Of course, Edith."

Her voice was soft, but her tone was strong enough to be the Queen of England's.

"Mistress, a tray for my lady would be most welcome."

Magge looked from him to Lady Emma. He nodded.

"Then ye'll not be needing the private room?"

Emma looked at him. She would attract too much attention in the great room. Could he be so churlish as to suggest she eat alone?

Aye, since the alternative was to dine in there with her, away from everyone's watching eyes.

"My lady will take a meal there. Or she might prefer a tray as well?"

Her eyes widened, making the blue flash as brightly as blood against freshly fallen snow.

"My lady," she said mockingly, "prefers to dine in the hall."

"No."

Both Edith and Magge watched their exchange, which was unfortunate but unavoidable.

"I've been charged with your safety, my lady. And I don't believe—"

"I'll have the cellar prepared," Magge said as she ambled away, not waiting for an answer. "For two."

Perhaps his father was right. "The fairer sex held more power than mere men could ever dream of," he'd often said. He could rule two great households in two countries, but not an aged innkeeper and a petite Englishwoman.

"Very well," he said. "As for a chaperone—"

"My lady doesn't require one," the maid said. All eyes turned to Edith, whose words tumbled from her all at once. "What I mean to say is that she often finds herself in situations . . . that is . . . she doesn't much care for . . . oh, never mind."

As if by way of apology, she glanced at Emma, whose smirk was anything but angry.

"Poor Edith. Go up to our room; I will be fine." Emma turned to him. "Shall we, then?" she asked, lifting an eyebrow in an obvious challenge.

Garrick glanced at his men, who'd already seated themselves in the great room. He led Emma toward the back of the inn. The door to the storage room was already open. He'd used this room on more than one occasion, having frequented The Wild Boar since he was young. It was normally used as a private meeting space. The smell of thyme wafted from the staircase, preferable to the musty stench of most below-ground rooms.

Magge had already placed a board across two cut-out barrels, and a pair of three-legged stools sat off to the side, awaiting their use. As she lay a linen tablecloth on top, Garrick's eyes began to adjust to the dim light. The cellar had been sufficiently transformed, but it was still darker than abovestairs despite the tallow candles that had been lit throughout the room. It was only when Magge winked at Garrick before making her way back up that he felt the full impact of their arrangement. This kind of intimacy was exactly what he'd intended to avoid.

So much for avoiding the lady. Tomorrow he would be better prepared.

Emma had begun to shrug off her hooded cape, and his arm moved forward automatically to take it from her. He placed it, along with his own, atop a set of wooden crates.

A noise from above drew their attention. It was not Magge who was coming down the stairs, but a serving girl who placed a tray laden with food and drink on the board. Before Garrick could even offer his thanks, she was gone.

"Shall we?" Emma moved first, sitting prettily on one of the stools after fanning her riding gown out beneath her.

He sat on his own stool, watching her face, so full of expression.

"You didn't tell Lady Sara we'd already met," she observed.

Garrick poured them ale from the pewter pitcher. "You had the opportunity as well, my lady."

Emma rolled her eyes. "Emma. I thought we'd established as much in the stables."

"That was before I knew—"

"Knew what?" Her question, asked innocently enough, brought a rush of desire as fierce as the edge of a Saracen's blade.

Knew you were his sister. Knew you were untouchable.

"Before I knew your identity," he said.

Garrick shifted his attention to their modest meal. Two trenchers, roasted rabbit, and an unidentifiable soup that look edible enough.

"An earl." She shook her head in apparent distaste. *That* was a first.

"You don't approve?"

Something in her expression answered him before she uttered a word. "I'm sitting in a storeroom with you, am I not?"

He glanced around the room. "You could not have dined in the hall."

"I disagree." She took a drink, her eyes peering at him from above the rim of the mug.

By God, she is lovely.

"I heard from the men earlier that you've been to Acre?"

He didn't comment on the change of topic. "Aye. I have."

"What was it like? Did you meet the king?"

"It was bloody and hot. Not unlike King Edward."

She laughed. Not the kind of laughter he was used to hearing from a lady but loud and unselfconscious. It was the kind of laughter that made a man want to join in. Even Edward would not have been immune, though he was not the sort of man to laugh at any kind of joke that featured him as a punch line.

The thought made him oddly uneasy. Edward was known to enjoy the company of beautiful women.

"Tell me how you came to be at Kenshire, Lady Emma."

When she took a bite of rabbit, he spied, for the briefest of moments, the pink tip of her tongue as it darted out to catch the spiced meat.

"'Tis a short tale, really. When Clan Kerr took Bristol, my brothers and I went to live with my Uncle Simon and Aunt Lettie. They could hardly support us all, so Geoffrey and my other uncle, Hugh, took to reiving while my other brothers complained about staying behind with me. Then Sara's father sent for Hugh, and Geoffrey went along . . . and, well, you know the rest. Everyone in England has probably heard the story."

"You've never grieved."

She went so still that Garrick wished he could retract his words. "I don't condemn you for it. I understand it all too well."

Her head, slightly bowed, snapped up.

He'd uttered the words unthinkingly, leaving himself with little choice but to share his own story. "I lost my father in battle."

They'd fought many battles together before that fateful day in a foreign land, in a foreign war. "In Acre," he clarified.

Emma didn't say a word after that. They ate in silence. When they finished the meal, Garrick was about to stand, to escape the confining space that brimmed with her presence, her smell, the draw of her soft skin. But Emma stopped him from pushing his stool away.

"Nay," she said. "Not yet."

CHAPTER SEVEN

*S*he'd thought last evening's meal was trying, but sitting next to Sir Garrick Helmsley in a crowded hall was like riding a horse in an open field. Thrilling, yet simple, and assuredly safe. Dining alone with him tonight, however, was more akin to riding while standing . . . up a mountain . . . with her eyes closed.

"What I meant to say is . . ."

What exactly did I mean to say?

"Why do you travel to Scotland?"

She really could have thought of something more profound. Although, "I don't want to leave just yet even though your high-handedness is exactly what I would have expected from an earl" would surely not do.

Emma, you can be such a dolt.

Garrick raised the pitcher slightly, and she nodded. Keeping her hands—and mouth—busy was helpful. Though she could think of other ways she'd like to keep her mouth busy . . .

Oh Emma, what is wrong with you? To imagine kissing the earl!

"As you know, I travel to my holding in Linkirk."

He had said as much, and she had no doubt it was true. Although he hadn't said much, he had a way of making every word sound important. And yet, she had no doubt he was holding something back.

Emma had been raised with three brothers. Her second eldest brother, Bryce, was even less talkative than Garrick. Emma had the opposite problem. Every single thought she had spilled from her head right out through her mouth. But even if she didn't understand her brother's reticence, experience had taught her that his lack of words didn't mean he lacked for thoughts. He was just better at keeping them to himself.

A trait her escort apparently shared with her brother.

"And you said your mother is there?"

His crossed arms told her this was a topic he wanted to talk about even less than his time in Acre.

"She returned two months past, as soon as word of my father reached her."

"Returned?"

"My mother is Scottish."

When the corner of his mouth turned up ever so slightly, Emma realized she had not hidden her surprise very well.

"Her father was the former Earl of Linkirk. As his eldest daughter, my mother inherited the title and one-third of his holdings. The title was passed down to my father through her."

"And now to you."

His expression gave nothing away. Inexplicably, she thought of when their hands had touched in the stable. Had she dreamt about that last night? Aye, she had. And she'd woken contemplating how a simple touch in her dream had been so full of meaning. His face was the first thing she'd seen in her mind upon awakening this morning.

"And now me."

"Sara mentioned possible trouble?"

Before he said a word, she knew he was not going to tell her. Perhaps she dug too deep and the matter felt too personal to him. Indeed, she was right, but he continued to look at her.

What is he thinking?

Everything about him was hard. Or, at least, she imagined it would be. Including his expression. Everything except the dark waves that curled just slightly around the nape of his neck. Emma wanted to touch his hair, to run her fingers through it as if it were her right.

"My maid cannot travel," she blurted.

When faced with his confused expression, she attempted to explain. "I do that often."

"Do what?" It was his tone, she decided, every word was delivered slowly, deliberately. That was what made his words seem so important.

"Talk about too many things at once. I told her it was not a good idea. Edith has always wanted to see Scotland, so she could not be dissuaded. But I knew so many hours in the saddle would give her some trouble."

Garrick appeared to consider the problem.

"Imagine," she said. "That she'd have so little experience riding with Eddard as her father."

"Eddard?" That had clearly managed to surprise him. "I didn't realize he had a daughter."

"Well, neither did he for quite some time. Which may explain her lack of interest in horses. A few years back, a woman whom Eddard had, um . . ."

He cocked his head. "Sought out the service of Venus?"

It took her a moment, but when she understood, she shivered as surely as if they were still conversing in the cold stable at Kenshire.

"Cold, Emma?"

Of course not. In fact, it was quite warm down here in the cellar. "Nay."

"I thought I saw you shiver."

He was a churl to say such a thing. "Your eyesight must be poor."

"I don't believe it is."

Did he know how he affected her?

Just because she didn't like the way he'd ordered her to leave the great room didn't mean she was immune to his charms. The Earl of Clave was perhaps the most good-looking man in all of England. Was it any wonder that she noticed?

"I'll leave a man behind to bring her to Dunmure when she's ready."

A man? Her? What had she done to convince him to leave her behind?

Oh, Edith.

"Is that safe?"

"Safe?"

Oh dear, how would she say this?

"A strange man. With my maid?"

He lifted his brows as if mocking her.

Arrogant earl.

"He is not strange to *me*," he said. "And 'tis no different than you being down here alone. Or traveling to Dunmure with me and my men."

He had a point. "I do believe my brother will not be very happy to learn I traveled with you unchaperoned."

"Yet you sit here with me now."

"You insisted."

"Your safety is my only concern."

"Your *only* concern?" She hadn't meant it that way. Nor had she meant to put quite so much emphasis on the word "only." Her point, or rather the point she'd intended to make, was that he seemed just as concerned about being in control as he did of her safety.

But that was not how it sounded.

"Unfortunately, yes," he said bluntly.

With that, he stood. Emma had no choice but to do the same. Confused by his last statement, and still unsure of their plans for the next day, Emma mutely followed Garrick up the stairs and waited as he hunted down the innkeeper. The sound of laughter prompted her to peer into the great room.

Oh my!

The serving maids, in various states of undress, appeared to be doing more than serving ale.

"You see why I insisted," Garrick said, returning.

She ignored that.

"You're sure Edith will be safe? I will speak to her tonight to ensure she feels comfortable with the arrangement."

"Your maid is quite safe," he said. Something about the way he said "your maid" almost prompted her to ask if *she* was safe. But then Emma thought better of it. Perhaps she didn't want the answer to that particular question.

"Do you need a break, my lady?"

Garrick's men had been trained well. They rode through the snow, which had started earlier that morn and continued throughout the day, and though their leader stayed to the front of the group, the others were very solicitous of her well-being, and they'd asked her more than once if she needed a break. The answer was always, "Thank you, but no." When they finally did stop for a quick midday meal, a red-headed knight who was nearly as tall as Garrick but much leaner tended to her mount.

She missed Nella. Though her beloved horse had no longer been feverish yesterday morning, she'd been too recently ill for such a long journey.

After their repast, they navigated around Dod Law before heading due north on a path that would take them across the border and nearly straight to Dunmure Tower. Straight to Clara. Emma had been to the border before, but this was the first time she would be staying in Scotland for an extended visit.

As the day wore on, snow began to accumulate on the ground beneath them. Though the wide-open fields didn't lend themselves to shelter, they did encourage a faster pace. As soon as the incline flattened out, Emma maneuvered herself until she rode alongside their riding party's leader. If she couldn't navigate a bit of snow, then she'd not rightly earned her reputation as the best rider at Kenshire.

She'd tried, and failed, not to glance his way throughout the early part of the day. Anyone watching them would immediately know Garrick was in charge. He held himself up a bit straighter than the others. Though she couldn't see it now beneath his cloak, Garrick wore a thick, padded gambeson, the kind favored by her brothers. His nasal helm, certainly not an unusual sight, somehow looked more ominous on him than it did on others she'd seen wearing them. If she had not spent a lifetime among fearsome men, perhaps she would have thought better of provoking the Earl of Clave.

"Your slow pace is because of me," she called to him above the clomping hooves of the more than a half dozen destriers behind them.

"Slow pace?"

She could have told him of her intentions, but her borrowed mount, a strong Spanish jennet, was no match for a charger bred to overtake his opponents. A warning was an advantage she couldn't afford to give.

Emma spurred her mount forward, and she didn't hold back. The snow was soft and powdery, safe enough to gallop across even at this pace. It flicked up beneath them in every direction, the distant sound of hooves alerting her that she wasn't alone. Nella loved when the snow kicked up and hit her belly, and she laughed aloud thinking of the joy it brought her and her beloved horse every time they rode this way. Falling into a steady pace, she spied the thicket of trees a long way off in front of them. Could she hold off Lord Clave for that long?

Likely not.

But Emma would try her best.

The rhythmic sound of her horse's hooves lulled her into a confidence that she should have known would be tested. She was alerted to Garrick's presence by the loud snort of his horse behind her. She didn't dare spur her mount to a faster gallop with the snow, so it was not a surprise when the shadow over her shoulder became a mounted knight in front of her. That he didn't stop made Emma laugh again. She'd thought he would be angry, but instead he was playing her game.

He turned his head just slightly to gauge her position. She was gaining on him. Could she possibly overtake him again?

Alas, not today. He reached the edge of the woods and dismounted in what looked like one fluid motion. She reached him and did the same, pulling her hood back above her head with one hand and keeping the horse's reins wrapped up in the other.

"How did you do that?" she said, referring to his dismount.

"How did you?" he asked.

Training, of course.

Garrick pulled off his helmet and led his horse into the thicket. As they walked, the dimming sunlight began to fade, the canopy of the trees hastening the day's descent into semi-darkness. A lone bird called to them, or perhaps to his family. When Garrick moved off the road and tied his horse to a tree, she did the same. He reached into his saddlebag, pulled out a handful of oats, and divided it between the horses, who promptly ignored their handlers.

"Where did you learn to ride like that?"

She hadn't expected the admiration in his voice. Anger, perhaps. But not admiration.

"My youngest brother. And my twin. He was born with the 'gift,' as Eddard calls it."

"And it seems you were as well."

Emma's heart thudded. The same awareness of him that had assaulted her in the stables at Kenshire was present now.

"Thank you."

Sara had taught her to accept a compliment, a task that seemed simple but often felt daunting. "Where are your men?"

They listened for the sound of approaching horses, but the others were still too far for them to hear their approach.

"Coming along shortly, I'd imagine."

Emma wrapped her cloak more tightly around her. "What is our destination for this evening?"

Garrick's tentative smile continued to grow. "I'm surprised you've not asked before now."

Emma shrugged. "You are an earl. And Sara's friend," she said.

"What does that have to do—"

"Making decisions comes naturally to you. And if Sara trusts you, I do as well. So I hadn't thought to question our destination before now."

Only, it was indeed getting quite cold. "So where are we going?"

He didn't answer. And from the way Garrick was looking at her now, she wasn't at all sure she wanted him to. She'd been looked at this way before. As Geoffrey often saw fit to point out, more than one suitor had traveled to Kenshire to woo her. Some had been invited; most had not. All had a similar look about them, but none of the others had made her chest pinch like this. None of the others had made her wonder what they were thinking.

What did he see when he looked at her?

When she looked at *him*, she saw power. And strength. Too much so.

"Carharm Abbey."

Emma wasn't sure why she took a step toward him. It was as if a hand splayed against her back and pushed her forward. This was the same inexplicable draw she'd felt to him since the beginning.

"Oh." Carharm, on the English side of the border, was a sensible choice for shelter for the night.

She stopped, but he took a step toward her this time. And then another. When he was but an arm's length from her, Garrick took off his cloak for the second time since she'd met him.

"You're cold."

She opened her mouth to answer, to insist that he keep his cloak, for surely he was cold too, but no sound came out.

Emma swallowed as he reached behind her to mimic the same actions he'd taken in the stable. But this time, when his gloved hands moved to fasten the clasp at her neck, he was successful on the first attempt.

"Nay, my lord, you mustn't." She finally remembered to protest. "Garrick..."

He didn't move away from her. Emma took in a long, icy breath, bent her head back and locked her eyes with his. It was there. That pull, an undeniable force that compelled her to him.

"Garrick," she repeated, and when his lips parted, she knew.

He was going to kiss her.

Blast it... she couldn't breathe.

And then the ground began to rumble beneath their feet. Garrick stepped away from her, and though she was wrapped in no fewer than two cloaks, she was even colder than she'd been before.

With a final glance at her, he moved to his horse, opened the saddlebag, and took out another cloak. The heather gray material with dark green lines looked more like a blanket than a garment made for keeping warm. Once wrapped up in it, he took out a circular clasp and fastened it about his neck.

Had she wanted to avert her eyes, Emma would have been unequal to the task. Her sister-in-law was fond of telling her she could do anything she liked—run a manor, ride her horse faster than any man. Emma had begun to believe it... until now.

For even if the king himself had ordered her to look away

from Garrick Helmsley at this moment, she could not have done it. When he turned to her, she did not look away. Perhaps she should have. Instead, Emma watched as he spoke to one of his men. She watched him walk toward her and vaguely heard his request to assist her. Laden with two cloaks, one quite large and definitely too long, she accepted his offer.

And for the remainder of the day, Emma could think of nothing other than the moment before his men had arrived. The moment when Garrick had stood beside her, his lips parting slightly in a gesture that left no uncertainty.

He had been about to kiss her.

And she'd been prepared to allow it.

CHAPTER EIGHT

inally, their destination lay ahead. He'd managed to avoid her at the abbey the evening before, spending the night with his men. Now, after ensuring she was safely installed as a guest at Highgate End, and with any luck, he'd be able to do the same tonight. After he left Emma at Dunmure Tower tomorrow, he would continue on to Linkirk and try to forget about the beguiling companion who'd haunted his thoughts since their unusual meeting at Kenshire's stables.

Though they'd made it safely across the border, Garrick would not relax until they reached Clan Scott land. Hell, he wouldn't relax until Emma was delivered to her destination. To think he'd nearly kissed her . . . *kissed her* . . . yesterday. He'd promised Sara to protect her. And though it had not been spoken of directly, he'd vowed to Geoffrey not to touch her. And yet, had it not been for his men's arrival, he may have broken that unspoken vow a mere day after giving it.

Kissing Lady Emma Waryn was the worst idea he'd ever had, save for convincing his father to come with him to the Holy Land. When she rode past him yesterday, his heart had nearly stopped . . . until he remembered Emma was an expert horseman. She was an excellent rider, and her laughter—so full of glee—had rung in his ears long after she'd outstripped him. Due to Bayard's training and his very real practice overtaking enemies when both of their lives depended on it, both horse and rider had used their skills to catch her.

The almost kiss was the exact kind of foolhardy, rash action he'd warned himself against these past weeks. Unaccountably, he'd almost done it anyway, and from the look in her eyes in that moment, she knew it.

Luckily, his men had saved him from such folly.

"We're on Scott land now, my lord?" said James.

"Aye." He spied the castle ahead of them. Highgate End. Home to the chief of a clan as old as any along the treacherous border.

Garrick rode ahead and was met, as expected, by Graeme de Sowlis's men. After a brief conversation, they led him across the lowered drawbridge. His men and Emma followed him into the outer courtyard where the stables were kept. Linkirk had been formally allied with Clan Scott well before Garrick's father was named earl. Graeme de Sowlis's ascension to chief was something else Garrick had missed while he was in Acre, serving Edward on a crusade to the Holy Land. He, along with over a thousand men and more than two hundred knights, saved thousands of Christians under siege from Baibars.

Dismounting and handing the horse's reins to a groom, Garrick followed another servant through the modest gatehouse and into the inner courtyard as his men were led to their own quarters. The main keep, a circular stone structure old enough to need repairs, looked unaltered by the change in leadership. Impressive, foreboding, solitary.

Their traveling party entered directly into the great hall, where their host stood waiting for them. Graeme de Sowlis looked more like a groom than he did a clan chief. More affable than most and as deadly with a bow as any, the famed warrior bowed when he approached.

"An earl in two countries and a celebrated crusader. Sir Garrick? Linkirk? My lord? Which title do you prefer, Clave?"

Garrick took Graeme's hand, glad to be out of the cold for the night. But when Graeme peered beyond him, his eyes widening, Garrick knew *she* had entered the hall. Their day apart had come to an end.

"May I present Lady Emma Waryn? My lady, I give you Graeme de Sowlis, chief of Clan Scott and second of that name."

He could not avoid looking at her now. But when he did, his body immediately responded even as he tried to stop its reaction. She curtsied prettily to Graeme, who bowed. The twisting in Garrick's gut made him wish they'd stayed elsewhere for the night. According to some, Sowlis had broken as many hearts in Scotland as Garrick had in England before he left on campaign.

A fine time to remember that particular rumor.

Some said Graeme had once been betrothed to Catrina Kerr, now married to Emma's brother. Others said theirs was a friendship only. Garrick had never asked Graeme for the story, nor did he care to do so.

What mattered now was that Sowlis was unmarried . . . and so was Emma.

Why was such a woman still unattached? Of marriageable age, Emma could not be wanting for suitors—and Sowlis appeared anxious to join their ranks.

"The pleasure is mine," their host said. And he looked as if he'd meant it. "Fiona will show you to your bedchambers."

Graeme nodded to a maidservant. The woman took Emma's cloaks, both of them, and then approached Garrick. Divested of their cloaks and gloves, they followed her down a long stone hallway and up a circular flight of stairs lit with oil wall torches. Garrick attempted not to look at Emma, especially when they stopped in front of her bedchamber.

Garrick cursed under his breath when the woman then led him to his chamber . . . right next door. He hardly noticed the room, his thoughts still on the woman who would be sleeping in the next room over. He could, and should, join his host and the men in the hall for the meal. But would he be able to endure an entire evening in Emma's presence?

He sat on the bed, lost in thought, until a knock landed on his door. He opened it to reveal their host, looking more like a man befitting his station than he had just moments earlier. Was this for Emma's benefit?

"I'd speak to you before we dine," he said.

Stepping back to allow him entry, Garrick poured two goblets of wine from the service set that had been left on a small oak table near his bed.

"Your steward is to be commended," he said. Though the man couldn't have had much warning of their arrival, a fire had been roaring in the hearth of the sparse but well-appointed room in anticipation of his arrival. Rosewater and wine had been left out for him to cleanse with. Common in the Holy Land, it was less so here.

"My condolences for your loss," Garrick said.

"And to you for yours."

They drank a toast to their departed fathers, and Garrick was reminded of the condolences he'd exchanged with Lady Sara at Kenshire. Though her father had been old and ill, surely it had not made her loss any less painful.

So much death and more to come, at least here in the borderlands.

"He fought hard, and fought well. Our clan mourns him still, but he left this world fighting for what he believed in," Graeme said. "Peace. An established border. His clan's survival."

Garrick remained silent. He couldn't say his own father had done the same. They'd fought for Edward's cause, not their own. Though he'd be named a traitor if he shared such thoughts aloud.

"You wanted to speak to me."

"Your charge . . ."

Emma.

"How did you come to escort her here, without a chaperone?"

He and Graeme had spoken of women in the past. They'd even made jests about who would be bound by marriage first. But this was different. This was Emma.

"I stopped at Kenshire to offer condolences to Lady Sara, and it seemed her sister-in-law needed an escort to Dunmure."

"To Alex Kerr?"

"To his wife."

"I see."

"Her lady's maid was unable to ride after our first day of travel. She's behind us still, and if you can receive her, she'll likely arrive in just a few days."

"Hmm . . ."

He knew what was coming next. But that didn't make it any easier to hear.

"Is Lady Emma spoken for?"

The hand at his side tightened.

"You will have to ask the lady herself."

Whether it was his tone or his expression, Garrick wasn't sure, but Graeme immediately picked up on the feelings Garrick had been trying to deny for days.

"Is she spoken for by you?"

Yes!

Beyond Graeme's predilection toward the company of fine women, which was much like his own, there was nothing that would not recommend him to Emma, something that filled Garrick with an uncomfortable feeling of jealousy. And yet he could not lie.

"Nay, she is not. I travel to Linkirk to secure my own betrothal."

Graeme's eyes widened. "Your own?"

He ground his teeth, wanting the conversation to end. Quickly. "Aye."

"Your mother." Graeme knew the situation well.

"She has arranged it, aye. The Earl of Magnus's daughter."

Graeme whistled, and it took every ounce of fortitude Garrick possessed not to roll his eyes.

"Do you think such a match necessary?"

Garrick shook his head. "Nay, but my mother believes so. Inverglen had become difficult to control in my absence."

His uncle, the Baron of Inverglen, hated Garrick for the same reason he'd hated his father. They were both English.

"Foolish bastard. The title was never his. *Could* never be his."

There was one way. "Without my mother. Without me?"

Graeme narrowed his eyes. "Do you think he means to—"

"Nay. If I thought he'd risk my mother, do you think she'd be alone in Scotland?"

"Garrick, by God, if that man so much as gives your mother an untoward look . . ."

This was what he'd liked about the Scottish chief from their very first meeting. He took his sworn loyalty as seriously as any man. It mattered not to Graeme de Sowlis that an Englishman had inherited the title of Earl of Linkirk. An ally in the true sense of the word, the man would no doubt go to war on his behalf. Which, luckily, his betrothal to Magnus's daughter would avoid.

"To alliances," Garrick said, holding up his cup.

"New," Graeme said. "And old."

That was exactly what worried him.

Emma attempted to slow her pace as she barreled down the corridor in Graeme de Sowlis's home. For as long as she could remember, she'd been told that she walked too fast, spoke too fast, though none of it was said with malice. Her brothers merely liked to tease her; Emma's parents, God rest their souls, had hoped to school her; and Aunt Lettie and Uncle Simon, well, they'd long ago given up on changing her ways. They'd said so in the kindest way possible, of course. She loved her family, and was eternally grateful to have their love in return.

But none of them quite understood her.

Emma wanted to live. Every moment. Every day. Each night she lay in her bed and imagined how she could eke out a bit more joy the next day—for one thing her parents' early death had taught her was that there may not be a next day. Before she'd gone to the market on that fateful day, her mother had kissed her cheek and said, "Until later, my love."

Later had never come. Which was why she was so unwilling to wait for anything. To follow anyone. She slowed her pace a bit, but not *too* much, until she came to a corridor with two possible routes. Perhaps it had been foolish to send the maid ahead, whether she liked to do for herself or not.

"I can find my way," she'd said stubbornly. Clearly, she'd spoken without thinking, as usual.

Now was it this way? Or that?

"To your right, my lady."

Emma didn't turn around. She'd recognize that voice anywhere. Instead, she focused on the flickering of the wall torch that lit the path before her. He was directly behind her now, his presence a tangible warmth behind her.

She peered around her shoulder then. "My thanks, Lord Clave."

"Garrick."

Emma picked up her skirts once again. She'd only taken two additional gowns. This one, a bright crimson with a straight neckline just slightly lower than the others, was one of her favorites. Whenever she wore it, Emma felt pretty. She felt like a woman and not a girl. Sara, bless her, had commissioned it to match a similar one of hers that Emma had always admired.

"Of course," she said, beginning to turn around until he stopped her with a hand on her sleeve. Even through the thick layer of material, Emma could feel the warmth of his touch. Or maybe she was simply imagining it.

"May I have a word first?"

When she turned fully around to face him, his hand dropped. He looked as regal as he had that first night in their hall. Every bit an earl. Including . . .

"You shaved," she blurted.

When he smiled, Garrick's eyes crinkled ever so slightly at the corners.

"I did."

She'd liked that bit of hair on his face. It had made him look a bit less polished. More approachable.

"Forgive my impertinence," he started.

Emma's breath quickened. She didn't want him to kiss her.

Yes, you do.

"Are you spoken for, Lady Emma?"

"Nay, I am not," she managed to say.

He didn't look happy about that. Which made no sense. Why would he—

"Graeme de Sowlis," he said, still frowning.

Emma didn't understand. "What of our host?"

"He inquired about you."

Garrick's gaze was so intent that it took a moment for his words to sink in. Graeme de Sowlis? Was he asking for Graeme?

Oh, what a fool I am. Well, good. Garrick was the exact type of man she most assuredly did not wish to marry. She had no use for an earl twice over, a man who was powerful in two countries. No doubt he'd expect to control her and aught she did.

"I see."

And she did. She must have mistaken the look in his eyes the previous day. Emma had very little experience with men, save two kisses. One had been with the only suitor she'd seriously considered. That flirtation had ended the moment the gentleman had spied Sara in her women's breeches one day while visiting

Kenshire. The look of utter horror on his face had advised her more surely than anything he could say or do that he was *not* the man for her. By her request, it had been the last she'd seen of him.

"But I don't believe . . . that is . . . I promised Sara and your brother to protect you—"

So he did not want her, but neither did he want her with Graeme. It was not his words but his tone that told her as much. Bryce often used that exact same tone, and it was always intended as a warning.

Well, Emma had never been the type to heed warnings.

"Thank you for your concern, *Garrick*."

She spun around, intending to show the earl exactly what she thought of his "protection," but he reached out to stop her. This time, he forced her to face him again.

"Emma, I didn't mean—"

He pulled her toward him so quickly that Emma only realized what he was about when his lips touched her own. They were so soft but firm. He released his grip, allowing her to pull away, which she did not.

Heat shot through her like a leather horsewhip. It came from nowhere but consumed everything, its effects utterly unavoidable.

When he touched his tongue to her closed lips, Emma didn't know what he wanted. She opened her mouth just a bit, intending to ask, and his tongue swept into her mouth.

Something deep inside her knew what to do, and she touched her tongue to his.

She was lost—even more so when he abruptly pulled away.

"I'm so sorry," he said.

She stared at the tip of his tongue when he licked his lower lip. Sorry? She certainly was not.

"I don't understand, Garrick."

"I should not have done that. Will you accept my apology? That was inexcusable."

"A stolen kiss—"

68

"I made a promise. More than one, in fact. Emma . . ."

"Fine. I accept. But I don't understand—"

"That way." He nodded to the corridor on her right. "We're likely to be missed . . ."

When it was evident he wasn't going to say anything more, Emma turned away and continued through the passageway. What the devil was that?

Graeme de Sowlis has shown an interest in you.

He could have just as easily said *allow me to melt your insides first before we join our host for supper.*

Their corridor spilled directly into the hall. As Garrick had predicted, the evening meal was well underway. Their host stood at the other end of the room, alone on the raised dais. Perhaps two dozen or so men sat scattered throughout the room. Just a few ladies, likely the wives of the clansmen who served the chief.

The chief stepped down and walked over to her, taking her hand in his and leading her to the dais. She snuck a glance at him as they walked. Handsome, no doubt. He looked to be about the same age as Garrick, nine and twenty or so. Young, for a chief. And an earl. But if the man had taken a special interest in her, Emma couldn't sense it. Though his courteous manner was what she'd expect for a man of his station, he seemed to look at her as he would any guest. Garrick must have been mistaken.

When they sat, she glanced around the hall, Garrick on Graeme's other side.

"It looks much the same as Kenshire's hall," she said.

"Not so grand as that, my lady," Graeme said.

Though they were but a day's ride from the border, she'd already sensed the suspicion of those around her. Such trepidation was to be expected. It was much the same in England, although less so at Kenshire. Being intermarried to a Scottish family had a way of tempering the usual contempt between the English and the Scots.

She took a sip of the soup, which was a fine barley, one of her favorites.

"I met your brother, once."

Emma couldn't help but smile even though the memory was anything but amusing. "Aye, when he and Toren Kerr attempted to lop off each other's heads. I heard about that meeting."

As an ally to Clan Kerr, Graeme de Sowlis had been there for the fight between her brother and Toren, the man he'd considered his greatest enemy. Luckily, Catrina had put a premature stop to the fight. Otherwise it would have ended with one of them dead.

Emma suddenly remembered something Catrina had once told her.

"You and Lady Catrina . . ." She snapped her mouth shut before realizing she'd crossed a line. Leaning forward just slightly to catch a glimpse of Garrick, she immediately wished she hadn't. The look he gave her was anything but encouraging.

She focused on their host instead.

"I am so sorry if I've caused offense—"

"Nay, apologies are unnecessary. Catrina and I were very good friends."

"Were?"

"Are good friends," he said. "I've met your brother since that day."

She looked up in surprise as the soup was cleared and trenches of roasted duck were placed in front of them.

"Just a few weeks past, in fact. As neighbors, your brother and I have much to discuss with attacks seemingly on the rise. After spending two nights at Bristol, I can see why Catrina married him."

"You can?"

She supposed it was uncharitable of her to sound so surprised. After all, *she* loved her brother. And, unaccountably, Catrina did as well. But his disposition was typically not so easily understood by strangers, and there was no denying that his clash with the Kerrs had very nearly led to someone's death.

"He is quite intelligent," Sowlis said. "And very loyal to Catrina. I'm happy for them both."

Emma did not detect the slightest hint of untruth or malice in his statement. Indeed, he seemed quite sincere. How could a man who was once betrothed, or at least nearly betrothed, to a woman be so casual about her decision to marry another? What an extraordinary man Graeme was!

Blast it. She'd accidentally looked at Garrick again. He looked decidedly unhappy. Emma leaned back and tried to forget the feel of his hand on her arm, to forget the sensation of his lips parting her own with . . .

"My lady, more wine?"

"Aye," she said to the cupbearer.

"Sir, beggin' your pardon, but the mistress asks if you can see her after the meal."

"Is it about our visitor?"

"Aye—"

"Pardon me." Graeme pushed the solid wood chair away from him and stood. "My grandmother twisted her ankle and is unable to join us. And we're expecting visitors she's most anxious about. I'll be but a moment."

He bowed, leaving Emma to gape at his back as he walked away. Although the main dish had been cleared, it was still extremely unusual for a host to leave during the meal. But then, if his grandmother was ill . . .

He was looking at her. She could sense his gaze, and when she turned to confirm that Garrick was indeed watching her, a flush crept up her neck.

"My lord," she said, quite politely.

"Emma."

Could he see her flush? Did he even know he was doing this to her? Did he bite his lip only when he was deep in thought? Annoyed? She couldn't guess his mood.

Well, she wished he would stop. Every time he looked at her with that intent, focused gaze, she forgot to breathe. It was quite disconcerting. And she could dispense with the use of her given name as well. It sounded so intimate when he said it.

"Why did you do it?" If she'd learned anything from Sara, it was to speak what she was thinking.

Garrick's eyes narrowed. "He is my king."

"Pardon?"

"I would have preferred to stay in England, but—"

"Nay, why did you—"

"Agree to escort you? Truth be told, I owed a debt to Lady Sara."

Warmth flooded her, though she told herself it was only from the wine. "Garrick, you know what I—"

"Because I've thought of nothing else since the moment you stood up from tending Nella, your gown sprinkled with hay. No cloak. Nothing to recommend you against the cold. Just you."

He remembered Nella's name, a silly thought that spread another wave of warmth through her.

She should not have spoken so bluntly.

"It was wrong, Emma. Stupid. I should tell you—" He looked up as their host approached.

"So serious, Clave. Is all well here?"

Graeme looked from her to Garrick and back. Emma tried to smile but wasn't sure if she quite managed it.

"Splendid," Garrick said as their host once again sat between them.

"Smile, Englishman. You're about to be wed to a Scottish lass. A lucky man indeed."

He said it so casually that it took Emma a moment to register the words. And then another moment to recover.

Garrick had come to Scotland to be wed?

Her vision blurred, the men and women before them combining into one large mass of people. She stared straight ahead, knowing that both Graeme and Garrick would know what she was thinking if she looked to her left. They'd know that she cared. She shouldn't. Garrick was not the man for her. He could marry whomever he pleased. Really, perhaps this was for the best. But none of those thoughts prevented her from turning her head away.

And then she remembered the kiss. The blasted man had actually dared to kiss her, knowing he was to be wed to another. She did turn to look at him then.

Garrick was speaking to Graeme, but wasn't looking at his host.

He was staring directly at her. Watching. Waiting for her reaction? Her eyes narrowed and told him exactly what she thought of the news.

Married.

The devil take him. And his Scottish lass too.

CHAPTER NINE

*G*oddamn Scot.

Though he was angry with Graeme, he had only himself to blame. He'd been about to tell her about the betrothal last eve, but their host had rejoined them at a most inopportune time and shared the news for him.

They'd arrived at Dunmure at midday, and though his men were anxious to keep moving, he'd refused to leave without speaking to her again. He'd summoned her to Dunmure's solar for a private conversation. He knew he owed her an explanation, but the words eluded him. What in hades had he been thinking in that hallway? Garrick was not in the habit of seducing innocents, and Emma certainly qualified as innocent. The only coherent thought he remembered having was that *he* wanted to be the one to teach her. To hold her. To claim her as his own.

Garrick's father had been everything to him, and the great man's nobility and loyalty had always motivated him. Upon his death, Garrick had vowed to put an end to his impulsiveness—the rash actions that had gotten him into trouble in the past. That very quality had driven him to join Edward's cause . . . and to convince his father to do the same. The guilt of that was a constant weight, made even heavier by the knowledge that his mother had tried to convince him of his folly. Now he was failing his parents again.

"You wanted to see me?"

He spun around, light streaming in through a shuttered window in Dunmure's solar. As lovely as ever, Emma stood before him in a new pale-yellow gown, its sunny color a stark contrast with her dark hair.

Last eve, Emma had retired early from dinner. He'd briefly considered going to her chamber, which was, after all, directly next to his own. But he'd just as quickly dismissed the idea. Nothing good would come of such an impropriety. Instead, he'd lain awake until the fire had completely died out in the hearth, thinking of his father and mother. Of his impending marriage. And, most of all, of her.

He'd risen before dawn, spent some time in the training yard before sunrise, and arrived at the morning meal to find Emma's seat from the evening before empty. Graeme had implored him to return on their way back to England. So he could court Emma? He'd noticed the way the man had looked at her.

Hell, who could blame him? Emma demanded attention everywhere she went, and rightly so. His men were enamored. And not just because of her beauty. The lady had a way of brightening a room with her very presence. Something about her seemed to beg those around her to *live* just a bit more, although she seemed wholly unaware of her effect on everyone.

"I'm surprised you came," he said quietly. "There is the matter of our return trip to discuss. I will send word, of course. In two weeks, perhaps?"

She folded her hands in front of her. "Very well, my lord."

She'd reverted from "Garrick" to "my lord" since Sowlis had blurted out the true purpose for his voyage to Scotland.

"I did not attempt to hide it from you," he said. Which was

true, even though he *had* hidden it from her. "I am to be betrothed. Not married."

She looked at the bare stone walls rather than at him. Emma was angry.

"As I said, I should not have kissed you. It was—"

"Would you at least care to explain why you did so knowing you are about to be married—pardon . . . betrothed—any day?"

She spoke so evenly that Garrick could only guess at her mood.

There was no other recourse than honesty.

"'Tis my mother's wish for me to marry. My uncle resents that an English lord inherited the earldom through her, even though the title is hers, was my father's, by right. She believes a match with Magnus's daughter will secure my claim. He's a powerful border lord that none, not even my uncle, will challenge."

"And the kiss?"

"Was a mistake."

"I see."

But she didn't. Not really. Her doubt was written across her face.

He remained silent, watching her expression turn from anger to resignation.

"Very well."

"Nay, Emma. It's not," he said in frustration.

She clearly didn't understand. Hell, how could she possibly understand when he made no sense, not even to himself?

"I kissed you because I wanted to." Just as he wanted to right now. That and so much more. "Why are you not married?"

"Pardon?"

"Why are you not married?" he repeated. "You are the sister of an earl. The most desirable woman I've ever met. Just last night you had a great Scottish clan chief clamoring for your attention. And I am sure he has not been the only one. Why?"

He didn't think she'd answer. Nor did Garrick know why he'd

asked. But she surprised him, this woman, just as she did nearly every time they were together.

"I would love nothing more than to have my own household to run. To have this"—she motioned around them—"and make my own decisions for once. But I haven't found the man who will allow it. Great clan chiefs. Mighty border lords." She made a decidedly unladylike sound. "Powerful earls"—she shrugged—"do not interest me. You are all too enamored with your own ideas to care for someone else's."

Her meaning was clear. If a match between them were possible, she'd not have him anyway.

Which was just as well. The question was a foolish one.

Garrick bowed, as anxious as his men to leave Dunmure Tower for Linkirk. "I understand. Good day, Lady Emma."

Though his feet felt as if they were made of the same molten iron that forged the sword at his side, Garrick walked out of the solar. Away from Emma.

And toward his future.

Emma sat on a bench in an alcove inside Dunmure Castle and tried not to watch him leave. Her reunion with Clara was everything she had hoped. Now, of course, it was time for her escort to move on.

Betrothed. Married. It mattered not. They were practically one and the same.

"Emma, I can't wait to . . . Emma." Her friend rushed over to sit next to her. "What's wrong?"

Clara's face was slightly rounded, and her mid-section showed signs of her pregnancy. The lady of Dunmure radiated happiness. Her brown hair, once as short as a lad's, now hung about her shoulders, and her light brown eyes sparkled.

"Oh Clara, 'tis so good to see you."

She wrapped her arms around her friend, and they sat there just so until Emma finally pulled away.

"I'm fine. May I?" She nodded to her belly.

"Of course," Clara beamed.

Emma laid her hand on the slight swell of Clara's stomach, but she could feel nothing other than the soft velvet of her friend's gown. She'd laid her hand like this countless times on Sara's stomach when she was with babe, and her little Hayden had eventually begun to move.

"Just wait until he or she begins to protest in there," Emma said with a grin.

Clara's eyes widened. "You can't feel it? My wee one is moving right now."

Emma pressed her hand a bit harder but couldn't feel any movements. "Nay, nothing." She took her hand away "Now you must tell me everything about Dunmure. And Alex. And the babe. I want to know it all. How do you like Scotland? Do the people treat you well? If they don't just because you're English—"

"Emma, you haven't changed a bit." Clara repositioned herself on the bench. "And we've weeks together. Your escort said at least two. But first"—she cocked her head—"you *will* tell me what's wrong."

While Emma loved Sara like a sister, she'd known right from the beginning that her friendship with Clara would be different. She could, and would, tell Clara anything.

"Garrick."

"The earl who brought you here?"

"Nay, the other Garrick. Of course the one who—"

"Stop." Clara laughed. "He is quite handsome. Very . . . earl-like."

"Earl-like?" She knew what Clara was trying to say and couldn't resist laughing at her description.

"Alex told me of him when we learned he was to escort you

here. You know Linkirk is an ally to Clan Kerr. 'Tis only one day's ride from here."

"Aye, I know."

"So . . ."

"So . . ." She might as well be out with it. "He kissed me."

"He what?" Clara scrunched up her face. "But he is to be wed to—"

"Precisely."

Clara's eyes widened. "Oh dear. Emma, please tell me that is all he did."

Emma couldn't resist a bit of teasing. "Or what? You'll be forced to toss my sheets with virgin's blood on them into the fire?"

They both looked toward the hall not far away from where they sat in the stone corridor. The cushioned seat overlooked Dunmure's courtyard, the precious glass window a rare delight.

Bursting into laugher, they both spoke at once.

"I can't believe you did that."

"I'm glad I was there that morning." Emma continued, "You . . . Sara . . . Catrina. Do any of the women in our family do things in the conventional way?"

"By conventional, if you mean marriage *before* the marriage bed, nay, I don't believe so. Although"—Clara turned serious—"I don't recommend as much for you. Especially if . . ."

"You've no worries there. As you said, he is to be married."

"Into a family as powerful as any here along the border."

"Aye."

"And an alliance that will end the Baron of Inverglen's mad claims to Clave's earldom here in Scotland."

She should not be surprised Clara knew of such things. Her friend, who had spent years running from possible political revenge in England, was very much involved in the politics of her clan and the happenings at the border.

"So I've heard," Emma said.

Clara took her hand and squeezed it. "Then you know without it, Clave's uncle will almost certainly gain enough support to start a clan war. One he will not likely win. But a war nonetheless."

"I suppose I didn't know that."

"Emma, look at me." If her friend was attempting to make her feel better, it wasn't working.

"When Clave's father died, his uncle wasted no time in attempting to take back the earldom. All know it. His mother came to Scotland to protect her son's rights. And if there *is* a war, we will be forced to take sides. Clan Kerr can no longer remain neutral. Not with our alliance to Kenshire and the Waryns."

"I understand," Emma said.

"So if you are upset about losing the Earl of Clave to Lady Alison, then we shall find you another reason to be sad. Or, even better, one to be happy."

Lady Alison.

Forget about Lady Alison. And, more to the point, forget about Lord Clave.

"You know how I feel about men like that," Emma said, forcing a glib expression. "I've taken too many orders from my brothers to spend the rest of my life taking more."

"Aye, but—"

"So he kissed me. And perhaps I wanted him to. But it matters not."

"Good."

"Lady Alison can have him."

"Aye, and all his earlishness with it," Clara said.

Emma pushed away thoughts about that, that perfect, knee-melting kiss, and hugged her friend again. "'Tis good to see you Clara. I feared my brother would never allow me to leave before spring."

"And you, Emma. Now let's go see what trouble we can muster."

CHAPTER TEN

*T*wo weeks and a day after she'd arrived at Dunmure, Clara and Emma sat in the same alcove as they had on the first day. Two weeks of sharing and laughter that Emma would cherish always.

"Everything is ready for him."

Emma looked up, wishing Clara could come with her. "I'll miss you desperately."

"Can you imagine? The next time we meet, I'll have a wee one for you to greet."

"Oh, no you will not. I will return before she's due to arrive."

"Emma, 'tis not an easy journey. There's no need—"

"That's quite enough. I'll decide whether there's a need."

The door creaked open. "He's here."

Emma looked at Alex, a man just as tall as Garrick but with shorter, lighter hair. Though he would no doubt make for a fearsome enemy, the Scots warrior had only smiles for his friends. He'd been nothing but kind to her on her extended visit. Emma had always liked Alex. Perhaps because she'd sensed from the start how much he cared for Clara, although the course of their relationship had been complicated by Clara's disguise. She'd pretended to be a lad, a squire, for years to escape possible retribution for the role her father had played in the revolution against the king. Finally, Alex's love and her friends' encouragement had allowed her to live as herself, unafraid and proud.

From observing the two together, Emma knew Alex was as charmed by Clara's quirks as she was. He plotted with their cook to make at least one of her favorites at every meal, not a difficult feat as she had many of them.

"I'm so happy for you," she said to neither of them in particular.

By now, Alex knew of her "indiscretion," and he had not hesitated to offer his opinion, which was—unsurprisingly—much the same as Clara's. Luckily, she'd nearly gotten that kiss out of her mind. Instead of thinking about it every waking minute, she only did so when other thoughts didn't occupy her.

Well, it was a start.

But she didn't look forward to their return journey, especially since Edith had sent word that she'd be returning to Kenshire instead. The short rest at the inn had not been enough to hearten her for the journey. Emma was surprised her brother hadn't made an appearance at Dunmure. He would not be pleased to think of her traveling alone with the earl.

But it hardly mattered. Garrick was now a betrothed man.

She stood with such force the bench would have likely toppled if it weren't for Clara still sitting on it. "I'm ready," she announced.

If she had to leave Dunmure, she would do it on her terms. Which she would inform the earl about as soon as possible. They would not be alone together during their journey for any reason. She would eat with his men, and not alone like a woman accused of witchcraft. After their return to Kenshire, there would never be any need for her to see him again.

"Emma, what are you planning?"

"Planning?" She pulled Clara up to join her. "Whatever do you mean?"

"Alex . . ."

"Aye, wife?"

He pulled Clara to him by the hand, and the happy couple looked at Emma as if she were about to do something foolish. Just the opposite, in fact.

"Lady Emma," Alex said in the exact same tone her brothers used when they intended to order her about.

"Alex Kerr," she countered. "I am a grown woman who is well aware that Garrick Clave is neither available nor desirable. As such, you've nothing to fear."

All three of them turned to the open door when a loud cough announced the presence of the very man Emma had spent two weeks trying to forget.

Sod it, as Catrina would say.

"My ladies," Garrick said. "Pardon the intrusion, but I was told I could find you here."

Clara and Alex began talking at once, but Emma simply stood there, attempting to breathe normally—or at least pretending that she could. He was much more handsome than she remembered.

Emma managed to gather herself enough to follow Garrick and Clara out of the room.

Alex, who'd hung back, whispered to her, "I know that look, Emma."

She made a face. "Of course you do," she shot back. "'Tis the same look you gave Clara, and she gave you in return, when you thought no one was looking at Kenshire. And though I can't very well see my own expression, I'd imagine 'tis very much at odds with my insistence that Garrick means no more to me than the stones beneath our feet."

Mayhap it was due to Alex and Clara's strong bond, but Emma found it easy to confide in him. Talking with Alex was just as comfortable as talking with her brothers. Nay, more so, for he was not quite as protective of her.

"Emma, stop."

She did, allowing the earl to be led away by her friend.

"I've been thinking about Sowlis."

"You and Clara seem to think an awful lot about him. 'Tis something you have in—"

"Marry him."

"What?"

She would not have been more surprised if Alex had dropped a war hammer on her toes.

"He is a good man. I've known him for years."

"Aye, because your sister was to wed him. And everyone seems to forget the man didn't exactly—"

"He and Catrina were friends. Toren refused the match because he's a stubborn arse. But it's a good thing he did. Both he and my sister will now admit they were never truly in love. They were merely accustomed to the idea of their match. And Graeme . . ." He looked toward the hall and then back at her. "A more honorable man does not exist. He might be pressured to marry a Scottish lass, but—"

"Alex, this is madness."

"Nay, it is not. I know you want independence. And that no potential husband compares to your brothers—"

"My brothers?"

"'Tis why you've denied so many, is it not?"

"Alex Kerr—"

"I don't blame you. Though I despised them once, I do not any longer. Just the opposite, in fact. But Garrick Clave is not for you. And if there's any truth to what he says about Graeme—"

"He was just warning me away."

"And he did so for a reason. If there is interest there, Graeme is powerful enough not to need permission. Clan Scott will accept you. It's a good match, one your brothers will condone. Think on it. Spend some time with him to see if you will suit."

Think on it. Marrying a clan chief, moving to Scotland . . . "I could see Clara often."

"Aye, you could."

Emma shook her head. "Alex, I must go." She smiled, grateful for his concern even though she'd not heed his advice. "Thank you."

"I care about you, Emma. Enough to have had an interesting discussion with your protector. I believe he—"

Alex stopped since they'd arrived in the great hall, where Garrick stood waiting with Clara.

She took a step toward him and stopped when her legs wobbled.

"Everything is ready, my lady," he said, indicating they should leave. Now.

Earlish. Very much so.

Trying not to notice the perfect contours of his face, Emma went to Clara and wrapped her arms around her dear friend.

"I love you," Clara said. "Take care, little sister."

Though her friend was just a few months her elder, the endearment had stuck.

"Love you back," she said.

Clara leaned in to whisper in Emma's ear. "He *is* quite cute."

Leave it to her friend to offer that truth even when it was impossibly useless.

"Aye, he is," she whispered back.

She pretended not to see him as she strode over to Alex, gave him a kiss on the cheek, and then marched out into the cold. So grand was her exit that it took a moment for her to realize she'd forgotten—

"Your cloak?"

Garrick came up from behind her with the offending garment in hand. She'd intended to mount and ride all day without speaking a word to him.

Blast it.

She lifted her chin and tried really, really hard not to notice the scent of pine as he reached around her and, not for the first time, covered her against the cold.

"It seems I've made a habit of this."

She would not speak to him. She would not speak to him.

Emma finally looked him in the eyes.

Oh God . . .

"So you're betrothed, then?"

He finally buckled the clasp and took a step back. Thank heavens. Now if only she could take back her words. She was supposed to act like she did not care.

Emma's stomach lurched at his expression before he even answered.

"I am."

She turned away, but not before he saw the look of deep disappointment on her face. A look *he* had put there. He watched as she mounted and joined his men, riding away from Dunmure. He eventually did so himself, taking the lead, and ignoring the flakes that had just begun to fall. Another blustery January day.

Aye, I am betrothed.

Garrick had been greeted at Linkirk by his mother. Still quite beautiful despite her age, she looked no worse off for the tragedy she'd endured. The only difference he could see was a few gray hairs replacing some of the brown ones. She said not a word, their shared grief palpable in the empty hall of her childhood home. Linkirk Castle stood as tall and proud as any along the Scottish border. Not as sprawling as Kenshire, but with enough buildings, including a centuries-old keep, to make it one of the borderland's greatest treasures.

"I'm glad you've come," she said, walking through the lower corridors at Linkirk, the sadness in her voice pinching at Garrick's chest.

"Of course, Mother. Where else would I be?"

Indeed, where else but in England, where he belonged? He'd often wished growing up his mother would be content at Clave, but Scotland had always sung to her. A song as lilting and lovely as any, she'd often said. He'd visited often enough, at least once or twice each year, but its steward was truly the lord here. Linkirk's battle scars gave testament to its vulnerabilities. There were no tides to protect it, and it was closer to the border than Clave. But despite the dangers, this was home, his mother often said.

Either way, it belonged to him as surely as Clave did.

"Have you seen Uncle?"

"Nay, nor my sister. They dare not show their faces here after the blasphemies they've been spouting."

"Tell me."

And she did. The moment she learned of her husband's death, Lady Joan had traveled to Linkirk. The whispers began within a week. Inverglen wanted Linkirk for his own. It should never have gone to the English earl, he said to anyone who would listen, and certainly he and his wife had a better claim to it than the English boy who already had an earldom. The refrain surprised no one now that Garrick's father was dead.

"You've made arrangements?"

Lady Joan nodded. "Her father should be arriving any time. The betrothal has already been negotiated. Much of this is a formality. Your uncle will not dare to continue his absurd claim once Magnus's daughter is family."

So it was done.

He was to marry a woman he'd never met. A woman he wouldn't meet before the wedding.

Lady Alison's influential father, the Earl of Magnus, had arrived the next day with a retinue of men three times larger than the one Garrick had brought from England. A show of force, though Garrick wasn't sure why such a thing was necessary.

It became clear after he spent some time with the man.

Mean. Unrelenting. Powerful. Garrick had interacted with plenty of men like Magnus. Men who felt an unrelenting need to display their wealth and power. He'd fought for one of them in the Holy Land, and there was none more powerful than King Edward —save his father, the King of England.

Garrick had been home just a few weeks before coming to Scotland, and his only stipulation was that the wedding be delayed until the following month. The earl wasn't pleased, but he'd agreed to give Garrick time to get his affairs in order.

"Garrick, we cannot afford a delay," his mother had said to him later that day, pulling him into the solar for a private conversation.

"A betrothal is as binding as a marriage. It matters not."

He'd told himself the delay was necessary. He needed time to acclimate. To become the Earl of Clave and of Linkirk in truth.

But is that the real reason?

The thought had plagued him so much, he'd nearly sent a message to Magnus to recant. But the very idea was preposterous. And unnecessary. As he'd said to his mother, the betrothal was just as binding as a marriage. Breaking such an agreement with a man like Magnus would mean war.

Then he saw *her* again, and his question was answered immediately.

Nay, it was because of her.

He'd made the betrothal agreement to secure his mother's inheritance. Signed his name to the papers to make it official. And yet, he'd found himself setting a furious pace to Dunmure this morning. His men must have thought him crazed.

I am a grown woman who is well aware that Garrick Clave is neither available nor desirable. As such, you've nothing to fear.

He had not meant to overhear their conversation.

Neither available nor desirable.

He was not available. But if Emma thought to convince herself she didn't desire him, she was doing a poor job of it. Garrick knew women nearly as well as he knew his way around a training yard. And every sign told him the feeling was mutual.

"Shall we stop, my lord?"

Garrick, deep in his own thoughts, hadn't realized they'd already ridden for several hours. "If the lady requires it."

At sunset, they would likely have to accept Graeme de Sowlis's invitation. As much as he despised the idea of bringing her back there, Emma's warmth and security needed to be his priority.

He stopped and waited, getting only a glimpse of her long cloak between his men. When they continued to ride rather than stopping, Garrick wasn't surprised. Not only was Emma skilled at horseback riding, she was tough. Most other women would have begged for a reprieve by now. But Emma stayed with them regardless of the weather or terrain.

They pushed hard and were rewarded for their efforts. They arrived at Clan Scott's land well before dusk, and Garrick sent word ahead to the chief.

This time, their host stood waiting for them in front of the doors of the great keep.

The chief looked behind Garrick as they approached.

He looked at *Emma*.

"Come, hurry inside," Graeme said. "You must be freezing." He clasped Garrick's arm in greeting and leaned in to add, "Get inside quickly."

The alarm in his voice evident, Garrick looked at him more closely. The man was worried about something. "What is it?"

"Rumors only. We'll speak on it later."

Since they were clearly secure this deep behind Graeme's defenses, Garrick could not imagine why the chief appeared so anxious.

He tried, and failed, not to look behind him at the men. Or, more precisely, at Emma.

He watched as she joined them at the door, sparing him not a glance. Graeme greeted her as prettily as a man who was courting a lady. Truth be told, an alliance between Waryn and Sowlis made too much sense for his liking.

Garrick allowed himself to be led to the same bedchamber he'd occupied on the way to Dunmure. Having no desire to witness Graeme and Emma together, he instructed the hand-maiden that he'd take the evening meal in his room. Garrick wasn't surprised when the chief himself knocked at his door not long afterward.

"You'll not join us for the meal?"

"Nay, I will not." Garrick wasn't feeling as gracious as he should toward their host. It wasn't Graeme's fault that he was in this hopeless, unhappy situation.

The other man looked at him a bit strangely, but he didn't comment. He entered the room despite Garrick's failure to invite him in.

"There've been rumors of a raiding party for the past two days," he said, closing the door behind him.

"You've scouted for them, I assume?"

"Aye, of course. The scouts found nothing untoward. But I'd like to send additional men with you, at least until you cross the border."

"If you feel it's necessary, I will of course accept them."

"You'll take extra caution with Lady Emma."

He resisted balling his hands into fists. "Of course."

"I trust your visit to Linkirk was productive? How is your mother?"

"As one would expect of a woman recently widowed."

"And your future wife?"

"She did not make the journey."

Graeme raised his brows. "Poor Garrick. If it's any consolation, I hear Magnus's daughter is much prettier than he."

"Ah, well then I look forward to our wedding," he said.

Graeme laughed like a man who was not being forced into

marriage. "You'll not reconsider?" he finally asked. "'Tis a sure agreement?"

"As long as your intentions toward Lady Emma are honorable."

Graeme's jaw clenched, but Garrick didn't care if he'd gone too far. Her safety was more important than his host's sensibilities.

"That you ask is an insult."

"You've noticed her extraordinary beauty." It wasn't a question.

"I have eyes, Clave."

"And she is unwed."

"My clan would not be pleased."

"But they would support you."

"You already have your answer." Graeme smirked as if he didn't suspect Garrick's feelings for her.

Again, Garrick's jaw clenched. His instincts had been correct. Which was the reason he should join them this evening to ensure the chief's behavior was beyond reproach. But the thought of watching a courtship between the two sickened him.

"Aye," he choked out.

With that, Graeme patted him on the back and left the chamber.

Another knock just moments later announced a serving girl carrying a wooden tray laden with food and drink. He took it, offered his thanks, and promptly began to drink.

Pacing the room, he ignored the food and reconsidered his position. He should go down there. He needed to ensure her safety.

Emma is as safe with Graeme de Sowlis as she is with any man.

Then he should ensure . . . what? That they weren't making plans to wed even now? As if he had any right to stop such a thing. He himself would be wed before long.

Garrick tore off his mantle and surcoat, all but the cream linen undershirt, and continued to pace back and forth. He had to get out of this chamber. And go where? Darkness had fallen. All of the castle's inhabitants would be at the meal.

The last time he'd felt this cornered, Garrick and four of his men had been cut off from Edward's forces. Alone, they'd faced a relentless attack on all sides.

Garrick's father had been killed three days earlier, and guilt and grief had turned him into someone he was not. Whereas he was usually a controlled fighter who relied on his training for victory, he'd acted the part of a savage that day, exactly what their royals had accused the Saracens of being. Except he had never been convinced the enemy deserved that epithet.

Later, he had heard one of the other survivors tell the story to the men who'd rescued them. To hear him tell it, Garrick alone had killed nearly all of their attackers. That he could not remember any such thing scared him still.

He replaced the goblet on the tray, his hands shaking with the memory of that day.

When someone knocked on the door moments later, Garrick pulled the heavy wood toward him forcefully, swinging it open as if it were a piece of parchment.

Garrick opened his mouth to send the intruder away, but the words never left his lips.

Emma.

CHAPTER ELEVEN

*W*ell, if she was going to do it, she might as well do it right.

Emma had just returned from the evening meal with their kind, gracious host. They'd spoken of her visit at Dunmure and Graeme's history with Clan Kerr. The chief had only fond words about Catrina, which made her think that perhaps Alex had the right of it—the pair had never been a love match.

Graeme de Sowlis was an easy man to speak with, and she found herself laughing at his tales of past antics, some of which rivaled some of her own.

Aside from not being English, he was the perfect potential suitor for her, someone about whom her brothers would surely have no complaint. If she was protected, they were happy. It was a refrain she'd heard from Geoffrey on more than one occasion. But Emma wanted more than just protection. More even than easy companionship and shared humor.

Emma relaxed when she realized Garrick wasn't coming. But as the evening wore on, she began to feel badly about her treatment of him. Aside from that kiss, which he'd apologized for on more than one occasion, he'd acted honorably in the face of . . .

well, if she were being honest, her animosity. He owed her nothing.

Though Sowlis had nothing but kind words for the earl and his family, he'd given her escort nothing but scowls. Something told her that she was the reason. Did he sense that Emma forgot to breathe every time the earl ventured into the room?

It couldn't possibly be Garrick's fault that the very power and confidence she claimed not to want in a husband nonetheless attracted her like a blacksmith to molten iron. Mayhap she should apologize to the man. Of course, this was neither the time nor the place for such a gesture. She could, and should, wait until the morning. But patience had never been a favored virtue of hers. So before she thought too long on it, Emma stopped at his door instead of her own. She knocked on the door and stared at the iron pattern of lines crisscrossing it, which made it appear more ornamental than practical.

It swung open so fast she hardly had time to prepare her greeting.

She swallowed. This had been a bad idea.

His face was no longer cleanly shaved. Eyes flashing, he opened his mouth to speak, but nothing came out. He looked half-wild. White hot desire pooled inside her, threatening to suffocate her. Emma couldn't speak even if she'd remembered what to say.

"Lady Emma."

His voice, low and seductive, beckoned her inside, despite everything.

"I'm sorry." She'd finally remembered her intention.

"Sorry?"

"For avoiding you. For acting so foolishly to someone who only meant to help me."

His hand lay high on the door, propping it open. Her gaze fell to the opening in his shirt, but she immediately caught herself and looked back up to his face.

"You've been avoiding me?" he asked. She knew by his hint of a smile that he teased her.

"Mayhap a bit." She'd said she was sorry, which was all she'd really come here to say. It was time to leave. But why didn't her feet listen?

"Why?" If anyone ever accused her of being overly direct, she'd point them in the earl's direction.

"Because . . ." How precisely should she answer that?

"Because I am neither available nor desirable?"

Oh God . . . he *had* heard them. Every last lying word.

"No. I mean, aye. What I mean to say is . . ."

"You were wrong about one thing." The light inside his chamber flickered as he spoke.

She didn't know if the guest chamber next to him on the other side was occupied, but she lowered her voice just in case. "Which one?"

She knew not why she'd spoken at all. She already knew the answer. He was most definitely not available—his betrothal to the Scottish earl's daughter ensured it—and he *knew* she desired him. She'd allowed him to kiss her after all . . . nay, she'd kissed him back.

"You said I was neither available *nor* desirable," he pressed.

His eyes narrowed, giving him a predatory appearance. Nay, not predatory exactly. Just consuming.

"And you are betrothed."

"Aye, my lady. 'Tis an unfortunate fact."

Unfortunate?

"As for being desirable, I don't believe it matters under the circumstances."

Blast it! She'd just admitted she desired him. Which was not much of a revelation at all, of course.

"Perhaps not," he said. "But that's not what I refer to."

Now she was confused. Emma had only come here to apologize. And she'd done that, so it was time for her to—

"You said one other thing to Alex and Clara."

Emma tried to swallow again, but her throat was too dry. The tightness in her chest was getting worse. Why did he have to be so blasted good-looking? So self-assured yet intense.

And what else *had* she said? Emma couldn't remember. She'd told Clara—

"You said there was nothing to fear from me."

Oh. That.

"But you already know that isn't true."

"It's not?" She refused to believe him. Emma had no idea what the stirring deep inside her meant, but it was certainly not fear.

"It's not. And I mean to show you why."

To hell with restraint.

There was only so much of it to be had, and Garrick had used up his share during that hellish meal. While it was true he had no desire to see Emma and Graeme together, it may have been preferable to imagining it.

He stopped thinking. He broke every rule of his training, both on the battlefield and off, and pulled Emma into the room. Closing the door behind her, he restrained himself enough not to kiss her at least. Instead, he gave in to another impulse and reached up to touch the hair that lay across her shoulders.

"Beautiful." Silky, as he'd imagined. "Are you nervous?"

"Nay."

"You're not afraid of me, Emma?"

"Nay," she said, her voice both strong and sensual.

"I am," he said. "Afraid." He'd never spoken such a raw truth in his life.

"Why?" She tossed back his earlier question.

"Because this cannot be." He dropped the strands of hair, which fell back onto her gown.

"Then why did you pull me in here?"

Rather than wait for an answer, Emma reached up and placed her palm on his cheek. His body jolted as if it had been asleep for a lifetime. Her touch branded him.

She held her hand there for a moment longer and then moved her thumb just slightly. With that simple touch, so innocent and slight, his cock hardened as if she'd just offered to climb atop him.

God's gates.

Nay, he'd never be allowed entry to heaven. But if hell had gates . . .

"For the same reason I kissed you before."

Emma dropped her hand, and they stood there staring at each other. Every instinct told him to reach for her, pull her toward him. Kiss her, ravish her. Make love to her until she moaned with every pleasure he could show her. But there was a thin ribbon of restraint left in him yet.

"Why did you allow yourself to come inside?" he asked.

"You know why."

Oh God. "Emma, this is so wrong. More so than the kiss I stole in that darkened corridor. I am to be married. You are an innocent under my protection. Not deserving of this treatment from me. If we were to be discovered here . . ."

"You're right," she said. "About everything, save one."

If only that one thing were the state of his matrimony.

"I am deserving of this. Have you ever desired a woman before?"

Had he? Garrick wasn't sure.

"Aye," he managed.

"Then how is it wrong for me to desire a man?"

It was not wrong that she should desire him. It was wrong that he should act upon it. But rather than say as much, he found his body moving toward her.

"One kiss."

She nodded.

Garrick reached for her then. When he wrapped his arms around her, he groaned as if he were already inside her. She fit perfectly against him, their bodies melding together as if they'd been made for each other. Garrick lowered his head then and captured her lips with his own. He wanted her more than he wanted to breathe. When he opened his mouth and she followed his lead, Garrick groaned again, the feeling of her hesitant tongue touching his too poignant to ignore. He delved deeper, trying desperately to get even closer. Maddened by the taste of her.

Garrick's hands gripped Emma's gown at her back, pressing her more tightly to him. Their fervent pitch increased. He backed her against the door, her hands no longer around his neck but clinging to his hair. She pulled, her grip tightening as his tongue swirled in her mouth, mimicking another notion. Her mouth was soft and wet against him, her breasts pressed so tightly to his shirt that Garrick could almost feel her nipples through the fabric.

He wanted more.

He broke the contact, moving his lips from her mouth to her throat. She lifted her head as he licked and kissed a trail lower and lower. His tongue teased the soft spot between her breasts just near the fabric that kept him in check. He wanted to tear it off her, take her into his mouth, and give her more pleasure than she'd ever dreamed of.

He was going to ravish her.

Garrick pulled away, his breath coming as quickly as hers. He'd been about to do something beyond foolish. Something that didn't bear consideration. She stood against the door, her hair tousled every which way, her lips swollen with his kiss.

He wanted to be inside Emma. And he'd very nearly made it happen.

She was as passionate as he'd expected. Untamed. Unabashed.

Utterly perfect.

"Emma, oh God. I nearly . . ." He couldn't say the words aloud.

She was his charge, and rather than protect her, he'd nearly taken her.

"What was that? It wasn't just a kiss."

Goddamn right it wasn't. "I don't know what that was, Emma."

"But you've—"

He shook his head, trying to make her understand.

"Emma, I don't know what that was," he repeated. "When you look at me. When you touch me . . ."

He turned and ran his hands through his hair.

Damn.

"So that's it, then."

Garrick turned back around. Emma attempted to tame her hair.

"It?"

"That is what makes Sara and Geoffrey look at each other so. 'Tis why Clara risked her life to protect Alex." She shrugged. "Well, now I know."

He really shouldn't tempt fate, but Garrick took a step toward her anyway.

"You don't." He tried to explain. "That was more. It was . . . something. I've never . . ." He'd never felt that way before.

"Do you think it will be like that with Magnus's daughter?"

It was as if she'd taken the pitcher of wine and dumped it on his head.

"No, I don't." He knew with a certainty he didn't question that it wouldn't be like that with anyone else. Ever.

"And if I were to marry Graeme?" She wasn't saying it to be malicious. Garrick knew her better than that. It was simple curiosity, but by God, he would have strangled the Scots chief if he stood here now with her. If she ever kissed him like that . . .

"Why would you ask such a thing?"

She shrugged "I don't know. It's just—"

He reached her in one stride. Garrick took her face in his hands and looked her directly in the eyes until she returned his gaze. He waited, watched. Lost himself in the blue depths in which he could almost see his own reflection. She would know one thing before they parted.

"Emma Waryn, listen to me. And listen well. Neither you nor I will ever feel that way again in our lives. With anyone."

Garrick had enough experience to know the truth of it.

And despite knowing their futures were headed down different paths, he wanted to do it again, lose himself in her willingness to embrace life, consequences be damned.

He dropped his hands. He couldn't stand this close to her. "Go."

He turned. And waited.

"Emma. This can't be. Go." Another few moments, and he'd disappoint his mother. Break two promises. Possibly start a war.

Thankfully, all of that was averted when she opened and closed the door with nearly the same force as he had used earlier.

What the hell just happened?

CHAPTER TWELVE

*H*e felt the change before the men surrounded them.

It was as if the very air they breathed had gone sour. When he'd fought alongside Edward, who'd been stupid—or brave—enough to ride beside the men on the front lines, his king had praised his instincts, proclaiming they'd saved them all more than once. And now those instincts were telling him danger was near.

He shouted to his nearest man.

"Ride back to Sowlis. Now. Avoid the road. Tell him we may be under attack."

Though the other men who'd heard him looked around as if to question his sanity, the knight to whom he gave the order did not. Trained well, he spurred his horse around and fled.

"Surround her!" he shouted, the quick glimpse he caught of Emma terrifying him more than any battle in his life.

His men did so just as the first sounds of horses' hooves reached their ears. Within minutes, more than twenty, perhaps as many as thirty men—double their own number—charged toward them from the rear. Garrick had already moved into position at the front and strained to see the banners of their visitors. None. No markings to name them friend or foe.

Which made their situation much worse.

Though they were not fully armored, the attackers did wear maille, which meant they'd come prepared to fight. If these were reivers, they were well-armed ones. Although they were outmanned, Garrick would not have been overly worried, except for one thing.

He couldn't look back at her now, but if these bastards so much as came near Emma, he was certain he'd lose his grip on control and send every one of them to hell.

"I am Sir Garrick Helmsley, sixth Earl of Clave and third Earl of Linkirk," he shouted.

"Then you are the man I'm here for," said their leader.

"We've no quarrel with you. Nor with your men." Garrick took off his gloves as he spoke—the only preparation he dared to make. To reach for his sword would be to invite battle, though it did appear that such a conflict might be inevitable.

A bird's call echoed over the sound of Bayard's snort. He must calm the situation.

"I cannot say the same."

He had not heard the man's faint accent before, but this time it was clear. The leader was Scottish, a borderer, and seemed to know him. Without warning, his opponent spurred his mount forward. Garrick pulled his sword from its sheath and yelled, "Defend! Protect!"

Just like that, he and his men were engaged in battle. Another man reached Garrick before the leader could. The sound of clanging swords behind him forced his sword arm to move as if possessed by the Devil. He'd slain the man, or at least unseated him, before he was able to look behind him.

They'd taken Emma far enough away to avoid the fighting but not so far they could be cut off from aid. Good. Though the ground glistened with freshly fallen snow and the air cut through his chest like a blade of ice, all else was the same. Though the men and the weapons were different, the screams sounded the same. It mattered not if they were at the Scottish border or on an open field in Acre. However, he and his men were outnumbered this time.

But not for long.

He heard their shouts even before the borderers turned their backs on Garrick and his men. Graeme de Sowlis had arrived. But how could he have gotten here so quickly?

Cutting down two—no, three—more men, Garrick fought his way to their leader. But before he could dismount, intending to capture the bastard, the cowards fled. Those who were left scattered in every direction. The trees, though many were bare, would make it difficult for his men to cut a straight path to any one man. As quickly as they'd come, the raiders were gone.

Turning Bayard around, Garrick rode as quickly as the destrier would allow back to the circle of men. "She is well?" he asked anxiously.

"Aye, sir."

He couldn't see her. Garrick *needed* to see her.

"Let me through," he shouted, and they did. Parting to either side of him, the wall of mounted knights revealed a proud but shaken young lady.

"Emma? Are you hurt?"

He knew she was not. Could see it for himself. But he needed to hear it from her lips.

Garrick jumped from Bayard and reached her in just a few strides.

"It's over," he said, stating the obvious.

"What happened?"

Emma, who still sat atop her horse, was covered in a thick cloak and hood, only her face visible.

"I don't know," he said, reaching his hand up to her.

She took it. "Who were they? And why did they attack us?"

He squeezed her hand, the first contact they'd had since last eve.

"Garrick?" Graeme said from behind.

He let her hand go and turned around to see more than fifty of Graeme's men with him.

"How did you get here so quickly?" Garrick asked. "And with so many?"

"We were already on our way to you. They were spotted by the extra scouts I stationed along our borders after the rumors reached us yesterday. Though it seems they are not rumors after all. Who were they?"

With one last quick glance at Emma, who nodded in answer to his silent question, Garrick allowed himself to be pulled back to the scene of the battle. More than five of the attackers lay dead. None with any markings upon them.

"I would ask you the same question. They are your countrymen."

Graeme kneeled down by the body lying closest to him. "You're sure?"

"Aye. Their leader spoke to me briefly before they attacked."

"Did he know you?"

"Aye. They knew well my identity."

"The blood." He pointed at Garrick's mantle. "It's not yours?"

"Nay."

"My lord fought like Saladin himself. Killed most of these men," Henry de Crecy, his captain, bragged.

He should have known better. Garrick was proud of his men, but individual feats had no place in battle.

"Sir Henry—"

"Apologies, my lord. It's just that I'd never seen anything like it, not even in . . .." Henry finally realized Garrick was still not pleased and stopped talking.

"Do you think these are the raiders you've been hearing about?" Garrick asked, turning back toward Graeme.

The chief shrugged. "Possibly. I've never seen any of these men before, but they don't appear to be reivers. What reason could they possibly have to attack you?"

As if a spark had lit inside him, Graeme looked up abruptly, meeting his eyes.

"Nay. He wouldn't," Garrick said.

"You're sure?"

Garrick's uncle hated him as much as he'd hated his father before him. But to murder him? And that wasn't all. He'd have to kill Garrick's mother to claim the title. To be caught performing such a treasonous act risked everything, and the man was hardly destitute or driven by desperation. The man's wife, Garrick's aunt, had received one-third of her father's lands—just as all the sisters had. The only thing his mother had claimed beyond that shared inheritance was the title. Would a man really go so far just to be called earl?

Garrick didn't like his own answer.

"Can you spare men to Linkirk? To send a message to my mother? Just to be safe?"

He would send one of his own, but Garrick wanted the remainder of his retinue intact to best protect Emma.

"Of course. And I will send others with you to Kenshire."

"That isn't necessary, Graeme."

"It may not be. But they're coming anyway."

Graeme looked behind him and Garrick followed his gaze. So he'd sent them for Emma. "I need to get her to the abbey."

"Of course. I will take care of this." Graeme gestured to the bodies that littered the dirt road in both directions and the two men that had been taken captive.

Garrick stuck out his hand and Graeme took it.

"Thank you."

"Garrick, I'm sorry this happened here—"

"'Tis not your fault. You saved me and my men. And Emma."

The flicker of emotion in the man's eyes—interest and protectiveness and speculation—was painful to Garrick. It made him recall the chief had pulled Emma aside for a short conversation before they'd left that morn. What had he said to her? Garrick released his hand, doing his damnedest to shove the thought of a courtship between Emma and Graeme from his mind.

"If you learn anything—"

"I will send word."

Garrick moved back to Emma, who still looked shaken.

He held up his hand to her. Without a word, she allowed him to help her dismount. Garrick whistled to Bayard, who came to them on command. Unbelievably, Emma then extended her hand, and Bayard placed his head under it. It was as if he were comforting her. Or just the reverse.

Mounting, he lifted Emma up in front of him. He nodded to his men and then left the bloody scene of battle without a backward glance, telling Emma to close her eyes as they passed the bodies. Whether she listened or not, he wasn't sure. All Garrick knew, or cared about, was that she was safe.

He certainly wouldn't think about how tempting she felt in front of him—like she was practically sitting on his lap.

The abbey. Must get to the abbey.

Emma shook her head, trying to clear the sound of screaming horses and clashing blades from her ears. Certainly she had heard such sounds before in a battle she'd witnessed at her aunt and uncle's home. But today she'd heard a man scream as he died. It was an awful sound, worse even than the pained neighs of the innocent horses. She *did* close her eyes, as Garrick had instructed, but only after she spied a black and white courser, its legs bent at an unusual angle that could only mean it was dead.

This was the danger Geoffrey had warned her about. Of course, she'd known better than to doubt him. She and her brothers had lost their home and their parents—something that had brought them face-to-face with the harsh realities of the borderlands. But even she knew this battle was unusual. Those men hadn't been intent on taking a keep for their king. Neither were they reivers who'd hoped to steal from them. They'd seemed intent on killing.

"Who were they?" Shivering despite the heavy layers atop her, Emma turned her head just enough for Garrick to hear her.

"We don't know." He didn't elaborate. So much like her brother Bryce.

"I heard what you said to the chief. Were they Scottish?"

Along the border, English and Scottish were nearly indistinguishable by sight. But they were still north of the border, so . . .

"I believe so." Again, nothing more than a terse answer to her question.

"'Twas brutal," she said, thinking once again of the glimpse she'd gotten just before she closed her eyes.

"Battle is never a pretty sight."

Nay, she supposed it wouldn't be.

Emma pulled her cloak tighter about her neck and adjusted herself.

Garrick sucked in his breath.

"Too close?" She edged away from him as much as possible given their close quarters.

"Nay." He reached around her, still holding onto Bayard's reins, and pulled her back.

She wasn't sure what to say. Every time she opened her mouth to speak, the words seemed silly. Insignificant. Nothing could encompass what she was feeling after the night before. After the battle.

The silence stretched on until the steady sound of their travel began to lull Emma's eyes closed. She'd hardly slept, thinking of—

"What did Graeme say to you?" he suddenly asked.

Her eyes popped open. "After the battle?"

"Nay, before you left. I saw him draw you aside."

Ah, that. "He asked for permission to visit Kenshire."

Garrick's arm tightened, just slightly, but enough for her to notice.

"And?"

"And I gave it."

Emma wasn't sure what Geoffrey would think, but Graeme de Sowlis was a good man. A *single* man. "There was no reason to do otherwise."

Certainly not for you.

"Emma, I—"

"You asked why I haven't married," she blurted, not sure why she should tell him anything. It was not as if she needed to explain. And yet the words continued to spill out of her. "Every year for as long as I can remember, my father and brothers would travel south to the Tournament of the North. They'd talk of its splendor. Of my brothers' victories. Of the prizes and jousts, the melee. And every year, I'd ask to accompany them."

She thought of standing in the courtyard at Bristol, watching them all ride off without her, their excitement palpable.

"I could tell they felt badly about it. None ever mentioned the horse race."

On the third day of the tournament, a horse race, the largest one in England, determined the "jewel of the crown." The winner could pick any horse he desired from the royal stable. Even though the king no longer attended the tournament, their representatives continued to do so, taking with them some of the finest horseflesh in the world.

She'd dreamed of being there, of seeing such fine animals race. Her daring had its limits—she'd never imagined herself in such a race, but she'd longed to be around it. Maybe to have one of her brothers enter so she could have someone to cheer for.

"They apologized every year, of course. But all of them agreed, Neill included. It was no place for me. 'Twas too dangerous."

"But you must have been young—"

"The same age as Neill."

"Your twin?"

"Aye."

Emma closed her eyes and tried to imagine, as she had so many times, what it must have been like. The horses everywhere, the excitement of the race.

"Father loved me," she said. "And my brothers love me still. Geoffrey will be enraged when he finds out what happened today. He's spent a lifetime trying to protect me . . ."

"Emma?"

"Aye?" She had been trying to forget his face. To forget that the warm body behind hers belonged to him. But that was impossible to do when his voice, so intimate and familiar, was whispering in her ear.

"What does this have to do with you not being married?"

She'd gone and rambled again. It would have been best if she'd never tried to explain. "I want what Geoffrey and Sara have," she said. "And my brother Bryce and his wife. But . . ."

"But?"

Emma watched as a single snowflake dropped onto the horse's head. It dissolved, ceased to exist. Forever.

"I want to go to that tournament more."

It was the best she could do. He likely didn't understand, but what did it matter? He didn't have to.

"And Graeme?"

"He is a clan chief."

"Which, I take it, is a bad thing?"

"Well, of course it is. He's accustomed to leading men. Giving orders. The exact kind of man—"

"You don't want to marry."

Aye. But she'd given him permission to court her anyway.

This time the silence between them stretched out for so long she thought perhaps Garrick had fallen asleep. But of course he had not.

"Maybe you can have both."

It took her a moment to understand what he referred to.

Emma turned around. Bad idea. Garrick was looking at her with such concentration he probably didn't realize he was biting his lip. But she couldn't take her eyes from that. He had such lovely lips. If only she could—

"He is a good man. An honorable one. Aye, he's a clan chief, and likely as protective as your brothers, but that doesn't mean he won't give you independence."

"Would you?"

Blast it! She hadn't meant to reveal more of herself to him.

"Nay."

His response was so quick, so terse, that she didn't doubt him for a minute. Garrick would have her locked up in her bedchamber if they were married. Well, that might not be such a dreadful thing—

"But then, it's not me you're considering for a husband."

She turned back around. *Of course not. You are already betrothed, oh great lord of England and Scotland.*

Blasted earl.

"Pity." He said it so softly, Emma thought for a moment she'd misheard it. But when he tightened his grip again, his hand shifted up just slightly to rest beneath her breasts.

An accident?

Nay.

A flutter began in her stomach and moved down to where she sat upon the horse, her legs wide open and her thighs touching his under their cloaks.

Three more days of this torture.

CHAPTER THIRTEEN

*G*arrick ignored his captain.

He trusted the man. Had put his life in his hands during more than one battle. Having fought the same enemy under the same intelligent but often misguided king, they understood each other on a deep level.

But at the moment, ignoring him was preferable to listening to him.

"Lord, if I may be so bold," his captain had said after pulling him aside in the entrance to The Wild Boar, "shall I tell Magge you'll not be dining in the storeroom tonight?"

Two days. For two damn days he'd avoided her as much as possible given that he could not bear to let her ride alone after the attack. And after one more day they would find their own futures, separately. He with a Scottish wife he'd never met. She at Kenshire, or perhaps as the wife of a Scot herself. Their connection, their kisses—he may have been right to tell her there was something very special about them. Hell, he *knew* it was true. But it mattered little compared to his desire to secure the Scottish earldom peacefully, and to accept his mother's inheritance without broken alliances or bloodshed. He would keep his mother safe. A feat which would have been easier had she agreed to come back to England with him.

"*I* will tell her," he finally grumbled to his captain.

It would seem Magge had taken it upon herself to secure private rooms for him and his captain as well as for Emma. She had prepared the storeroom as well, assuming he would request the same arrangement as before.

Impossible.

After ensuring Emma was shown to her room, where Magge would retrieve her later, he and his captain retired to theirs to clean after the long journey. As soon as he was done with his ablutions, he hurried downstairs to find the innkeeper.

"Magge," he called out as he wandered into the great room, which was just beginning to fill with patrons for the evening. She was nowhere to be found.

Until a plump form sidled alongside him.

"Magge takes care o' her favorites, she does."

"The very reason The Wild Boar thrives."

Whereas other innkeepers around these parts often resorted to brute force or bribery to keep their establishments safe, Magge accomplished the seemingly impossible with only her wiles and reputation. She could be a mother or a seductress. An innkeeper or a brewer. Magge could be whatever her patrons desired as long as they kept their fights away from the inn. English, Scottish—it mattered not to her.

"I appreciate the extra care—"

"Well, ye be an earl in two countries now."

She didn't care about any of that.

"I'll have the real reason, love."

She shrugged, looking past him at one of her serving girls. "I liked your father."

He laughed. "Of course you did. Everyone did."

"And yer just like 'im."

How many times had he heard that before?

"Now go see how nice I made it for you an yer lady. A shame her maid ne'er made it to you," she said with a wink.

She pushed him toward the door that led to the storeroom.

"Magge, this is not—"

"Well, ye gonna make her eat in there?" She gestured to the great room, where a serving maid's bosom nearly toppled onto the guest she served. "Go now, it's all set up for ye."

He could lead a few hundred men into battle, but this one woman, twice his age or more, shoved him down the stairs with no difficulty.

When he reached the bottom, Garrick knew why she'd insisted on the arrangement. The room appeared much as it had before, but the tallow candles had been replaced with beeswax ones. A gift, most likely, since no innkeeper could afford such a thing. Many noble households could not.

Again, two barrels held a plank that served as a makeshift table, already weighed down with roasted venison, bread, apples, and cheese. A pitcher of ale and two mugs sat next to the food. The space was warm, but not too warm, thanks to its location directly next to the kitchens.

"Nay, I'm sure 'tis not necessary," a voice above him said. "I'm glad to take the meal—"

"Hush now, you, or I'll tell your brother ye didn't listen to ol' Magge."

She'd just begun to descend the stairs. Garrick could see the bottom of her deep green riding gown. The same one that had been pressed against him all day.

"You know my brothers?" Every time Emma spoke of one of her brothers, her voice took on a softer tone, something that made him smile.

"I do. Most especially the older two scamps who love to tease and torment your poor ol' host."

Emma chuckled. "That sounds like them. 'Tis their good fortune to have a sister who does no such thing."

"Ha," Magge cackled. "That's not what they be tellin' me. An I look forward to your youngest brother's return."

Apparently giving in to the inevitable, just as he had, Emma continued to walk down the creaking wooden stairs. Every step was sweeter than the one before it. First he saw the slim waist that he'd held in his arms. Then the breasts he longed to touch and tease. Then the tips of the black hair he'd touched first with his fingertips.

Emma. So beautiful she could hardly be real.

But she was.

And she froze at the sight of him.

Garrick nodded to where Magge presumably still stood at the top of the stairs.

Emma smiled, a conspiratorial smile that made Garrick's stomach twist into a knot.

The door to the storeroom finally closed. Was Magge tempting fate on purpose?

"I suppose we should eat," she said. "We've been given little choice in the matter."

He had no appetite for anything but her.

Garrick stood and pulled out her makeshift seat. The silence was punctuated by muffled sounds from abovestairs. They did eat, or at least Garrick tried his best. How his friend Conrad would laugh at him if he saw him now. The great Lord of Clave, hardly able to eat because of a woman.

He was utterly and completely . . .

What? Lusting for her? Nay, it was something more.

"I can't stop thinking of those men," she said quietly. Battle. A safe topic.

"You'll likely not rid yourself of the image for some time."

"Do you? Rid yourself of the image of the men you've killed in battle. After so many—"

"The number matters not. I still think of the first man who ever met the end of my blade." He took a swig of the beer Magge brewed herself. "I was but ten and two. My father and I traveled to York for a tourney. I remember being worried about the squires' joust, my first. Instead, I should have worried about the mercenaries on the road intent on proving themselves against mounted knights. Though my father instructed me to run, I could not. This was what I'd been training for. The man I felled was twice my size, but I knew how to overcome poor odds."

He could still smell grass, wet from a recent rain shower, from that day so long ago.

"The blade didn't slide into his body as I'd imagined. But when it did, he fell immediately and never posed another threat to me, or anyone, again."

Garrick had never spoken of the incident aloud before, but he found it easy to tell her. His father had berated him for not following orders. One or two of the men had said, "Well done."

But that had been it.

"For some time afterward, I saw the man's face. Or what I thought his face would look like. His great helm revealed nothing, but my boy's mind thought he must be ugly and scarred."

"Do you see his face still?"

"Nay."

"So someday I *will* be able to banish those horrible images."

Garrick wanted to tell her there were pleasurable ways of distracting oneself from thoughts of the battle, but he bit his tongue.

"Let's speak of something else," she said.

Emma's mind moved as fast as her body did on horseback.

When neither of them said anything, Garrick thought to tease her.

"Just not of the battle. Or my intended. Or Graeme. Or how angry your brother will be when he learns what happened. Let me see, shall we talk about . . ." He trailed off and took another sip of his beverage.

"That kiss?"

He choked then, nearly spitting out the fine ale that somehow made its way down his throat.

"Hardly a delicate topic," she said.

"But a fine one, nonetheless."

"Indeed?" Her eyes danced with the merriment of knowing she'd unbalanced him. He'd certainly not expected the suggestion.

"What precisely, my lady, would you like to discuss concerning said kiss?"

"Hmm." She lifted her finger to the corner of her full mouth. "Shall we discuss the first one, or the second? I believe the second." As if having made a weighty decision, she said, "The second kiss. Aye, let us discuss that."

He set down his mug. "Gladly."

"I've been kissed before, of course."

The words immediately conjured a vision of Graeme de Sowlis bending his head to her, claiming those—

"But they were nothing quite like yours."

They?

"How were they different?" Garrick struggled to keep his voice neutral.

"Well," she narrowed her eyes. Damn if she wasn't trying to remember them. Multiple past kisses with different men.

"For one, I'd never opened my mouth before. Your tongue . . ." She'd reached the limit of what propriety would allow her to say.

A shame.

It was a shame there were different standards for what the two of them could discuss. And that she'd felt the need to stop.

"If you never kissed a man using your tongue," he said, "then you've never been properly kissed."

"But—"

"Before me," he clarified.

"Did you kiss your intended?" she blurted.

"Did you kiss Graeme?" he shot back.

This was a dangerous game they played.

He inhaled, the scent of burning wax overpowering the stores of wheat surrounding them.

"Why would I kiss Graeme?" she asked it innocently enough, giving him his answer.

"Sometimes admirers will—"

"I never said the chief was a suitor."

"So he is not? He expressed no interest—"

"I didn't say that either."

"So he *did* express interest."

Of course he had, Garrick admonished himself. The man had asked for permission, as if it were his to give, to visit Kenshire Castle. To properly court her.

"You never answered my question," Emma said.

They looked across the table at each other, Garrick wanting nothing more than to pull Emma onto his lap and show her a proper kiss. Ensure that no matter who came after him, it would not be the same.

"I didn't even meet her," he said, his tone neutral.

"Oh."

Did she seem pleased by that news?

Neither of them said another word as they continued to pick at the meal.

When they were both finished, Garrick pushed himself away from the tray and stood. "If you're ready?"

Emma stood as well and wordlessly turned toward the stairs. This was it. The last time they were likely to be truly alone together. She had just put her foot on the first wooden step when he stopped her.

Garrick, this is not a good idea.

As soon as she felt the tug on her arm, Emma knew she was lost.

She had little experience with men and even less with desire, but she'd begun to understand both a little more over the course of the meal. To be around Garrick was to experience a constant state of desire. Her rapid heartbeat was so strong she imagined everyone could hear the pounding in her chest. The need to look at him whenever he was in the same room was almost overpowering. The utter lack of control, not that she had much to start, over what came out of her mouth.

Around him, Emma felt like a witless fool. She'd never be as controlled as Sara, but she strove to emulate at least a shred of her poise.

Not with Garrick near.

The very thin thread of control she had clung to these last days was about to snap. He was pulling her back toward him now, and she'd not stop him.

When she slammed against his hard chest, Emma wanted more. She pressed against him, wrapping her arms around his neck as his head descended, his lips covering hers. Their tongues performed a wild and erotic dance.

As he pressed into her, Emma's knees buckled. Rather than pull her back up, Garrick allowed her body to fall backward onto the stairs, his hands cushioning the initial impact. She half sat, half lay against the stairs as Garrick moved on top of her. He cradled her head with one hand, leaving the other free to explore.

And explore it did.

No part of her wanted this to end or cared about tomorrow. This man, pressed against her, showing her what it meant to be desired . . . this was all that mattered.

"This cannot be," he murmured against her ear while at the same time nipping the sensitive flesh there. The warning seemed more for himself than for her.

In response, she pressed her hips against him, easily able to feel the thick column through the folds of her gown and his tunic and hose. It wasn't quite in the perfect position, though, and she squirmed to make their bodies match.

"Oh God, Emma, no . . ."

But his words didn't match his actions. For as soon as they were perfectly aligned, he pressed his body against hers and kissed her again. He circled his hips against her, and Emma did the same, their bodies moving in rhythm with their tongues. With his free hand, he covered her breasts and squeezed so gently Emma thought perhaps it best not to interfere.

But she wanted more.

She arched her back to feel her hips and breasts more firmly again him.

Garrick responded by squeezing again, this time harder. His thumb ran across the tip of her breast.

"Gown, shift . . . it matters not. I can feel your tips beneath me."

His hand moved even lower, then inside her gown, dipping under the layers of fabric to cover her breast. When he took her nipple between two fingers and squeezed, Emma broke the kiss. It was an overwhelming surge of sensations. His tongue, his hand. The pressure of him against her.

"What is—"

"Shh, just feel."

Then all at once, his hot breath against her neck, his body and hands against her—pushing and circling, squeezing and pinching —everything started to vibrate and intensify.

"I—" Emma tilted her head back and allowed herself to let go. When she did, a flood of pleasure washed through every part of her body like a tidal wave, but concentrating down *there*. She began to shake, her fingers clasping onto his tunic as the tingling became a steady throbbing.

"Look at me, Emma."

She did. He watched her, waiting for something, she knew not what.

She couldn't breathe. Emma tried to inhale a deep, calming breath, but she couldn't. Her breaths were shallow and fast. Her grip tightened, and Garrick's intense gaze only made it worse.

Then, with the smallest of smiles, he pressed her hips into the stairs below and squeezed her breast with his rough, strong hand.

And she was undone.

"Look at me."

Doing so made her shudder—not just there, but everywhere—and she struggled to form a coherent thought.

Eventually, the throbbing dulled and retreated like a cat slinking back after it received its treat. Everything relaxed . . . her grip, her body. Everything but Garrick.

He didn't move.

"How did it feel?"

"Like . . ." She shuddered.

"There's more," he said. "Much more."

He stood and pulled her up with him. Garrick wrapped and held her face in his hands as he'd done that first night. He ran his thumb across her lip, and she touched her tongue to it without thinking.

Garrick was not hers.

She took a step back, and his expression immediately dropped. He knew what she was thinking. What she was about to say.

"Garrick—"

"I will not keep apologizing, Emma. It's wrong. Very wrong. But I want you more than I've ever wanted a woman. And that is the truth."

"But not enough."

Try as she might, Emma couldn't control her thoughts. If she could, she'd tell them to stop wanting more of this man she couldn't possibly have.

"Emma—"

"Nay, ignore me. I'm just a tad . . ." She looked down at her gown and pulled it back up to where it belonged. "Overcome."

He was quiet for a moment. "As am I."

So there. They had both made a mistake. No harm done.

"Garrick—"

"Emma—"

She would never know what he'd intended to say. The door opened, and Emma spun around to see a servant standing in the doorway. They'd come so close to being caught . . .

"Pardon, ma'am. Shall I take the tray?"

Emma licked her lips and began to ascend the stairs. "Aye, you may."

She didn't look back.

CHAPTER FOURTEEN

*T*hey arrived at Kenshire well after dark.

Though they were cold and wet from the snow-storm that had caught them just as they rode into view of Kenshire Castle, Garrick had no wish to stay the night. But if the look on his men's faces were any indication, they had no other choice unless he wanted to tell them, "We traveled through the night because of a certain raven-haired woman who enflames my senses and makes me want to forget the Earl of Magnus and his daughter even exist."

"Emma," her brother called from the courtyard as they made their approach. Apparently not content to wait for his sister to enter the keep, Geoffrey bounded toward her. She'd ridden separately for most of the day. On Caiser property, Garrick knew there was no need for them to ride together. And as much as it had pained him to watch her walk away, he didn't think arriving with Waryn's sister snuggled between his legs would help defuse what would likely prove to be an extremely tense situation.

"I'm fine," she said, allowing herself to be engulfed in her brother's arms.

They'd not spoken since the night before. They'd ridden

together for a time this morning, and he'd opened his mouth more than once, but nothing had come out. Instead, he'd concentrated on the road ahead, on watching the coming storm, on anything that would get his mind off of the feel of her body pressed against his. Off the wide, joyful smiles she gave his men when they teased her, Emma taking their jests in stride.

Though she didn't actively seek attention, his battle-hardened knights could not resist her smile. They laughed when she stuck out her tongue to capture snowflakes on it and demanded they do the same. And when they'd stopped around midday to rest the horses, Garrick hadn't been surprised to feel the *clunk* of a snowball hit his back. Not the kind that fell apart when it landed, but a wet and hard bit of ammunition tossed by a minx who tugged at his heart every time she was near.

He'd been just about to mount Bayard at the time. Though she'd packed it up well, his gambeson absorbed most of the impact. Even so, he immediately knew what it was. He'd seen her toss them at some of the men, who refused, after looking to him for approval, to toss them back.

The brutes hardly knew their own strength and would likely injure the poor woman.

"I saw you warning away the men," she yelled to him.

"If we want to reach Kenshire by dark—"

"You don't have time to toss a snowball?"

The men looked at him and then Emma and back again. He'd like to toss her into his bed and be done with it. But a snowball? "Nay."

He turned and another landed square on his neck, its wetness already seeping into his tunic. Exactly what he deserved for taking off the cloak.

When Garrick spun back around, he found Emma holding her stomach in laughter. More than one of his men wore a smirk.

If she wanted a snowball fight, then by God he'd give her one.

When he lowered his gloved hands into the snow, just enough

to form a decent-sized ball, he caught the look of surprise on his captain's face.

Garrick wasn't known for his frivolity, after all.

He'd stopped the men because he feared they would accidentally hurt her. Aye, the legs should be safe. He took aim and threw his missile gently, connecting exactly where he'd intended.

By now the others were fully mounted, watching, but Garrick knew it wasn't over. He didn't wait for her to come at him this time, but instead bent down to form another ball. He stood, pulled back his arm, and was pelted square in the face this time.

Emma laughed so loudly Garrick was sure the men who'd attacked them in Scotland would hear and come finish the job they'd started.

He reached her in a few short strides, grabbed her arm, which was already prepared to finish him with another snowy bit of ammunition, and held it in the air.

"You, my lady, are a menace."

"You, my lord, have poor aim."

Garrick would like to show her how untrue that statement was—and he very nearly told her so—until he remembered the men were watching them from all sides.

"I'm afraid we'll be forced to call a truce." He let go of her arm.

"Truce? More like a win for the fairer sex."

At that simple word, his cock stirred and hardened. Her ability to affect him so was unparalleled.

"Very well, a win. What is to be your prize?"

Though he'd said it low enough for her ears only, Garrick regretted the words as soon as they left his mouth. There was only one prize he wanted to give her.

Rather than say something else equally as foolish, he turned and walked away.

They hadn't spoken since, but he couldn't stop thinking of that moment. Her laughter. The snow crystals collecting on her long lashes.

"Clave, we need to talk," said Geoffrey.

Garrick was equally as anxious to speak with the earl.

Without a backward glance, Emma rushed past him toward the stables, leaving them to make their way to the keep.

"How is Nella?" Garrick asked.

"Emma will be pleased to learn she is doing just fine. Whatever ailment afflicted her seems to have disappeared." If Geoffrey thought it odd for him to inquire after Emma's horse, he didn't say so.

Garrick breathed a bit easier at the news. He'd only remembered the horse's condition as they passed through the gatehouse. Her nervous posture had reminded him. Knowing how much she cared for her beloved horse, he'd hoped, for her sake, the animal had recovered.

"I'm glad to hear it."

Instead of leading him into the great hall, Geoffrey brought him directly to the solar, where they sat in front of the hearth.

"What happened?" Arms crossed, eyes blazing, Geoffrey Waryn was not a man easily dismissed.

"We were attacked."

"I know you were attacked. Everyone knows. Who was it?"

"I don't know. The enemy bore no markings of any kind."

"But they knew where to find you. Knew who you were."

"Aye."

"Reivers?" Though Waryn was clearly angry his sister had been exposed to harm, his tone was evenly measured.

"Nay."

"Trained?"

"Aye"—the door swung open unceremoniously, admitting Lady Sara—"and Scottish, or at least one of them was."

"Was it Inverglen?" Lady Sara asked.

He bowed, but Sara dismissed his formality with a wave of her hand.

"Possibly. But my mother contends my uncle has accepted the

title is mine." At Sara's arched brows, he amended, "Now that I've been formally betrothed to Magnus's daughter."

A look passed between Sara and her husband that Garrick couldn't decipher.

"You must be thankful your mother arranged such an advantageous match," Geoffrey said.

Thankful that my mother will not be forced to endure further disappointment after Father's death? Aye. That the match should pacify my English-hating uncle? Aye. But thankful to be betrothed to a woman I do not know? Nay. I can never be thankful for that. Not now. Not since Emma.

"Aye, Sara. I am very thankful," he managed to choke out.

Geoffrey began to pace, his fists clenching and unclenching as he circled the room like a caged animal. "She could have been killed. Whoever did this—"

"Will forfeit their lives for it when I find them," Garrick finished. "I'll hold a council of the border lords at Clave."

The vehemence in his voice did not go unnoticed.

Sara leveled an assessing look at him. "Garrick—"

"My lady, I must apologize for—"

"Apologize? Garrick, you kept Emma safe."

The earl very nearly growled. Spinning about on his foot to face them, he said, "Which would not have been necessary had she not—"

"*Geoffrey.*" Sara's tone suggested this was not the first time they'd had this conversation.

"Fine. But I want to know who did this. If they were merely thieves . . ."

"They were not." Though Garrick still didn't know who was behind the attack, he was sure he and his men had purposefully been targeted. "They intended to kill me. If Sowlis hadn't come so quickly . . ." Garrick refused to finish that thought. "I do wonder why they risked an attack so close to Scott territory."

"What matters most is that Emma is safe. *You* are safe. Thank you," Sara said. "Thank you for your escort and for all that you've done for her."

A vision of Emma under him on the stairs of the storeroom flashed through his mind.

"No thanks are necessary. She is . . ." He had to be careful here. "A delightful young woman."

Geoffrey's lips quirked. "Delightful, aye."

And also spirited. Full of life and humor and warmth. An amazing woman, he should have said.

"Speaking of Emma, I'm sure she's waiting for us in the hall," Sara said. "Garrick, you haven't had time to refresh yourself. Come."

She led him from the solar through a familiar corridor toward his guest chamber. He could not refuse to dine with them, which meant he would see her once more. One last time before he left at first light for Clave.

Thankfully, she would not be alone. What could possibly go wrong in the presence of her family?

———

Garrick already knew it would feel like both the longest night of his life and the shortest.

This is it. After you leave, you will never see her again. Or if you do, it will be as a married man.

Freshly dressed, Garrick walked toward the hall as if to the gallows, each step heavier than the last.

Kenshire's hall was even more spectacular at night with dozens and dozens of candles lighting every crevice, their glow casting shadows on brightly covered tapestries depicting the Battle of Hastings, the stories of King Arthur, and other well-known tales.

"Pardon, my lord." A young man, perhaps seven and ten, had bumped into him at the entrance to the great hall, forcing

Garrick's attention away from the high wooden beams overhead.

"Good eve," he replied.

The boy beamed up at him, his expression familiar. It was the same look Garrick himself had once given knights bigger and more powerful than him. Though it was far from typical for a young man of his status, Garrick had not been sent away to foster. His father had personally trained him, just as he'd trained Conrad and several other men who were now earls, barons, or knights in their own right. Many prestigious men had sent their boys to train with the legendary Earl of Clave, and Garrick was glad for the friendships he'd formed because of it.

The boy bowed. "Reginald, my lord." He stuck out his chin. "Lord Kenshire's squire."

"Pleased to make your acquaintance," he said. "You're a lucky lad to train with such a man."

Reginald was already nodding before Garrick finished. "Very much so. He is the strongest, fiercest, and bravest warrior in all of England."

Garrick raised his brows.

"Beg pardon, my lord," the lad said, his cheeks turning pink. "I am sure you are just as strong and—"

"Fear not, you're within your rights to say such a thing. And I'm sure you're quite right about the earl."

Faced with Reginald's puzzled expression, he explained, "Though Clave is a neighbor to Kenshire, I've just returned to England—"

"From fighting alongside the king in the Holy Land," Lady Sara finished from behind him.

Reginald's eyes widened.

"You fought with King Edward? What is he like? When will he return to England? Who—"

"Reginald," Sara said. "Poor Garrick would like to—"

"Nay, my lady," Garrick said. "I'm glad to answer this fine

young gentleman's questions. The king is quite tall, as I'm sure you've heard," he said, grinning at the lad.

Reginald nodded vigorously.

"And strong. Edward fights as well as any knight I've seen."

"He does?"

"Aye, lad. And he's quite intelligent too. As for when he will return? That I cannot tell you. When I left, he remained in Acre—"

"Why did you leave?"

"Reginald," Sara warned.

"My father was killed in battle. I returned to ensure my mother's safety."

"And to claim the earldoms of both Clave and Linkirk," Sara finished.

"You are a Scottish earl too?"

"Aye, Reginald. Sir Garrick is one of England's finest warriors. And comes from a family as dear to the Caisers as any."

Her last comment was directed at him, he knew, not the boy.

Long, long ago he had been as impressionable as young Reginald. If only life were still that simple. Back then, his biggest worry was whether or not he'd be able to remain on his feet in the training yard the next day.

Garrick had planned on saying something, either to the lad or to Lady Sara, but the words escaped him. Emma had just walked into the hall, emerging like a wood nymph from the corner of the room.

He'd become accustomed to her modest travel gown, but there was nothing modest about her this eve. Resplendent in a bright blue velvet gown, its sleeves nearly hitting the floor, she sauntered toward him. Her hair was as wild and untamed as ever, a delicious contrast to her courtly dress.

Garrick forgot to breathe.

He abruptly remembered Sara stood by his side and held his arm out to her. "My lady."

Sara took it and allowed herself to be led to the table on the dais. If the Fates were kind, he would not be seated next to Emma this time.

The Fates were not.

Garrick continued to stand until Emma reached him. Holding out the cushioned chair she'd been assigned, he tried to avoid looking at her. But as she sat, he could smell the scent that was uniquely hers. His cock stirred, reminding him, as if he needed a reminder, of their meal the previous evening.

Garrick ate and drank in silence.

"You're quiet this eve," she said finally.

A trencher of roasted meat and carrots was placed between them.

"Your brother watches us."

She turned her head just slightly before glancing back at him. The blue of her gown made her eyes look darker tonight. Though still very blue, they looked more serious than he was accustomed to seeing them.

"He knows nothing."

"Emma—"

"I will never say a word, Garrick. You know that, I'm sure."

He concentrated on his drink. It had never occurred to him that she would. But something about the finality of her words stirred him.

"I would speak to you one last time," he blurted.

She didn't hesitate. "I will come to you."

"Nay, 'tis too—"

"Garrick." She gave him a look similar to the one Sara had given Geoffrey in the solar earlier. The kind that said, *I know best, and you well know it.*

"Do you not agree, my lord?" Sara interrupted. "Geoffrey believes his brother should remain in training even after he is knighted. I think he should come home to Kenshire. Where do you think a young knight belongs? Fostering or with family?"

He considered the question. "I think it depends, my lady."

Everyone waited for him to expand upon his answer. "My good friend Conrad came to us at one and ten. Had he stayed with his family, I do believe his mother would have coddled him. She does so even now that he is fully grown."

Sara frowned. "I understand a mother's desire to protect her own."

"I mean no offense. His mother is quite unusual. I mean to say, I understand why most parents choose to foster their children. But as you know, I myself was trained by my father."

"You were?" Emma asked.

"Aye." He spoke to all three of his hosts. "He was one of the most skilled knights in all of England. He fought by King Henry's side on more than one occasion."

"And his reputation was only overshadowed by yours once you came of age," Sara said generously.

"I agree with you," Geoffrey said. "My own father fostered me as well, but out of necessity. Only after the sheep trade turned Bristol from a poor baron's holding to a property with a lucrative income did we have the funds to send my brother Bryce to Huntington."

"Has Neill discussed wanting to come back north? He's said nothing of the sort to me," said Emma. She seemed disappointed, hurt even.

"Nay," Sara was quick to answer. "But he was just knighted this past year. Give him time."

"And Sara has taken it upon herself to worry for him—" said Geoffrey. His words were said with an indulgent smile.

"Only," Emma interjected, "because we continue to hear whispers of his name. I don't believe there's a single tournament he's not entered."

"A worthy activity for a man in training," Garrick said.

"And nearly as dangerous as battle," Emma said in a quiet voice. In those few words, she revealed all of her worry about her brother, her twin.

"I can understand your concern, but every match ensures he is more skilled. Protects him for when the broadswords are not blunted." Garrick looked straight at Geoffrey. "Mayhap Emma could attend the next Tournament of the North to see for herself what Neill is facing?"

Emma stared at him in shock. Geoffrey's eyes narrowed, and Garrick knew he had overstepped. But he didn't care. The way she'd spoken about that horse race she'd never seen had stayed with him. Despite what he'd said to her, he wanted her to see that race. Was attending risky? Perhaps. Especially after their attack. But a life without risk was a life not worth living at all.

"We shall see," Geoffrey said, turning his attention back to his food.

Garrick caught the conspiratorial look between the two women and tried not to smile.

He actually relaxed for a moment until he remembered his earlier conversation with Emma.

I'd speak to you one last time.

What had he been thinking? And what would he possibly say to her that had not already been said? He would find out soon enough.

CHAPTER FIFTEEN

*E*mma hated the dark. Every time she was forced to face it, she felt the need to run and run and run, as if something terrible would materialize behind her. Somehow the stables didn't qualify. But these abandoned secret passageways that hadn't been used since . . . well . . . since she'd used them to smuggle a cat inside the year before.

Little had she known the animal was about to give birth. Her brother had never loved cats, so she'd hidden the mama and babies in her chamber. After trying, and failing, to care for four newborn kittens unnoticed, she'd finally informed Geoffrey of their new addition.

She continued through the passageway, careful step after careful step, until she arrived.

Though Garrick had seemed to regret the hasty invitation moments after issuing it, she could not. She'd been trying to conjure a way to speak to him just once more before he left. Though there was nothing further to say, she could not imagine waking up to find him gone without a final goodbye. Or a "thank you" for all that he had done.

Aye, that was it. She would thank him for escorting her to and from Scotland.

She had not finished knocking when the door opened.

She stepped into the chamber and placed the lantern, its single candle flickering, on a nearby stool. The sparsely furnished room was warm thanks to a fire in the corner.

"I've never been in here—"

"You should leave."

He had that look about him. A warrior's look. But it no longer frightened her. The tick in his jaw begged to be touched. He *wanted* it to be touched. It was why he was so desperate for her to leave. She'd come to say goodbye, aye. But she'd also come to feel his arms around her one last time. To be cherished by his lips, kissed like she was the one he would marry.

At some point in these last days, her fears about marrying an earl had begun to melt away.

Emma had not stopped thinking about their encounter in the storeroom even for a moment. Or how he defended her—so fiercely—in battle. And then at dinner, when he'd prodded her brother to take her to the tourney.

Aye, this was a powerful, forceful man. An earl in two countries.

But he was also Garrick.

Her Garrick.

"If you don't, I will dishonor you, Sara, your brother, my mother—"

"Your mother? Not your intended?"

They stood close enough to touch, but neither reached out. It was as if they both knew the flames, once sparked, would not be doused.

"My mother wants this marriage. Deserves it, after I—" He stopped.

"After you what, Garrick?"

He shook his head.

"What? You can tell me. After you—"

"Killed my father." Clearly, he was as surprised he'd uttered such words as she was to hear them.

"How could you possibly—"

"It was my idea."

He swallowed, and Emma didn't move. She was afraid to do anything that might stop his lips.

"I'd fought alongside Edward before. When he decided to join the king of France in the foreign campaign, I received the summons." Garrick ran his hand through his hair and made a sound. A painful, strained one utterly unlike anything she'd heard from him before.

"When you received the summons?" she prodded.

"He'd been saying for months he felt useless. Age had begun to claim his body. He'd slowed down, but he was still one of the finest warriors I knew." He frowned. "I wished to prove it to him."

She waited for him to continue, still unmoving.

"I encouraged him to come with me. My mother begged for him to stay. Neither of us listened."

And so he thought it was his fault his father had been killed. This was the weight he carried on his shoulders.

"Garrick, you didn't—"

"If I hadn't talked him into coming, he would still be the earl." He looked at her with such pain in his eyes. "I would be—"

"Garrick Clave, listen to me."

When she grabbed both of his hands, a jolt ran through her. The spark in his eye assured her that he felt it too.

"You did not kill your father."

He tried to pull away, but Emma would not allow it.

"You say he was the strongest man you knew. *Not* the kind of man to be swayed against his will."

"But he may never have—"

She used Sara's tone. "You did not kill your father," she repeated. "The day my parents were killed, I asked my brother to take me to the market for new ribbons. My uncle Hugh decided to join us, so two of the best Waryn fighters were not there to defend Bristol when it was attacked. For years, Bryce blamed himself for leaving. But it was not his fault. It was not my fault. Your father's death is *not* your fault, Garrick."

She reached up and cradled his face as he'd done to her twice before.

"Please believe me. I speak from experience."

His eyes widened, and he leaned down and kissed her. His lips moved over hers like a bolt of velvet, soft and sensual. Emma kissed him back, and for the first time, it was she who moved to deepen the kiss. She opened for him, and he took her invitation. His tongue moved over hers, pulling her with him, drowning her under a wave of passion that forced her arms around him.

His lips moved from her mouth to her neck. She lifted her head and allowed herself to lean back into his arms, arching her body against him.

"The sweetest taste in the world." His mouth moved lower, kissing her collarbone and the soft flesh beneath it.

But then he stopped and pulled her into his arms. He held her tightly to him, much as he'd done on their rides these last few days. But this time, there was nowhere for her to fall.

Or was there?

She turned her head sideways, laying her cheek on his chest. Inhaling deeply, Emma pushed even closer to him.

"I can't let you go," she said.

"Tonight?"

Nay, that was not what she had meant.

But saying more seemed silly. He was to be married. He was a man of honor and he'd made a pledge.

"You are an extraordinary woman, Emma Waryn."

She moved even closer to him.

I love you.

The words sat on the edge of her lips. Nothing had ever felt so right. Because it was true. Emma had seen love before. Her brothers had found it, and now she had as well. But her story would not end happily.

He pulled away to look at her.

"Love me, Garrick." It was not what she wanted to say, but it would have to do.

"Emma, no, I—"

"The way you did that night."

Wrapped in each other's arms, they stood motionless, eyes locked.

Emma waited.

"I am a virgin still," she said, breaking the silence at last. "And will be one when I leave. What harm is there—"

"What harm? Emma, we should not be here. Your brother—"

"Is sleeping with his wife." *The wife he loves.* "My maid knows what to say if either of them—"

"Your maid knows?" He pulled away then, and the look of horror on his face made her smile.

"Of course she does. Edith knows everything. And I trust her with my life."

Trust me with yours.

He took a moment to consider the idea. Did he not have any friends whom he trusted implicitly? But there was no time to think on it further. No time to ask him. His expression changed in a moment.

"I want nothing more than to make you scream with pleasure," he said, his voice husky.

He was going to do it.

"To watch your face," he said, reaching for the ties that bound her gown together in the front, "and feel your soft flesh beneath my fingers."

As the ties loosened, her chest felt unaccountably tighter rather than the opposite.

She'd changed into a simple undertunic and kirtle, which threatened to come undone at any moment.

At last, it was completely untied. The neckline, wide enough to fit over her shoulders, was easy prey for him. Garrick tugged with both hands, widening it even more. He guided her arms through the sleeves until the royal blue material lay in a puddle at her feet. She stepped over it as Garrick kicked the discarded kirtle to the side.

Wordlessly, he lifted the ivory undertunic over her head. She reached up her arms to assist him as if it were the most natural thing in the world.

Everything but Garrick ceased to exist.

Standing before him in nothing but a shift, Emma moved to cover her breasts, which peeked out behind the thin material. Garrick would have none of it. He grabbed her wrists and guided them behind her back. Still holding them there, he moved toward her.

He kissed her, first on the lips and then the neck, and moved lower, his lips trailing a path between her breasts, where the material dipped and allowed him access. When he stood and released her wrists, his movement was so sudden Emma didn't have time to prepare.

And she definitely needed it.

He lifted his loose shirt up in one swift motion. Tossing the offending garment aside, he stood motionless, watching her with an intense gaze.

She'd imagined those muscles, had felt them beneath her fingertips, but she hadn't spared a thought for the scars. An angry scar ran from his right shoulder to his collarbone. It was the most pronounced, but certainly not the only one. Each ridge was punctuated with battle scars, one precariously close to his heart.

He must have known she wanted to touch him. Garrick took her hand and guided it to his expansive chest, covering her sprawling fingers with his own. When his muscles twitched under her fingertips, she squeezed lightly, just enough to ensure he was quite real.

When Garrick released her hand, she explored, trailing her fingers down to his stomach. The sound that escaped his lips emboldened her.

He closed his eyes.

She grew bolder yet.

Wondering if she could arouse the same feelings in him that he'd stirred in her, Emma stepped forward and kissed the area just beneath his neck.

"Emma—" He pulled her against him, her chest slamming against his own. But this time, there was little to separate them, and when she wrapped her arms around him, it was flesh her fingers found.

His mouth lowered to hers, but this was nothing like the last kiss. This one was hard and insistent and filled with need. She opened for him, her body pressing against him—closer, closer, closer—of its own accord. When she felt his hand lifting the bottom of her shift, Emma welcomed the touch.

Still, her curious mind was a light, and she started to ask, "What are you . . . ," only to stop, mesmerized by his expression. She momentarily forgot about his wandering fingers, focused instead on the corner of his mouth, where he bit his lip. But he didn't let her forget for long. Without warning, his hand cupped that most intimate part of her. She met the question in his eyes with a slight nod.

She trusted him.

And then his fingers were inside her.

Emma didn't have time to be shocked. She tried to hold his gaze but could not. She closed her eyes and tilted her back.

"Garrick . . ."

"You know what to do."

She opened her eyes as the pressure increased between her legs. She held on to him, her knees weakening.

"I don't." The slow, sensual smile made her feel as if she were Garrick's prey. Well, if he wished to consume her, she'd allow it.

"Your body knows."

And it did.

It pressed and circled against him as he continued to watch her. The pressure was nearly unbearable.

"I can't."

"You can, Emma."

Her whimpers reverberated through the empty chamber. She couldn't stop them. Couldn't stop thrusting against him.

When he moved his hand against her this time, she could no longer hold on. Her body exploded as her fingers clenched against the hard muscles of Garrick's shoulders. The rippling sensations spread from her core to every other part of her body and only intensified when she opened her eyes to find him still watching her.

She licked her own lips then, unable to swallow. Or speak. It was like before, but stronger, more intense. And only when the throbbing began to ebb did Emma remember to breathe.

He withdrew from her then, the loss so poignant she wouldn't allow it. She reached for his hand, wrapped it around her back and kissed him with her newfound love, raw and unequivocal. Garrick lifted her then, cradling her in his arms, and strode over to the bed. He tossed her onto the bed and climbed atop her, his weight a delicious pleasure.

"I'm going to do it again," he warned her just before he lifted her shift and made good on his promise. This time, with him lying partly above her but to one side, she was able to grip him more firmly. No longer startled by his touch, she was prepared for it when he entered her again.

Emma knew what to do this time. And when his mouth captured hers, his tongue mimicking the movements down below, she couldn't hang on for long. She let go nearly immediately, her cries muffled against him.

"My beautiful Emma."

Oh God!

That pushed her over the edge. A cliff she fell from willingly, never hitting the bottom. With Garrick's help, she soared, her knuckles painful from clutching him so tightly.

"Never."

When she finally came back down, her feet once again planted on what felt like solid ground, she realized she'd said the word aloud.

"Never what?" he asked.

Good question. She'd never experienced anything quite like it? *Nay. I never want to let him go.*

Garrick rolled to the side, realizing he was likely crushing her. He closed his eyes, attempting to get control of himself. His cock was hard, throbbing, aching to be touched. To glide into her as easily as his fingers . . . nay, that wasn't helping.

Stop thinking of it.

He needed to think of something, anything, but the passionate response of the woman lying next to him. If he so much as turned toward her . . .

"Garrick?"

"A moment, if you please, Emma."

He took slow, deep breaths, willing himself to gain control. He had no choice. There could be no relief for him. Not here. Not with her.

Never.

What had she meant?

"Are you well?" she asked.

He still couldn't look at her. England. Scotland. Acre. He'd never been with a woman who aroused such a passion in him. What would it be like to . . . *Garrick, stop.*

CECELIA MECCA

"Did I do something wrong?"

That did it. The horror that Emma would think such a thing, even for a moment, finally enabled him to gain the control he desperately needed. This time, his heart, not his manhood, stirred.

He turned onto his side, propping his head on his elbow. "Wrong? Never."

She was so incredibly lovely. She'd pulled down her shift, and a good thing because his wandering eyes could not stop gazing downward. What would it be like to have those legs wrapped around him?

"You have that look again."

He groaned and pulled her toward him. "No more looks this eve, my insatiable minx."

They lay side by side, Emma's face just inches from his own. He caught himself from leaning his head forward to kiss her. It would only make it harder in the end.

"You'd best be getting back."

"Aye," she said without moving.

"Garrick," she whispered, her hair tickling his cheek. He moved it to the side, trying not to look at her. "That felt really good."

And there it was again. Desire welling inside him, pulling at him, encouraging him to . . .

No. He could not have her.

Emma was not his.

"I'm glad to hear you say so." He pulled her tighter.

"I don't want to leave yet."

"Then don't."

Despite all the reasons he should tell her to go, he found he could not. He wanted her to stay too, but if they were ever caught, the fallout would be considerable.

Garrick allowed his mind to wander down that path. They'd have to marry, of course. His broken betrothal would enrage the Earl of Magnus, mayhap enough so to start a clan war. His uncle would use the incident to steal the title out from under him, and his mother would lose a husband and her inheritance in one fell swoop.

And yet Garrick still found himself reaching for the back of her hair, pulling the strands together, and moving them aside so that he could touch her neck. It was only an innocent touch, certainly nothing like . . .

Emma sighed.

And then he imagined her lying like this with Graeme. He pictured her atop him, her expression filled with the pure pleasure of release. A release given to her by another man.

No!

"I'm going to delay the wedding." Even as he said it, he knew the words made no sense. He had to marry. Would marry. A delay was pointless.

"I see."

She didn't ask why. Or what it meant. Instead, she moved her head to the side to give him better access to the exposed skin there.

Garrick flipped Emma onto her back and moved over her.

"Don't marry Graeme."

She blinked. "I have no intention—"

"He will ask."

The corners of Emma's lips lifted and her blue eyes sparkled with mischief. "You're being silly—"

"Wait until I send for you. Promise me."

"Send for me? Garrick, you aren't making sense. Why would you—"

"Your brother and I spoke of a meeting, a gathering of the border lords to determine the next recourse from the attack. I will host it. Find a way to come with him."

"That should not be a problem. But why?"

He shook his head, not understanding himself.

Or maybe he understood all too much.

"I can't make any promises. My mother expects a wedding. Magnus and his daughter . . . they are all expecting a wedding. But . . ."

He reached up and laid her hand on his cheek. His heart raced as the implications washed over him. What he was about to say could not be unsaid. But it was the truth, and he could no more keep quiet than he could resist bringing this woman every pleasure she deserved.

"If there's a way to stop it, I will."

Her hand dropped. Garrick, propped above her, looked down at the most beautiful, spirited woman he'd ever known. One who had captured his heart and soul in the short time they'd known each other.

"I love you, Emma."

Her eyes widened, and he wished the words back immediately. He'd never uttered them to a woman before, and in truth, he'd never expected to.

She cupped his face as if he were a newborn babe rather than a hardened warrior. "I love you too."

His chest constricted and his mouth went dry. Garrick couldn't get closer quickly enough. He leaned down and kissed her, every nerve ending in his body screaming, her lips all-consuming. He loved this woman with every part of himself, would give everything he owned to be closer to her, to be inside her, to show her the truth of his words. To make a life with her.

For now, he'd be content with a kiss, one that threatened to drag him into an eternal bliss from which he might never recover.

One that held promises he wasn't sure he could keep.

CHAPTER SIXTEEN

I love you, Emma.

The words came back to her before she was fully awake. She repeated them over and over in her mind. He truly had said them.

And more.

By the time Emma left his chamber, Garrick had vowed to set up a meeting, and nothing would stop her from accompanying Geoffrey to Clave Castle.

I love you too.

And she did. She didn't want to, of course, but she did.

She had been wrong. Love, it seemed, did not care about circumstances. There was no denying he was everything she didn't want in a man. He was an earl twice over. He gave orders as if he'd been doing so his whole life, spoke of the king as if he were just another man, owned more properties than Sara and Geoffrey, and could call two separate armies of men to battle. And yet her earl was also thoughtful and strong. He inspired the kind of loyalty she could admire. And whether it was logical or not, and it was most assuredly not as he was currently betrothed to another woman, Emma *did* love him. She hadn't asked him to break the betrothal. Emma understood the politics of his alliance. Indeed, she couldn't fathom a way for him to escape them. But if anyone could do it, Garrick could. He was smart and—

"Are you awake, my lady?"

Emma turned in the bed, pulling the covers toward her chin. "Of sorts."

It had been quite late when she'd returned, without incident, to her bedchamber. She hadn't felt the need to rise early because she'd already said goodbye to *him*.

"The household will be thinkin' you're ill."

She watched as Edith stoked the fire.

"I didn't even hear you come in to start it," she said.

"Roaming around will tire you out, to be sure." There was a teasing sparkle in the other girl's eyes.

As much as she wished to stay abed for a little longer, there was no need to keep her friend in suspense. "Come here and sit!" she said. "I've so much to tell you."

Edith picked up a stool and brought it over.

"Go on, then," she said, taking a seat. Her tone told Emma she'd been waiting, with varying degrees of patience, all morning.

"He loves me," she blurted.

Emma laughed at her maid's shocked expression.

"I can hardly believe it myself, but I feel the same way. I think I knew at the inn the other day. Or mayhap before, at Dunmure, watching Clara and Alex together. There's always been something . . . I can't explain it. But I told myself it didn't matter. And then I found out he was getting married. Maybe that's when I knew. I felt as if I'd been punched—"

"Slow down! I can hardly follow you—"

"But in the storeroom, when he did that, I thought, 'Well, Emma, now you know what desire is all about.' But love? Maybe it was a bit of both—"

"Did what?"

Emma could feel the heat rushing to her cheeks. She hadn't meant to say that, exactly.

"Never mind."

She rushed to change the topic.

"I know what you're thinking. 'But Emma, he's an earl. You've turned away every powerful man who's sought your hand. You want to be in control. To run your own household, aye, but also to have a husband who won't tell you that you can't go to a tournament, or that it's too dangerous to travel to Scotland. To be a partner, like Sara—'"

"Are ye finished talkin' to yourself?"

"Quite."

A sudden thought occurred to Emma, and she sat up so quickly she felt dizzy for just a moment. "Edith!"

"Aye, my lady?"

"He did not ask to marry me." She rushed to explain. "Of course he cannot. He is still betrothed. But he did not promise to marry me if he succeeds in breaking off the betrothal. Mayhap—"

"He said he loved you?"

"Aye."

"And that he would delay his wedding?"

"Aye, but you don't understand. 'Tis not just a wedding. His uncle resents that Garrick's mother inherited the title. And that his father, before he passed into the afterlife"—Emma crossed herself—"was the Earl of Linkirk. He could cause trouble. 'Tis why his mother encouraged this alliance with the Earl of Magnus's daughter."

Emma did not like Edith's expression. She'd expected excitement or interest, but she saw only doubt.

"So, you see, 'tis quite a tangle."

She jumped out of bed, no longer wanting to look at the doubt on her friend's face. "Come, I must speak with Sara at once."

"My lady," Edith said from behind her.

Something in Edith's tone enticed her to turn around.

"If what you say is true . . ."

"Aye, Edith, 'tis true. But Garrick knows better than—"

"My lady."

Her tone sent a shiver straight to Emma's core.

She knew at once what Edith would say. The voice in her own head, the one trying to push aside thoughts of how Garrick made her feel and memories of how sweetly he'd pledged his love sounded much the same as Edith's.

"Do you think it's wise to tell Lady Sara?"

"Of course. I share everything with her. She is—"

"Your sister-in-law, but also the Countess of Kenshire. As the countess, what do you believe she'll say?"

Emma had planned to tell Sara everything, hoping it would ensure she was included in Garrick's invitation to Clave, and then . . .

Oh dear.

Sara would say that there was no way Garrick could break the betrothal without facing repercussions. This could change the course of Linkirk's history. It could force neighboring clans, like Clan Kerr and Graeme's people, to take sides.

Emma wanted to be angry with Edith. She wanted to rail at her, at the Earl of Magnus and his daughter, and at their whole sorry situation.

But she would not, of course. It was no one's fault that she'd allowed herself to fall in love with a man who was promised to another.

No one's fault but her own.

"Have you gone stark raving mad?" Conrad asked. "What are you still doing here?"

He should never have told Conrad the truth.

Garrick had returned to Clave, the torturous ride from

Kenshire one of the longest of his life, despite the fact that it was but a few hours away. He'd arrived before the tide could wash away the footpath leading from the shore to the castle gates, allowing him and his men safe passage before the rising tide turned Clave into an island once again.

Looking out of the window of the same solar where he'd taken advice from his friend before his fateful trip to Scotland, Garrick tried to remember the man he had been then.

A son without a father. An earl, a man with as much power as any in Northumbria. But not enough, apparently, to control his own destiny.

"Garrick, think on it. You cannot break this betrothal."

"'Tis done, Conrad." Or it would be soon. He'd already sent a contingent of men from Kenshire straight back to Linkirk to change the date of the wedding and summon his mother back to Clave. They'd been less than pleased with the prospect of returning to Scotland so soon, especially since they were less than a day's ride away from home, but he hadn't dared send a sole messenger.

Conrad sat with his legs and arms crossed on the wooden chair Garrick's father had often occupied. His friend was a very different man from the former earl. Their loyalty and ferocity in battle, whether on the field or in a tournament, had united them. But any similarities between the two ended there.

"Why are you smiling?" Conrad asked.

Garrick couldn't resist. "You are unique, Conrad."

"And you are a dead man." Never one to circumvent an uncomfortable topic, much like Emma, his friend was direct and possibly correct. He knew what his decision might cost him.

"I've no choice," he said, trying to explain.

"Of course you have a choice. Marry the Scottish lass."

"I cannot."

As was his custom, Conrad was not intimidated by a look meant to silence him. "You must."

"I love her, Conrad."

His friend's eyes widened as large as two round shields. Earls did not marry for love. Even baron's sons, like Conrad, married for advantage.

But he could not do it. Not now that he knew Emma was out there, that he could love in such a fierce manner.

"She is . . ." He thought back to last eve. "Extraordinary."

"Garrick, if she were the Queen of England, it would not—"

"What is the one thing that annoys you most about me?"

Conrad snorted. "That you cannot visit the garderobe without a plan? That you overthink everything until you—"

"She is just the opposite. Emma is . . ." How could he explain her best? "She doesn't think, she acts. And everyone around her is better for it. Aye, she's beautiful, but—"

"And now you're a bard."

"There's something there. Before I knew who she was. Something, Conrad, I've never experienced with a woman. Like a pull to—"

"Start a war with your mother's relatives?"

Garrick clenched his fists. "You are a singular ass."

"Why did you agree to the betrothal?"

In a rare display of seriousness, Conrad uncrossed his arms and legs, and sat forward, his elbows propped on his knees, his expression somber.

"Garrick?" he pressed.

Why? He'd asked himself the same question so many times in the past weeks.

"Because you encouraged it," he shot back, still standing at the window.

Conrad didn't respond. He merely quirked an eyebrow, silently communicating that Garrick had a better answer.

"Why? You know exactly why! Because the alliance will secure Linkirk. It will tighten our ties to our northern neighbors, convince those who are not yet convinced that peace along the border is possible."

Conrad cleared his throat.

"Dammit, Conrad. What do you want me to say?" His skin tingled as beads of sweat began to form around his temples.

He knew the answer Conrad wanted. But he was still loath to think about it. Because it was the one thing, the only thing, that was keeping Emma from being his.

"Garrick?"

"To appease my mother."

He let the words hang in the air like a morning fog. He had agreed because it was what his mother wanted. And after his father had been killed because of him, it was the least he could give her.

You did not kill your father.

He'd begun to believe her. Because he wanted to believe her. But his father was dead, and he had now set a path in motion that would ruin his mother as well. She would be forced to return to England. She would lose the one bit of comfort she had left.

"Bollocks, Conrad. What have I done?"

CHAPTER SEVENTEEN

*H*e would make it right. Somehow he would make it right. Somehow he'd find a way to fix this without giving her up.

After his discussion with Conrad, Garrick did what he'd always done growing up on an island that wasn't an island. He waited until the water receded and walked the path from the castle gates to the shore, over and over again, taunting the rising tide as if conquering it meant conquering life itself. Every time he made it safely to the rocky beach at the foot of the castle, Garrick felt renewed.

His mother hated the practice. Especially now, during the winter months, when the frigid waters could kill a man as easily as a sword in the gut. But the tactic helped him think. And while the castle housed only his knights and sworn swordsmen, their wives and children, and Clave's servants, some of whom had been with the family since his birth, it still felt too crowded to suit him.

When Conrad had left the solar, delivering him a final pat on the back on his way out, Garrick had allowed himself a moment of pity before shrugging it off. His father would have faced this challenge as he had faced any other.

Audentes fortuna iuvat.

Those words were inscribed on the wall behind the lord and lady's table in the hall and engraved in both his shield and his father's. It was more than a family motto. His father had lived by it. Garrick had sought to do so as well.

And if fortune truly favored the bold, he would make Emma Waryn his wife.

When he finally made his way to the great hall the next morn, weary down to his bones, Mable immediately told him, "My lord, if I might say such a thing, you look . . ."

She rarely held back her words.

At two and fifty, Mable was everything her husband had been before her, and more. Her husband had served Clave as steward under both his father and grandfather. They'd all been shocked when the much older man had married Mable, a serving woman who'd already been widowed once. Ten years later, she'd become a widow once again. But his father had taken a chance and named her steward, and she'd never given him reason to regret it.

Garrick would do anything for this woman and her two sons. Despite her surly disposition, which his mother pardoned as the natural result of "doing the job expected of a man," she was a woman of deep loyalty and feeling. He would never forget that she'd comforted his mother after his father's death.

Though her hair had gone gray, Mable had an unwavering gaze that was unaltered by age. Most of the residents of Clave were either terrified of her or adored her as if she were their own mother.

"I need to send a message," he said, sitting down, alone, for the morning meal.

In his youth, he'd wanted to sit among his men, but his father had never allowed it. Even though the high table was raised less than an arm's length above the others, it was set apart from Clave's retainers as clearly as if it were in a different room altogether. Today he was grateful for the distance.

"To whom, my lord?"

He handed her the missives, not wanting to wait until after the meal when they typically conducted business of the day. "I've called a meeting for ten days from today. Clave must prepare."

Mable, who could read and write courtesy of the same tutor who had instructed Garrick as a boy, looked at the outside of each scroll.

"Nine lords and their families," he said.

"Aye, my lord."

"The attack I mentioned. This is a small council to discuss it."

"And establish yourself as our new earl," she correctly surmised.

Most of the men on that list would accept his new role with ease. At least two of them, hesitant allies of his father, would need to be convinced.

"At once, my lord." Mable did not move to leave.

"Is something amiss?"

"There are rumors."

"Of?"

"'Tis said by some of the men that you've changed the wedding, that you'll not wed till spring."

"That is correct," he said without clarifying. Though he'd hoped the envoys he'd sent back to Scotland would refrain from sharing the contents of the message with others, it had perhaps been too much to hope. He should have known better.

Mable was waiting for him to elaborate when their attention was drawn to the entrance of the hall.

Conrad had made his entrance. He'd have some company at the dais after all.

"'Tis said the Lady of Brookhurst is wanting her son home at once," Mable said, looking at his friend and shaking her head.

"Curious," he said. "Would you be anxious to have such a man at your side?"

Mable's cackle followed her as she walked away, leaving him in the company of the only brother Garrick ever had. An imperfect one, to be sure.

"Speaking ill of your best friend again, *Lord* Clave?"

"'Tis an early morning for you," Garrick said. "You're just in time to help me plan a council meeting."

"At Clave?" He popped a morsel of cheese into his mouth.

"Aye."

"And invited Kenshire, I assume?"

"Aye." He tried to ignore the sound of Conrad loudly chewing.

"And kept the invitations to the lords and ladies of each family, I assume?"

He forced himself to look directly at his friend as he said, "Nay."

Conrad sighed. "You invited their families."

"Aye."

"Including Lady Emma."

His silence was affirmation enough. He no longer wanted to discuss it. If anything, his resolve had been strengthened by his restless night.

If he could not go a day without her, how could he possibly spend a lifetime without seeing her smile? Without knowing Emma Waryn, both her luscious curves and her beautiful soul, as only a husband could do? It was unthinkable.

Impossible.

Garrick would make this work.

He had no other choice.

It was never going to work.

Sara couldn't leave the babe, and since the attack, Geoffrey had been more protective than ever. When Emma approached him in the great hall after he received the missive, the one she only knew about from Sara, her brother refused to so much as consider the possibility.

"Until we know who was behind the attack, I think it's best you remain here."

Lord, save her from older brothers.

"Besides, haven't you had enough excitement for the moment?" he continued. "What could you possibly hope to achieve at Clave?"

They stood in front of the mantel in Kenshire's great hall. This winter was more bitter than most, and the crisp air seemed to have permeated the stone walls of the castle, forcing everyone closer to the fires that burned in every occupied room.

"Achieve?"

Only two days had passed since she'd last seen Garrick, but it was two days longer than she would have liked. She spent most waking moments remembering their brief time together, the intimate moments that seemed so otherworldly now that she'd resumed her regular habits. How had it happened so quickly?

"A gathering of pompous old men sitting around trying to solve the border problems," he quoted her. Emma couldn't help but smile at Geoffrey's poor imitation of her voice.

"I do not sound like that at all."

Although the words *were* familiar.

"By your own criterion, there will be no marriageable men in attendance. This crowd is much too 'titled' for my baby sister."

Geoffrey was quite familiar with her thoughts on men with titles. Although he considered her reasoning absurd—he and her other brothers had only been a mite protective, to hear him tell it —he nonetheless accepted that her goals were different than most women's. He, of course, disagreed that she'd been coddled as the younger sister. They were only trying to protect her, after all.

"But he invited families as well," she tried.

"Peculiar, that."

Emma didn't comment.

"It's less than a half-day ride. What trouble could I possibly get into on Caiser land?"

That seemed to give him pause. Maybe she could convince him after all? Although it hardly mattered. Emma was going, with or without her brother's permission.

"No retort?" a soft voice asked from behind them.

Emma turned, grateful for her sister-in-law's support. "Good day, Sara."

"Good day, Emma." She walked to Geoffrey and leaned up for a quick kiss. "Husband."

Emma followed Geoffrey's gaze behind her. The hall was empty but for a handful of servants moving trestle tables into place for the midday meal.

"Faye is with him. Sleeping again."

Apparently satisfied, Geoffrey finally answered.

"You could get into trouble in your own bedchamber," he said. Emma's heart pounded. Her brother's statement was truer than he realized.

Sara gave him a chastening look and a slight nod, and to Emma's shock, he relented.

"Fine. But you ride next to me. And will remain at Clave until we return."

Spirits soaring, Emma grinned at Sara. "And where else do you believe I would go? Clave is, after all, an island."

"With the exception of twice a day during low tide."

"Oh, aye," she said. "When I can make a dashing escape, riding swiftly to the shore where I—"

"We've been invited to stay the night," he interrupted.

Emma froze. Sara had not mentioned that. She'd been wondering how it would be possible to steal a moment alone with Garrick, and now it seemed she'd have ample opportunity.

"Oh, there's Peter. Finally. If you'll excuse me." Geoffrey left her and Sara alone together before the enormous mantel.

"Emma? What is amiss?"

Her sister-in-law knew her well. For the past two days, Emma had vacillated about whether she should confide in Sara. Still undecided, she'd taken to avoiding her instead.

Emma shifted her weight. "Amiss?"

Today, Sara looked every bit the countess in her simple cream day gown, her hair in a jeweled filet. It made it more difficult to withstand her penetrating stare.

"Emma?"

"Sara?" she teased. She was just not ready to tell her all. In truth, Edith had scared her.

"I would never presume to ask you to reveal what you don't wish to tell," Sara said finally. "Shall we?" She gestured to the chairs in front of the mantel.

Once they were both seated, Sara turned to her and asked, "I know you've told the tale of the attack before, but are there other details you can remember?"

The memories still assailed her, but she'd much rather talk about that than discuss her feelings for the earl.

"I was so scared," she admitted. "And Garrick insisted I not look upon the dead, although I did peek. Everyone seems to think Garrick's uncle may be responsible."

Sara sighed. "He certainly may be. A horrid man."

"You know him?" Though she was unable to hide the surprise in her voice, Emma somehow refrained from asking more questions. There was so much she wanted to ask about Garrick—his family, his earldom, and Sara's friendship with him—but she didn't dare.

"I've never met the man, but I overheard my father and Garrick's father having a conversation about him once. They didn't speak highly of the man, and his attempts to undermine the natural succession of the earldom doesn't speak highly of his character." She sighed. "It matters not that Garrick is English. The title is his mother's by right. Why his uncle can't accept that fact . . . well . . . I suppose 'tis not so unusual."

She knew what Sara was thinking. Her dear sister-in-law had almost been harmed by a cousin intent on murdering her for the sake of her title and land. Thank goodness Geoffrey had been there to protect her.

"But I do know his mother," Sara said.

"What is she like?" Emma asked, too quickly.

"Fierce," Sara said, thankfully not appearing to notice Emma's eager response. "Determined. The only man along the border meaner than the Baron of Inverglen is the Earl of Magnus, the man she sought out for an alliance. His reputation is known well, even here."

"It is?"

"Aye. The relative peace we've experienced along the border these last years has lulled everyone into a state of unpreparedness that worries me at times. But when the border was less stable, if there was one man in the North all wanted as a friend and feared as a foe, it was Magnus."

Garrick's future father-in-law. Or the man who would have been his father-in-law. What would such a man do if his only daughter was jilted? Would he truly allow Garrick out of the marriage contract? Or would it mean war?

Oh dear.

"Enough talk of overeager men and their insecurities. Tell me, more importantly, about these rumors I've heard about you and a certain man who's taken a liking to you."

Emma's stomach flipped. "Sara, I can—"

"I've not met Graeme de Sowlis, but I've heard much about him from Catrina."

Graeme?

Emma felt so flummoxed she almost gave herself away.

"Well?"

She shook her head, unsure of how to respond.

"Do you fancy the man?"

"I . . . I'm not sure."

Sara appeared to think on that.

"Well, then perhaps we should invite him to Kenshire to get to know him a bit more. What do you say?"

Invite Graeme to Kenshire?

"Uh—"

"Think on it." Sara jumped to her feet. "Do you smell that? Cook has managed to find cinnamon." She took in a deep breath. "I do love that woman."

"Aye," Emma agreed as Sara walked away, presumably to find the source of the smell.

Graeme. Magnus.

This meeting at Clave couldn't come soon enough. Emma needed to speak with Garrick. She required answers that only he could give her.

CHAPTER EIGHTEEN

"Geoffrey, look!"

As they made their way across the cobbled pathway toward Clave Castle, Emma continued to point out evidence of the sea water that had swept through the area just a short time earlier. She reached down to give Nella a bit of encouragement.

"Seaweed. So very fascinating." He grinned down at her from his taller steed.

"Mock all you like, brother. But have you ever seen anything like it?"

Despite his casual tone, Geoffrey looked around them with an expression so similar to her twin's that Emma couldn't resist smiling. She knew what it meant without asking—Geoffrey was impressed by what he saw.

"You look so much like Neill right now."

They'd reached the shoreline, or where the shoreline would soon appear, and began to climb up toward the gatehouse.

"Is that right?"

"Aye. Or at least you look like the carefree boy Neill was, and less like the big brother who fought so hard to keep our family safe."

"That is all I've ever wanted to do, Em."

Despite his occasional high-handedness, Geoffrey really did care about keeping her from harm's way. If he was a mite over-protective since their parents' death, she could hardly blame him.

And her twin was no longer the sweet boy she remembered. His reputation continued to grow at the tournaments she could never attend.

"I miss him," she said, knowing there was naught Geoffrey could do about it.

"As do I," he said. "But he promised to visit this summer."

Emma hadn't seen him since his accolade, and now that he was officially a knight, she feared he was falling prey to the "tourney call," as Geoffrey called it. But he was always quick to remind her that he and Bryce had both done it and lived to tell the tale. Seeking validation and glory from one tourney to the next, each win sweeter than the last. But she remembered the wounds they'd suffered, the scares they'd given her mother and then, after Bristol was taken, their aunt, every time they left to compete.

Emma tried not to think on it. Instead, she concentrated on the circular stone structure that rose above them. Garrick was somewhere inside there. She would finally get to see him again.

She'd hardly slept the night before. After waking early to ensure Geoffrey would not leave without her, Emma had donned her favorite gown, a pale blue one that matched her eyes. Sara had visited her in her chamber, and her behavior had made Emma wonder, if only for a moment, if she knew the truth. Sara had looked at her oddly, opened her mouth as if to speak, but then closed it again.

"Beautiful," she'd finally said.

Edith had accompanied the group, and just a few hours in the saddle had reminded them all why Emma had ended up traveling to Scotland unaccompanied. For a marshal's daughter, Edith really wasn't a passable horsewoman.

In fact . . .

"Geoffrey, I don't believe Edith will make it up there."

The incline to the main gate, halfway up to the castle itself, was a steep one. The keep was, quite literally, built from the rocks that surrounded it.

They dismounted just as a man on horseback came down to meet them. Emma pulled her hood forward, trying to keep the wind from whipping into her face. The breeze rendered a cold day freezing.

Assuming it was the steward, Emma turned to find Edith being helped off her mount.

She took a few steps back to talk to her friend, dragging Nella's reins with her. "How could we have possibly imagined you'd be able to make it across the border?" she teased.

Edith stood up straight, as if to contradict Emma's words.

"I'm just fine, my lady. I—" Edith looked over Emma's shoulder. "Oh yes, I can see what you mean now. He is quite a bit more handsome than I remembered," she whispered.

Part of Emma had already known it was him. She could feel him behind her, and the pull that had always existed between them compelled her to turn.

Garrick looked at her in a way he most certainly shouldn't. It was a good thing her face was partially hidden by her hood.

The hair on his face slightly grown, his jaw set, Garrick exuded power. Dominance.

Desire.

He greeted her brother and then strode directly toward her.

Garrick bowed. "'Tis good to see you again, my lady."

He looked to Geoffrey, who nodded distractedly as he talked to one of his men. Having secured her brother's permission, Garrick held out his arm.

And she took it, trying to ignore Edith's sly smile as a groom took Nella's reins.

Despite the biting cold and unrelenting wind and the layers of cloth between them, the jolt of his touch strengthened Emma's resolve. She was exactly where she should be. No one had ever made her feel as such, and she doubted anyone would again.

Her heart thudded with every step she took toward the keep. So much she wanted to say, but none of it was proper.

"You made it."

She peeked at him and caught a glimpse of the water beginning to edge its way closer to the shore.

"Of course." Emma couldn't contain her amazement. "Clave is . . ." She looked up, beyond the gate that had just been opened to allow them through.

"Do you like it?"

"Like it? I love it. 'Tis the most beautiful place I've ever seen."

When he didn't respond, Emma looked back toward Garrick.

"It is now."

Emma's gown was too tight. Nay. The air was too cold.

She turned away, looking back at the others who followed them up the hill.

"We've much to discuss," he said in an undertone. Then, turning toward his guests, he gestured toward the entrance, a massive oak door that seemed to spring up from the rocks.

"'Tis almost as if the rock and castle were one," Emma said with wonder as she stopped and leaned down to inspect the construction. "Fascinating."

Men streamed past her and Geoffrey said to Garrick, "Her interests know no bounds."

Indeed, Emma loved understanding how structures were made almost as much as she loved horses. "When was this built?" she asked, standing. Then, remembering something, she spun to look down at the remainder of their party. "And the horses? Where will they—oh."

It seemed Nella and the others were being led down a path to their right.

"The stables are behind the keep," Garrick said. "Did you imagine she would follow you directly into the hall?"

The look on his face tugged on her heart. Despite his wealth and position, despite the horrible things he'd seen and done, Garrick retained a playfulness that had endeared her to him from the start.

"Well, no, I—" She swatted his arm. "You're teasing me."

The others had already made their way inside, Geoffrey and Edith included. But Emma was reluctant to do so. Once there, they would be separated.

He seemed to hear her thoughts. "We will find a way to talk."

Talk.

He said the word as if it were a curse. The implication that they would do more hung in the air between them.

"I look forward to it, my lord."

For a moment, she thought he might kiss her right there. The way he looked at her drove her mad.

"After you, my lady." He gestured for her to enter. If Emma had thought the castle's outer appearance was spectacular, the entrance hall leading to the great room was as exquisite as any she'd ever seen.

What Clave lacked in size, being trapped on an island, it made up for in splendor. It seemed as if gold sparkled from every corner, yet it was neither cold nor unapproachable. The Clave coat of arms hung prominently above a raised dais. The high wooden beams that crisscrossed above them shined as if they'd just been freshly cleaned.

The room was filled with strangers, men and a few women, all unknown to her. But apparently she was alone in that, as greetings abounded between the great border lords. Just as she'd suspected, Garrick was swallowed by his guests the moment he followed her inside, but a strange woman soon approached her. A lady's maid?

Before Emma could tell her she'd brought her own maid, the woman said, "Good day, Lady Emma. I am Mable, the steward here. Lord Clave asked if I—"

"Steward?"

It was incredibly impolite, but Emma could not contain her surprise. She'd never met a female steward before.

Mable was apparently accustomed to such a reaction and did not appear offended.

"Aye, my lady. Would you an' your lady's maid care to refresh yourselves from the journey?"

Emma glanced around the room. Another small party had arrived, and this time it was someone Emma recognized. Lord Huntington. Bryce had squired with the man, and though she had no opinion of him, Emma despised his now-married daughter. The woman had rebuked Bryce after learning he was a second son, thereby breaking her steadfast brother's heart. But no matter. If the woman hadn't acted so poorly, Bryce would not have met and married Catrina.

"Of course," she murmured to the steward, trying not to seek out Garrick in the crowd. She found Edith instead, and the steward led them through a long, well-lit corridor and then up a winding set of stone steps.

"This is the best chamber, beside the lord's and lady's, of course. The view, 'tis—"

Emma gasped. Upon entering the room, she was immediately drawn to the window. Though its shutters were only slightly open, she could already see why Mable had complimented the room. Even though the flowers were not in bloom, Emma could tell the area below the steep drop-off from her window was an expansive garden. Rocks intermingled with the remnants of plants, all of it leading down to the rocks that lined the coast. Beyond that, there was only ocean.

"The view?"

"'Tis mid-tide, my lady. You arrived just in time."

"I knew Clave was a tidal island, but to see it happening—"

Mable moved to the window and closed and latched the shutters. "My apologies for the cold air. I can't imagine why these were left open. On the other side of the castle, you'd see the causeway is just barely covered with water now. Within the hour, boats will bring the remaining guests."

Remarkable.

"I'll put my things here," Edith said, coming up from behind her.

"Nay."

Garrick's voice, so unexpected, made her jump.

"Mable, please see Mistress Edith to the servants' quarters."

The steward startled. "Aye, as you please, my lord."

Mable and Edith left at once, taking Emma's wits with them.

"What are you doing here?" she finally managed to ask. "Garrick, your guests . . . my brother."

He closed the door behind him as she spoke, and then reached for her before she could utter another word. She kissed him eagerly, feeling as prey to the emotions and desire churning inside her as the cobbled walkway was to the tide.

His lips moved over hers, his tongue insistent, and she met every thrust. She pulled him closer just as Garrick broke contact.

"I had to, Emma. I needed to know."

His breath smelled of mint. His scent was exactly as she'd remembered it.

"Geoffrey—"

"Will not miss me for a few moments. None know where you are but me."

He cupped her face in his hands. "God, I've missed you."

He kissed her nose. Her cheeks. Her eyelids. With every soft touch of his lips, Emma could feel the answer to the two questions foremost on her mind.

He still wanted her. He still loved her.

"Garrick, how—"

"We can't talk now," he said, already letting her go. "I must get back. After the meeting," he said. "At the meal, I need you to know, no matter what is said—"

"What do you mean?"

"No matter what is said—by me or your brother or any of the others. Emma, look at me."

She was trying to concentrate, but his touch was distracting. She was finally in his arms after dreaming of it for so long.

"I love you. Do you hear me?"

Aye. I do.

"Remember that. And I will come to you tonight."

She'd hoped for as much, and yet . . . "Do you think that's a good idea?"

He bit his lip, a simple gesture that banished any thoughts of whether or not it was a good idea.

"I think 'tis the best idea I've ever had. Promise me you will remember?"

He was worried about something.

"I will. But what—"

"I have to go." He squeezed her hands, and just as quickly as he had come, Garrick left, closing the door behind him.

Emma moved back to the window and unclasped the wooden shutters. She peeked out, allowing herself to imagine, just for a moment, a life here at Clave. As Garrick's wife. Could Garrick even make such a thing happen?

Oh God, she hoped so. Because the alternative was unthinkable.

The Northumbrian council of border lords had been a success. They'd discussed the attack, and those closest to the border had agreed to inquire further on his behalf. His English allies had all pointed their fingers firmly north. In this, Garrick was hesitant to disagree—he'd heard the man's accent, after all—even though he knew blaming the Scots was a much too common deflection.

The council had also agreed that the unprovoked attack pointed to a bigger problem. Though the Day of Truce, a once-a-month meeting between Scottish and English nobles at the border, had been established more than thirty years earlier, peace never felt assured in the borderlands. Raids were still more common than anyone would like. But it was only recently, since just before Garrick had left for the Holy Land, that circumstances had begun to change.

Establishing himself as the new Earl of Clave, strengthening alliances—Garrick would have considered it an exceptional day if it weren't for his inability to think beyond the woman seated just in front of him at dinner. The one who set his blood on fire. Emma was the reason he had called the council, in truth, and she was about to find herself at the center of an extremely uncomfortable scene if Lord Davenhill did not cease his appalling behavior toward her.

"You're staring. Again," Conrad said. His friend, seated beside him at the high table, had taken it upon himself to continually admonish him for all of the glances he'd been giving Davenhill.

With so many prominent men and women present, Garrick had left the seating arrangement to the very competent Mable. Of course she'd put the earls and their families closest to the high table, which meant Emma was seated directly below him. The moment she entered the hall for supper, Garrick had known the evening would be a very long one.

Dressed in a deep red gown, its neckline and sleeves trimmed in the same gold as the belt that hung loosely around her hips, Emma had entered the room to the stares of nearly seventy noblemen and women. Everyone had looked at her, including Conrad, and some had not deigned to hide their appreciation.

Her brother, clearly accustomed to his sister's impact on men, had stayed close until they sat, a most welcome gesture. Even now, he gave Lord Davenhill a look that would send most men cowering into a corner. But the cocksure widower continued to flirt mercilessly, undeterred by the angry stares angled at him from two directions.

"I don't like him."

"Clearly," Conrad said, pushing a mug toward him. "Drink. Before you do something you'll regret."

He tore his gaze from the scene before him. "Regret smashing in that bastard's face? Have you forgotten the rumors that he beat his first wife?"

"Alas, he also shares a border with Clave and is a favorite of the king. He'd make a poor enemy."

Garrick grabbed the mug Conrad had shoved toward him. "But I do see the appeal."

Garrick couldn't even manage the goodwill to smile.

Conrad continued, "The Earl of Kenshire is not a man to be trifled with. Judging by his expression, a brawl may break out yet, even if you don't start it."

Garrick resisted the urge to look. "Good."

He ignored Conrad's exaggerated sigh of frustration.

"So 'tis not enough for you to start a war in Scotland?" Conrad asked. "You've a mind to have one here as well?"

"I haven't started a war."

"So what exactly have you done? And don't say 'nothing.'"

Thus far he'd avoided speaking to his friend about Linkirk, but Conrad was not put off so easily. "I may have postponed the wedding. And I've asked Mother to return to England."

"And?" Conrad waited.

But there was nothing more to tell. "And I will speak to her upon her return."

"Dear God, Garrick. Please tell me you're not relying on an

appeal to the woman who stands to lose her inheritance if you back out of this agreement."

"Conrad," he warned.

"Garrick, please tell me Linkirk's future does not rest on a discussion with your mother. You must—"

"Not now."

Conrad, surprisingly, fell silent.

The meal finished, guests began to move from their benches to other parts of the hall. The harpist Mable had found in Clave's village continued to play, lending a harmonious atmosphere to the gathering. In his estimation, it was a scene his parents would have been proud of. If only he could enjoy it.

He looked, unable to stop himself.

Emma was staring straight at him.

Garrick stood, grabbed his pewter mug, and walked toward her. He heard Conrad's expletive, but his friend underestimated him. Garrick was capable of composing himself, even if he wanted nothing more than to eliminate Davenhill's grin with the back of his hand.

"My lady," he bowed. "My lord," he said to her brother.

Seemingly grateful for the excuse to leave the table, Geoffrey stood and offered a hand to his sister. "A fine evening indeed," he said, guiding her away from the table.

Garrick avoided Davenhill's gaze. The baron was likely furious with him for removing his entertainment for the evening. Good.

"I trust your meal was enjoyable?" Garrick asked as he led the way toward a brazier in the corner.

"Very much," Geoffrey said.

Emma simply smiled.

"And yours, my lady?" He let himself look at her, and the charge between them nearly felled him. How could Geoffrey fail to notice it?

"Delicious," she said.

His cock hardened, the implications of her answer clear.

Emma was a saucy minx, and she teased him, knowing he was in a poor position with Geoffrey between them.

"Then I am pleased," he said. "I was sure to have Cook dig deep in Clave's storeroom for the finest of spices for the main course."

He tried not to smile at the way her eyes darkened at his deliberate mention of the storeroom.

Garrick turned his attention to Geoffrey. "So were you pleased with the outcome of the council?"

"Very much." Geoffrey held up his mug for a toast. "Cheers, Lord Clave, on your day. It appears your return to England has been quite successful so far."

"Mostly so," Emma said.

Though her brother drew his brows together, Garrick knew what to expect—more teasing.

"On the return trip, that night on Clan Scott's land. You seemed vexed. Frustrated. I never did get to ask if all was well."

His thoughts immediately went to that night. How he'd opened the door to find Emma standing there, lantern in hand. He'd pleased her well and would do it again tonight.

Oh, she was bold.

"Ahh, that. I do recall now. It was something the chief said. Nothing of importance. In fact"—he tried not to grin—"it was so inconsequential I'd nearly forgotten it."

When her eyes narrowed, Garrick resisted the urge to laugh aloud. It really was too easy to tease her back.

"Speaking of Graeme de Sowlis," Geoffrey interjected, "I nearly forgot to mention." He turned to Emma. "Sara believes we should invite him to Kenshire. What do you think?"

Geoffrey's words landed between them like a sea-tossed ship thrown onto a shore of rocks, obliterating even the memory of any smooth sailing.

The Scottish chief was going to propose to Emma. Or, at the very least, pursue her.

No.

He'd told Emma to ignore whatever he said this eve for this exact reason. Somehow he had known Geoffrey would ask for his opinion of the chief. And he would not lie and slander a man he respected.

"I do believe Sara and I had that same discussion before I left," Garrick said. "As I told her, Sowlis should be considered."

Geoffrey took the words as they were given, as an affirmation of Graeme's good intentions, no more.

But Graeme de Sowlis would not marry Emma.

After tonight, there would be no doubt of it.

CHAPTER NINETEEN

*H*e'd intended to take her virginity tonight, but he couldn't go through with it. No matter how much he wanted her, it would be irresponsible to treat her as such. He would have to wait until they had an understanding.

"Emma?"

Garrick opened the door without knocking. The darkened chamber was lit only by a fire and two candles, so when she appeared in front of him, it was as if she'd been conjured from his dreams.

"I thought you may be sleeping."

His heartbeat thudded with every step she took toward him. Her velvet robe could have passed for a gown until she came closer. But now he could clearly see the slit that made its way from her neck to the ground.

"Sleeping?"

She reached out, hesitant and unsure.

He took the outstretched hand, pulled her toward him, and enveloped her in a kiss that was meant to claim. Garrick poured all of his frustration and urgency into that kiss. It terrified him how much he wanted her. He'd kissed more women than he could count, but never had he become so lost, so quickly. Never had the urge to be inside a woman physically pained him.

Overcome with the desire to see more of her, to feel her body against his, Garrick tore her robe off in one swift motion. He grasped Emma's hair at the nape of her neck, pulled her toward him, and ravaged her mouth.

She shoved at his tunic, and he broke contact with her for just long enough to remove the offending garment from his body. He threw it on the floor beside them, and then, at Emma's prompting, did the same with his shirt.

He pulled her toward him once again, and when her hands began their exploration, he knew he was lost. Drowning in a sea of passion, in the arms of the woman he loved, he could not get enough. He explored her backside, teasing both of them with the idea that he could lift the thin chemise over her head.

But if he so much as saw an inch of skin, he'd be lost. As would Emma's virginity.

"Emma," he murmured. "We need to talk."

The words were spoken between kisses. Garrick shifted his attention to her neck, flicking his tongue against the sensitive flesh there. Emma's soft moan prompted him to continue teasing and tormenting them both.

"Aye," he said, his mouth moving lower and lower. "Talk."

He loosened the ties at her front. Just a taste. One simple taste.

Undone, the ties fell to either side, widening the neckline just enough for him to reach in and lift a perfect breast toward his mouth. He brought his mouth down to taste her, and the rosy bud hardened against his tongue.

Bloody hell.

He tore his mouth away, intending to back up, but then he saw her face. Her swollen lips. Taking her lower lip into his mouth, he continued to torment them both. This time, the soft groan was his own.

"Talk," he said again once he'd finally managed to stop. A

nearly impossible feat. He took a step back, but the temptation to return to her, to take her in his arms again, was too strong.

Reaching down for the robe, he picked it up, draped it around her shoulders, and reassessed the situation. "Better."

"What are you about, Lord Clave?"

He didn't miss her gaze, which dropped as she spoke. His mind started to wander as he pictured her mouth on his chest, moving lower and lower as he had done to her.

Garrick reached down again, this time grabbing his own shirt and tossing it back over his head.

"Talk," he said again, as much to himself as to her.

His throat was dry, the air thick and heavy with the promise of what could be. He continued to back away, but it was still not far enough. Her sweet lavender scent overwhelmed him.

"Of course," she said, as if they'd been having a logical conversation rather than nearly ravaging each other.

"I cannot yet promise you anything beyond my heart." He swallowed. "But I came here with the intention of ravishing you."

Emma stood as still as the bed beside her.

"To make love to you as I've dreamt of doing since the very moment you stood, covered in hay, in that stable. There is nothing I want more. That I've *ever* wanted more."

"But?"

"But I can't."

"Can't? Or won't?"

"Does it matter?"

Emma opened her mouth to speak, but God help him, he couldn't let her. Not just yet. If she uttered even one word to convince him to carry out his original plan, he would do it.

"Is this really what you want, Emma?" he asked, desperate to make her understand. "Do you want a man promised to another?"

She lifted her chin, and Garrick knew he'd gotten through to her.

"I can barely keep my hands from you. But you deserve more."

And he intended to give it to her. "I don't want anything to stand between us when we make love for the first time. Not your brother. Not Magnus."

"Not your mother."

He could not deny it. She'd come to know him well. "Nor her."

"Then what will we do?"

He nearly did go to her then, but Garrick didn't trust himself.

"I've asked her to come to Clave."

She didn't have to ask who. "Before I left Kenshire, I sent a group of men back to Scotland to deliver the message that the wedding is to be delayed until spring. But I need to inform my mother before making any other decision. I've asked her to return to England for the time being."

He wished he had all of the answers now, but he didn't. "And the attack . . ."

"You believe it was your uncle?"

He shrugged. "Perhaps. Inquiries are being made. If it was him—"

"He will stop at nothing to gain the title."

"I will kill him first."

"You're serious."

Very serious. If he had put Emma in harm's way, if he had thought for a moment to threaten Garrick's mother . . .

"Garrick, please don't do anything rash."

"Rash? The bastard—"

"Might well be behind the attack. If so, allow the wardens to deal with it."

"Emma, you don't know what you're asking."

"I do. You'll remember I have three brothers, all of whom would put themselves in danger to protect what is theirs. But at least two of them have learned a powerful lesson. Trust in the process you're so willing to fight to protect."

She didn't realize what she asked for. To not seek vengeance? If his uncle truly was behind the attacks?

"As for us—"

"Just give me time to sort through it."

She didn't answer right away.

"Emma?"

"You heard my brother earlier. It seems Graeme is pressing his suit. If he—"

He reached her in two strides. "You will not marry Graeme."

"Perhaps we can discuss it rather than you ordering me about—"

"Promise me, Emma. You will not entertain him."

He didn't like the look on her face. A line of frustration had formed between her eyes.

"Promise me."

She shrugged off his hand.

"This no longer feels like a discussion."

The image of Graeme lifting Emma's hand to his mouth filled Garrick's mind, muddying his thoughts. "I will not leave without your promise."

He waited.

"I promise." She didn't look pleased, but he had her promise and her love.

It had to be enough for now.

───

"Tell me."

Her brother's voice, not Garrick's.

Emma had found shelter in a peculiar room on the ground floor of the castle, just next to Clave's great hall. She'd discovered the empty space just after breaking her fast. She'd spent the morning trying not to look at Garrick and not to be cornered by the overeager Lord Davenhill. Eager to escape it all, she'd wandered away and found this remarkable space. Housed inside a postern tower, the circular room had more windows than most, and none of them were arrow slits. Granted, the oriel windows were not in much danger of being attacked from the sea, but they were extremely rare on the ground floor. She rather liked them.

"There's nothing to tell." Of course, it was a lie. And her brother knew it.

"If Davenhill insulted you before I arrived—"

"It is not that pompous old goat."

"Old? The man is nearly the same age as I am. Ahh, is that a smile?"

She straightened her lips lest she allow her brother to be right about anything.

"Just as I said."

"Emma Waryn, you are bold."

She ignored that since he made it sound like a compliment. "Look at that view."

Her brother watched the gentle ebb and flow of the waves with her in silence.

"You'll catch a chill." Geoffrey moved to close the tall wooden shutters, but Emma stopped him.

"Just a moment longer."

Geoffrey shook his head. "Your blood must be warmer than most, sister."

Emma couldn't resist.

"Are you cold? Perhaps I could fetch you a cloak?" she teased.

He didn't appear amused.

"Emma, what is it?" he said, looking into her eyes.

She met his gaze without flinching. Emma trusted her brother with her life. Loved him fiercely.

But she could not tell him the truth. This was also the man who'd prevented her from seeing any of the horse races. Who chided her for wandering too far from the castle. Who thought she was still very much a child. Perhaps to him she always would be that little girl who wore ribbons in her hair. Emma couldn't dream of allowing little Hayden to be placed in harm's way, so maybe part of her understood.

"'Tis nothing, Geoffrey."

He frowned.

Emma didn't want to upset him, so she tried her best to smile. "I'm grateful to have come with you. Clave is beautiful."

When Geoffrey moved to close the shutters this time, she did not stop him.

"It is an impressive holding," he agreed. "And I believe the earl will prove a worthy ally."

At the mention of Garrick, Emma's heart skipped a beat.

"He is quite honorable."

Too much so.

"If only he were not already betrothed . . ." Though her brother attempted to sound casual, Emma knew him too well to be fooled.

He suspected the truth.

"His future wife is very lucky," she conceded.

Geoffrey continued to watch her. But she would not give him more than that. "Perhaps we should discuss—"

"Nay, I think we should not," she said.

He frowned, but she'd not be intimidated by his stare.

After a long, tense moment, he finally conceded. "We should be going."

"May I speak to Lady Emma first?"

They both turned at the sound. Garrick stood in the doorway, filling it as only he could. Emma stole a glance at her brother.

Aye, her brother knew the truth, or at least some approximation of it. Was it the way Garrick looked at her, or she at him? Or perhaps it was something else altogether?

Geoffrey inclined his head to her. Striding from the room, he stopped just before reaching their host. Emma was sure Geoffrey would say something to him, but instead he turned back to her.

"The others will be waiting."

With that, he was gone.

He'd left the doors open, of course.

Garrick took a step toward her, and then another. Emma wanted to weep. To scream. To laugh with the joy of being with him just once more.

"You took a chance," she said, referring to his request to speak with her alone. Though he'd not said as much aloud, the implication had been obvious to all of them.

"I will take another. And another. Anything to be with you."

She could tell he meant it.

"I would wrap my arms around you," she said.

Garrick shook his head. "If you did, I'd be forced to kiss you. I would make you mine this instant, Emma, if I could."

"I will wait," she said. "But how can I put off Sowlis's visit?"

"Find a way," he said. "I will come to you, I promise."

She believed him. And she knew in her heart she would wait for him. She'd wait an entire lifetime if necessary. Her love for him had caught her unawares, but there was no denying the force of it.

"I love you, Garrick," she whispered, the words coming as easily as if she'd said them many times before.

"And I love you, Emma," he said. "I will come to you," he repeated.

She didn't ask when. Garrick's task was a difficult one. But he had promised, and she believed him.

"I must go." With a final backward glance at the earl who had captured her heart, Emma walked from the room.

He'd asked her to wait.

And she would.

CHAPTER TWENTY

*N*early a week had passed since the council. Since he'd seen *her*.

Clave ran as smoothly as ever. Garrick's men benefited from the tactics they'd learned overseas and trained hard despite the cold, making him proud to be their leader. And his allies had all communicated their praise and ready acceptance of him after the meeting of the council.

Better yet, news had arrived just this morn indicating one of the men who'd been captured following the attack on Garrick's men had been turned over to the English warden, per Garrick's agreement with Graeme. The man had finally started talking. He'd admitted to being sent to waylay Garrick specifically, though he claimed not to know who'd hired him. The warden intended to hold the man prisoner until the next Day of Truce, at which point he'd be brought to trial for his crimes.

Another messenger had arrived. Garrick had hurried back to the castle from the training yard, eager to see if it was a missive from his mother. But instead of seeking the steward out directly, he found himself drawn to the same exact spot where he'd last seen her.

He returned to this place each day to feel closer to her.

"Pardon, my lord."

He closed the shutters. Mable had found him instead of him having to seek her out.

"A missive from the men you sent to Scotland." She held out the letter.

He quickly read the message and glanced up at her. The eagerness in her eyes told him she'd be reluctant to leave until he relayed the message. He knew why—Mable and his mother were nearly as close as sisters.

"The men are on their way back."

Mable waited.

"To England." He tried not to smile. He really had missed teasing their steward.

"I know, my lord, to England. When? With whom?"

"Posthaste. With each other, of course. Why, do you believe any of them would stay—"

"Lord Clave, you've got too much of yer father in you," she scolded.

He rather hoped so. "I would expect them within the week. And my mother travels with them."

"Very good, my lord."

Without another word, Mable snatched the missive from his hands. The edges of her mouth had tipped up just slightly enough to form a smile, though someone who didn't know her would not have noticed.

The sound of footsteps preceded Conrad's voice. "Mistress Mable, you are looking quite fine—"

"Save yer compliments for the ladies who think ye sincere," Mable said to him as he turned the corner and walked into the room.

Garrick chuckled, delighted to see there was at least one person who would not fall prey to his friend's charms.

"Mable is wise to your wicked ways," he said, knowing full well she could still hear.

"The men said you'd left training early. After you knocked every last one of them on their arses. Their words, not mine."

Garrick had seen the rider and hadn't wanted to wait for the news. But if he told Conrad as much, his friend would chide him for a fool.

"So your mother's coming?"

"God's blood, is there nothing you don't know about what happens around here?"

"You forget, great Earl of Clave and master of men, I know all. About everything."

Garrick crossed his arms. "Do you now?"

"Aye, and more than you, to be sure."

"What did the missive say, then?" Garrick asked.

Conrad didn't hesitate. "Your mother is on her way to England, spitting mad and ready to box your ears for delaying the wedding."

All likely true. "And the one from earlier this morning?"

"One of the captured men from the attack is squawking like a chicken now that you've turned him over to the warden."

"Then it appears, my friend, you truly do know all."

Conrad pretended to consider his words. "Nearly all. Except one thing." He paused. "How does a man manage to fall in love at nearly the very same moment he pledges his life to another? The timing does seem rather poor, even to—"

"You are an arse, Conrad. And I do believe your own mother has written yet again, asking for your return. I'm highly tempted to send you home."

"How would you know if Emma appeals when you hardly spoke to her—"

"Did I not tell you? I met up with the Waryns on their ride home." Garrick's look would have had lesser men cowering in fear.

Conrad merely grinned. "Nay, you did not tell me."

"I see. Well, it must have been because I had hoped you would forget about the chit."

"Conrad—"

"Woman. My apologies. The *woman* who will be responsible for your downfall."

They'd avoided the topic of Emma thus far, but it would seem his self-imposed muzzle had been removed.

"In fact, if you weren't in love with her, I would be very interested to—"

"I will kill you."

"If, my dear Garrick. *If.* But of course you are, in love that is, which makes her very much off-limits. Will you give up Linkirk for her then?" his friend pressed.

"You believe I will need to?"

Conrad's lips flattened. "It was very likely your uncle who was behind the attack. You know it as well as I do. Even if Magnus can be persuaded, or bribed, to let you out of the agreement, your uncle's pursuit of the title will be relentless. That he even dared the attempt on your life . . . I can only assume he sent those men before learning the betrothal was made official."

Conrad was just getting started. "Your mother's childhood home won't be safe, and it might not be safe for her to return to Scotland. At best, your uncle will continue to plague you. At worst, Magnus will join his cause. Lives will be lost, your kinsmen caught in a battle between siblings, and you—because I know you well—will not allow it to happen. You'll relinquish the earldom first. And aye, it will devastate your mother."

Garrick wanted to disagree. To tell Conrad he was wrong, about all of it—or most of it. To explain how it could work, and under which conditions he could retain Linkirk for his mother.

But he couldn't.

Edward had relied on him to win battles and save lives. He had sent for his mother for a reason. The plan he was about to set in motion would risk her inheritance, at best. Her life, at worst.

A vision of his mother bending over him to smooth an errant hair back into place crossed his mind. Then a memory of her pulling him off the training yard well after the others had finished, begging him to stop, to eat, to see reason. She'd always supported and loved him. And now he would repay her with this. After he'd already taken her husband from her.

Garrick was the worst sort of man alive, and when he looked into his friend's eyes, he could see his own thoughts reflected there. This would not end well. For anyone.

And yet, what choice did he have? Would it truly be better to spend his life in misery? Bound to a stranger he did not love?

"Let her go, Garrick."

Nay. Not that. Never that.

"Let her marry a man who isn't on the precipice of war. One who can keep her safe in a way you cannot do if you break off this betrothal."

The mere thought made him fist his hands at his side.

"If you love her," Conrad said, "you need to let her go. This is no way for a young woman to begin her married life. And you know it, Garrick. You know it in your heart, which is why you've avoided me since she came here. There's no other way."

Garrick frowned, wanting to deny his words.

But there was some truth to them.

Emma pulled her cloak tighter as she stroked Nella's sleek black coat. She'd taken her out for a short stroll earlier, careful to avoid the patches of ice that had formed since the last snowfall. The ride had allowed her time to think. To reflect on her recent trip to Clave.

To consider Garrick and their predicament.

She looked at the spot where he'd stood that day. Emma could remember precisely how she'd felt when she had realized it was not some stablehand who'd joined her, but a strange knight. A wickedly handsome one who'd pulled her toward him without speaking. Who had captured her heart, assailed her senses so completely that she'd hardly had time to consider what it all meant.

That she loved him, there was no doubt. Sara had once told her that love felt somewhere between sheer bliss and utter fear. She and her sister-in-law had stood together on the bit of shore by Kenshire, Sara's favorite spot, on the day Geoffrey was to return from Bristol. Though Emma had been convinced her brother was safe, the panic in Sara's eyes had not failed to move her. She'd wondered that day if his wife could love him more than she, his sister, did. She'd concluded it was just a different love. One less rational. More desperate.

That was the way she loved Garrick. But would it be enough?

"I thought I'd find you here."

Emma turned toward the entrance of the stables, expecting to see Sara bundled against the cold. Instead, her breeches peeked out from beneath a cape that was made for riding. Though fur-lined, it was a thinner cloak than she would have expected on such a frigid day.

"Have you already taken her out?" Sara asked.

Nella answered for Emma, the soft snort forcing a laugh from Sara.

"She's still restless."

Emma agreed. Perhaps Nella was reacting to her own mood.

"I did, but I'm not opposed to another ride. Nor does Nella appear to be."

"Before we go . . ."

The stablehand had followed Sara inside, but when she turned to look at him, he fled, closing the great doors behind him. Though Emma hadn't seen the look that had sent him running, she could well imagine it. This could only mean one thing.

"We've not had a chance to talk since you returned last week."

Sara knew. Perhaps because Geoffrey had told her, or perhaps she'd known all along. Emma was only ashamed she hadn't said anything earlier.

They spoke at the same time. "I would have told you—"

"You know you can talk to me—"

They both stopped. Sara walked toward her, stopping to greet Guinevere, her horse.

"Who told you?" Emma choked out.

"You did."

Emma thought back to their conversations and was fairly assured she had *not* told Sara about her feelings for Garrick.

When Sara smiled, she conveyed both confidence and warmth. A born leader. Lucky that, since Geoffrey needed a partner who would stand up to him. One who was just as strong and self-assured as he had always been. So it would seem Sara had guessed after all.

"When?"

"Before you left for Dunmure."

"But 'tis not possible. I didn't—"

"You didn't yet know you held an affection for him. But I could tell."

Emma thought back to the dinner. She remembered being appalled by Garrick's status, grateful that he'd agreed to look at Nella and . . .

"I knew how badly you wanted to see Clara. And also that Garrick was on his way to forge an alliance with the Earl of Magnus."

"But how could you have known—"

"It was foolish," Sara said, interrupting her, "of me to encourage you to go. I knew of Garrick's reputation. And could sense the connection between you at dinner."

Reputation?

"But I also know him to be an honorable man. One who would not lie with one woman when he was promised to another. And I also trust your judgment, Emma."

There was no conjecture in her voice. Sara was simply stating facts.

"His reputation?"

Sara rolled her eyes heavenward, as if trying to grasp a distant memory before it floated away. "He and Conrad have broken many hearts between them."

"Sir Conrad Anstead?" Emma had met him briefly. A knight who knew his own appeal.

"Aye. A second son known more for conquering women than enemies in battle. And Garrick's best friend. He's rarely left Clave since moving there to foster with the old earl."

Garrick had spoken little of Conrad. In fact, there was much they had not spoken of. She hardly knew him at all, really.

"I didn't worry, though I should have. When you avoided talking about Graeme—"

"Sara, I'm in love with Garrick." She blurted it out, knowing it would be easier to admit to all at once.

"I know."

"How could you possibly—"

"You've not been yourself since returning from Scotland. And I must say, I'm surprised. An earl?" A small smile quirked her lips.

Emma should have known there would be no censure from Sara. She should have confided in her earlier.

"I didn't intend for it to happen. I didn't even know the purpose of his trip, at first. By the time I'd learned . . ." She shrugged and looked up at the timber crossbeams above them.

"You've nothing to be ashamed of."

"Except being in love with a man promised to another. One who will very likely start a war when he—" She stopped. The look of alarm on Sara's face reminded her that her sister-in-law was also the Countess of Kenshire.

"What does he intend to do? Have you—"

"Nay, we have not," she said, though not proudly. It was not exactly her doing that she was a virgin still. "And I don't know exactly what he intends. Just that he asked me to wait for him. And for me not to encourage—"

"Graeme de Sowlis."

Emma nodded.

Sara began to pace, just like her brother, fresh rushes crunching under her feet as she walked.

"If he breaks the betrothal, Magnus will be furious. And his uncle . . ." She stopped and looked at her.

"Aye. Precisely."

"We need to find out if his uncle was truly behind the attacks. How far is the man willing to go to secure a title he thinks belongs to him? To Scotland?" Sara seemed to be talking as much to herself as she was to Emma. "I'll take care of Geoffrey. He asked just this morn if we should send for Graeme."

"What?" She hadn't meant to yell, but the word had burst out of her. "Sara, he can't come here. Please—"

"We'll make an excuse. If I simply tell him you are not interested in pursuing the Scots chief, Geoffrey will invite him anyway. Your brother still believes he can sway your thinking as easily as he did when you were a child. But neither do I want to lie to him. Perhaps a dose of the truth will do."

The implications of Sara's words began to penetrate.

"Are you saying . . . do you believe I should encourage Garrick then?"

Though she couldn't stop thinking of him, imagining a life with him, Emma had begun to doubt such a thing was possible.

"Of course." Sara's posture was that of a proud warrior about to head into battle—a battle on Emma's behalf. She actually looked offended. "What did you believe? That I would attempt to dissuade you?"

Emma declined to answer. She had not the first idea of what to say.

"Emma, I trust you to make your own decisions. Know your own heart."

"But he's betrothed!"

"Yet not married."

"To a woman whose father is a powerful man. A man who—"

"Is just that. A man. Nothing more."

"But his uncle. The earldom—"

"Garrick is not stupid. You'd not have fallen in love with him if he were. He can work it out."

Emma didn't know what to say. After a moment passed, she added, "He is an earl. You know how I feel about that."

"Are you trying to convince me or yourself that Garrick is not the one? Because I've seen the way you look at him, and he at you. You say you're in love, and I can only assume he's said as much to you."

Emma nodded.

"Then if he's a man worth fighting for, he'll find a way to make it work. Otherwise . . ." She didn't finish, but Emma thought she understood. "I will ask just once more, before we decide what to tell Geoffrey. Are you in love with Garrick Clave? Is he the man you want to marry?"

Emma didn't hesitate. "Aye."

Sara smiled. "You've made a fine choice. I've always wished a good woman would find a way to his heart. 'Tis a shame he didn't come to Kenshire before agreeing to marry Magnus's daughter."

With that, Sara walked away, presumably to get the groom.

For the first time since her return from Scotland, Emma felt confident about her future. Thank goodness Geoffrey had possessed the good sense to fall in love with Sara. How lucky they both were to have her in their lives.

Garrick would find a way. Their love would be enough.

In the meantime, it was a great day for another ride.

CHAPTER TWENTY-ONE

*E*mma was ready to scream.

She couldn't wait a moment longer. Another week had passed without word from Garrick. In some ways, life felt much the same as it had before her fateful trip to Scotland. The days were monotonous and long, except for her joyful rides with Nella. She'd headed out to the stables with the intention of taking a long ride, but the cold wind had rendered the day so frigid even her fur-lined hood made little difference. Perhaps she should rethink her afternoon, but Hayden was asleep and Geoffrey and Sara were locked in the solar, purportedly to make their way through a scroll of tenant disputes.

She'd planned to speak with her brother but hadn't the nerve to tell him the truth. Sara had spoken with him about Graeme, but otherwise, they waited for word from Garrick.

When a commotion at the gate caught her attention, Emma abandoned the stables in favor of inspecting what was happening at the gate. When she saw Peter, the steward, emerge from the keep and head in that same direction, Emma knew something was afoot.

She heard the approaching horses before she saw the men on

horseback. Though she couldn't see their faces from this distance, Emma could make out the quality of their mounts. Visitors. Nobles. Her mind raced with possibilities faster than her feet could carry her to the gate. She didn't see Bayard, but who else would be calling on such a day? They had few visitors this time of year.

The group rode into the inner courtyard just as Peter caught up with her.

"Do you know who it is?" she asked breathlessly.

The steward was barely visible beneath his enormous cloak. "I do, my lady."

Without elaborating on that most vexing answer, he raised his hand in greeting.

Emma's heart thudded harder with each passing moment, but as the small riding party came closer—she counted five men—she could still not make out any sign of Garrick. The men were all swathed in heavy cloaks and garments, but surely she would know him even from a distance. She drummed her feet against the ground, looking . . .

Their leader pulled down his hood, and Graeme de Sowlis stared back at her.

What in the devil was he doing here? She had told her brother she was not interested in the man, and besides, Sara had promised to put off a visit. Had Geoffrey gone behind their backs to make the arrangement? Why was he so eager to marry her off to a Scotsman?

"Good day, Lady Emma," Graeme said, jumping from his horse. "I had not expected such a welcome." He looked up at the sky. "In the courtyard."

A maidservant, rushing toward the castle to escape the cold, bumped into her, nearly knocking her down.

"Pardon, my lady," the girl mumbled. Then she looked up at Graeme—and very nearly walked into Peter because she couldn't seem to avert her gaze.

Emma didn't blame the girl. The chief, taller even than her brothers and Garrick, was indeed very handsome. His hair, which he kept shorter than most men, appeared darker today, but normally the dark blond gave him a boyish look that was completely at odds with his demeanor.

Straightforward. That was the best word she could think of to describe him. Well, straightforward *and* kind. All in all, a worthy catch for someone who didn't dream of another man.

"A common occurrence?" she asked as he dismounted.

His wink gave her the answer.

Peter ordered their horses stabled and, as was his custom, took charge of the men. Playing the part of the unwitting host, she escorted Sowlis into the great hall of Kenshire Castle.

Her brother appeared almost immediately, and the cad didn't look the least bit surprised. Of course he wasn't surprised. No doubt her wretched brother had arranged the whole thing.

"Welcome to Kenshire. You made it here without incident, I trust?"

The men clasped hands, and Faye, Sara's maidservant—who'd hurried into the hall after Geoffrey—took Graeme's mantle from behind.

"None at all. Thank you for the invitation," Graeme said, confirming her suspicions.

I am going to strangle Geoffrey.

Graeme walked further into the room, the hall opening up before him. He looked all around, turning in a circle, and whistled. "I've heard rumors of this place, but they do Kenshire no favors. The tapestries are magnificent."

The sound of rapidly approaching footsteps filled the air, and Sara, who'd just entered the room, said, "Thank you," a tad breathlessly.

Emma could tell from Sara's expression—and the fire in her eyes—that she was just as surprised by their visitors. For his part, her brother appeared quite cheery.

"I'll have Faye show you to your room. Unless you'd like a tour of the castle first. It is quite magnificent." Geoffrey smiled at Sara, who, to Graeme, must seem the vision of a perfect hostess.

"I would very much enjoy that." He turned toward Emma. "Perhaps my lady would care to accompany us?"

It was a simple question asked in expectation of a simple, and affirmative, answer. *Yes.* But if she encouraged him now, it would only be more difficult to deny him later.

"My apologies, I was just on the way to speak with the stable master when you arrived. Do enjoy your tour."

He did not appear at all displeased. The same could not be said for her brother.

Well, perhaps he should have consulted her first about this visit!

"My lady. Your ladyship," Graeme said to Sara.

When they walked away, Emma stole to the side of the hall with Sara.

"Faye," Sara said, "you will check on his men and speak with Cook about the meal."

Faye didn't move.

"Faye?"

The woman's eyes darted across the room, settling on the doorway through which the earl and the chief had just disappeared. "Cook already knows."

"Good," Sara said. Emma was sure she didn't want to involve the servants in her disagreement with Geoffrey. *Their* disagreement with Geoffrey.

"Thank you, Faye. That will be all. Oh"—Sara stopped her with a gentle hand on her arm—"have you heard from Hugh?"

Faye had married Emma's uncle Hugh not long after Geoffrey and Sara became husband and wife. Emma was glad for them and knew Faye was anxious for Hugh to return from Elmhurst Manor. But Hugh's help fortifying Elmhurst was much needed.

"Aye, my lady. He says 'twill be a fortnight, at least, until he returns."

"Thank you for your understanding," Emma said. "I know you must miss him, but Lettie and Simon are very grateful for his assistance."

"At least I don't have him tellin' me what to do. A fine man, but a mite stubborn, if I do say so myself. Beggin' your pardon," Faye said with a fond grin.

Emma laughed. "All Waryn men are quite so. Please, no apologies for saying it aloud." She turned to Sara. "Speaking of Waryn men . . ."

Faye bobbed a curtsy and moved on, for she was as wise as she was patient.

"I thought you didn't tell him?"

"What could he be thinking?"

They spoke at once, but Sara answered first. "I did not. But your brother is smart, and my guess is that he knows about you and Garrick."

"'Tis possible. Garrick did ask to speak with me privately the day we left Clave."

"And Geoffrey allowed it?"

Emma nodded. "So perhaps he—"

"Oh dear. Emma, you need to speak with him."

"About Garrick? Sara, you know him. He will—"

"Be understanding, I'm sure."

They looked at each other, and Emma found herself laughing despite the dire situation.

"Oh, dear sister," Emma said, using her best Geoffrey voice. "Why ever did you not tell me you've fallen in love with a man betrothed to another? What a fine match. Well done."

"Shh . . ."

Emma had as much desire to tell Geoffrey about Garrick as she did to spend her days learning to embroider. But she had no choice. She couldn't ask Sara to deceive him on her behalf, and neither could she put off a discussion of Graeme any longer.

"I will speak to him this evening," Emma said.

Sara nodded. "I should be there—"

"Nay, you've done enough for me. I will speak to him alone."

"That poor man, traveling here in such wretched weather for naught."

"'Tis your brother's fault for encouraging it," Sara said. "Though you must admit the man is quite handsome."

"Aye, very much so. Graeme de Sowlis would make a fine husband indeed. For someone else." Emma reached for Sara and hugged her. "Thank you for your help."

Sara glanced across the hall, and Emma followed her gaze. Faye had reappeared in the entrance to the kitchens and was waving for Sara to join her.

"Go. I shall see you at dinner."

Emma was so distraught that she was halfway to the stables before she realized she'd forgotten her cloak. She stopped, considered going back for it, but decided against it. She'd really only needed an excuse to avoid Graeme's tour of the castle. Besides, she wouldn't be there long. A quick visit with Nella and she'd escape to her rooms, avoiding Graeme before dinner.

"Good day, Reginald," she said to the squire as she stepped into the stables. He was unsaddling Geoffrey's horse.

"Lady Emma," he said. "Your brother asked that I exercise him. Have you seen my lord?"

"My brother is with his guest," she said, watching Reginald as he finished his work and left. She smiled. He really had begun to take on Geoffrey's mannerisms.

"The lad seems to appreciate a fine piece of horseflesh," a voice said from behind her.

It couldn't be. She spun around to confirm what her mind already knew. "Garrick?"

CHAPTER TWENTY-TWO

*G*arrick was here. At Kenshire.

Standing just in front of her.

She spun around, checking to be sure they were alone. Sure enough, no one was about.

When she turned back to look at him, he was leaning against the stone wall with his arms crossed as casually as if he stood in his own hall at Clave Castle.

"Emma, you really should learn to better prepare for the cold," he said. With that, he uncrossed his arms and began to take off his cloak.

She wanted to run to him, throw herself into his arms, but something held her back. It was the way he looked at her. She shivered. "Why are you here?"

He held out the mantle to her. "Because you are."

She walked toward him, turned, and allowed him to place the warm covering over her shoulders. And then he wrapped his arms around her. Even through the thick material, she could feel the power of his arms, firm and secure.

"What is Graeme de Sowlis doing at Kenshire?" he whispered in her ear.

"Is that why you've come?"

"Aye."

Again, she attempted to turn around. Again, Garrick stopped her.

"Why?" he asked. He sounded pained, the raw emotion in his voice stopping her from giving a glib answer.

"He was invited by my brother without my knowledge."

Garrick pushed the hood away from her neck, allowing him better access. His breath was warm against her flesh.

"How did you get in here?"

In response, he kissed her neck. Though it was the gentlest of touches, it sizzled through her body, her response to him as instantaneous as always.

He finally turned her around and captured her lips with his own. Garrick's mouth slanted over hers, his tongue turning the fire between them into an inferno. It licked at them, engulfing her body as she struggled to get closer to him.

How had he come to be here?

Did she care?

If they were caught . . . if Geoffrey found them like this . . . if Garrick started a war . . .

She ceased caring about any of the very real obstacles that stood between them. Nothing mattered but the man who held her, cherished her with his body and soul.

"When I learned he was riding toward Kenshire," he murmured against her lips.

"How did you know? How did you get in here?"

He held her head between his hands. Desire pooled in his eyes. He wanted her, and she wanted to give herself to him. More than anything.

"I do not want Graeme de Sowlis," she said. "I want only you."

He groaned, capturing her lips once again. "Oh God, Emma. I need you."

She pulled away but didn't break eye contact. "Don't leave."

But she knew he was not going to listen. She felt him holding back. Knew, instinctively, their time together was already coming to an end.

His next words proved her correct. "I can't stay. I shouldn't be here at all. But I had to see you. Had to be sure."

"I promised to wait for you."

"I love you, Emma Waryn. I *will* find a way for us to be together. But for now . . . I have to go."

"You're really leaving?"

He reached for her cheek, his ungloved hand running down her face. "I cannot be found here now, not with Graeme in attendance. But I had to see you."

"Garrick, you never answered me."

"I've scouts everywhere, on account of my uncle. When I heard Graeme was making his way to Kenshire, I snuck inside." He didn't smile. "Announcing myself would be as good as a declaration for you—"

"A declaration you cannot yet make."

"My mother will be at Clave any day. I must speak with her first."

"To get her permission?"

"Nay. To give her the courtesy of knowing that I intend to start a war."

"But surely—"

"It was my uncle."

She blinked.

"The attack. The men were hired by my uncle. All the more reason that my mother should be safely in England."

"Your uncle? Are you sure? How could he?"

Garrick tightened his arms around her.

"Aye, we're sure. The border lords' reach is wide. After the council, it was only a matter of time before someone learned the truth. The men were mostly Scottish, but one that was captured, an English mercenary . . ."

Emma didn't like the look in his eye. "Garrick?"

His jaw clenched.

"You spoke to him," she asked.

"Aye." This . . . this was the crusader. The warrior. The knight trained to kill.

"What will you do?"

Garrick sighed. "I will tell my mother about the attack and my uncle's part in it. I will break the betrothal, attempt to pacify Magnus without making a bitter enemy. And my uncle . . ."

She wasn't sure she wanted to know.

"He will pay for his actions."

"And Linkirk?"

He didn't answer. Garrick didn't care about his Scottish title. From what she had seen, he cared only for Clave, but his mother was another matter altogether.

"I have to go," Garrick said.

"Garrick, are you sure what you're doing is wise?"

His eyes narrowed.

"To break the betrothal, knowing about your uncle's role in the attack? He will never rest with you as the Earl of Linkirk, and if you're married to an English lady, you'll have no claim—"

"Except a legal one. Emma, the title is not his by right."

"But I will be responsible for—"

"You'll be responsible for nothing. Emma," he said definitively. "This is my decision. If my uncle was truly willing to go to such lengths knowing the betrothal was imminent . . . he's become careless. Foolish. And you—"

"Will be the ruin of your family."

He shook his head. "Nay, my uncle Bernard made the choice to destroy our family."

"But Magnus?"

The look on his face told her he was less hopeful than he pretended to be. There was a very real chance this would end in war, one way or another. Emma felt as if someone had reached inside her and torn her heart from her chest. "Garrick, you need to be sure. I love you. I can't imagine another week, nay, another day, without you. But I will not live with the knowledge that I was responsible for tearing apart your family."

She nearly collapsed under the weight of her own words, but it needed to be said . . . and she had not yet finished.

"Do not promise me anything."

"Emma, what are you saying?" Garrick's expression, one of disbelief, nearly made her change course.

"Speak to your mother. Open your mind and heart to what's right. And make the decision you need to make. Not for me. Not for your mother. But for yourself."

The words stuck in her throat like a dollop of molasses, but she would not take them back.

"Emma?"

"I did not ask Graeme to come here. I neither wish to marry him nor plan to encourage him. But while I hope with all my heart we'll find a resolution that sees us together, I won't depend on it." She took off his cloak and handed it to him. "I love you, even with all of your earlishness."

He looked at her oddly, but she didn't know how else to explain herself.

"But now I ask for a different promise."

"Emma. No."

"That you will make the right decision. For yourself."

"Emma." His tone was one she was sure he'd used on his men many times, but she wouldn't allow it to sway her.

"And consider my earlier advice. Allow the wardens to handle your uncle."

She had said what needed saying, and now she needed to leave. Immediately. Emma broke away, ran to the stable doors, and tossed them open. No one was about. She ran through the court-yard, past the entrance of the keep, and around to the back. She ran until her chest hurt, until she knew Garrick had not followed her.

Panting, she stopped beside the kitchens. Smoke billowed into the sky, its stench mixing with the smell of dirt and cold. She watched it climb into the air and disappear. If only she could do the same. The thought of sitting at dinner, entertaining their guest after what had just happened . . .

What *had* just happened? Garrick had come for her. Risked himself to see her. And he'd felt so good, so perfect in her arms.

But when he'd told her of his uncle . . .

His mother's life, threatened. The mercenaries who'd attacked them, dead or soon to be that way, even if Garrick did listen to her. Their time would come on the Day of Truce. This was *real*. It wasn't some tale told on a tapestry or a bard's song to entertain its noble guests. Garrick was risking everything for her, and she couldn't allow it, not unless he made the decision with open eyes.

What had she said? That he should make the best decision for himself?

What would he choose?

Emma tried to tell herself that it didn't matter. That she'd spoken from the heart but also used her head, something her eldest brother was forever encouraging her to do.

And if it meant she risked losing Garrick?

Oh Emma, what have you done?

"Garrick."

Garrick swung his sword into the pell, over and over again. Unlike the men he'd felled earlier, the wooden stake could not be injured. He thrust and sliced, closing his mind against all thoughts beyond the training yard, his sword, and the pell. His mother and uncle, Magnus, and Emma . . . the men who'd met the edge of his sword in battle—all fought for his attention in the background, but the constant motion helped hold it all back.

"Garrick."

He tightened the grip of both hands and was preparing to swing again when the shout finally penetrated.

"*Garrick!*"

After delivering a final blow to the pell, Garrick allowed his sword to drop.

Conrad and a dozen other men stood to the side of the training yard, watching him. Though they were unsheltered from the elements and likely cold, there were no scowls or complaints. Those who had been with him in Acre knew the importance of training, and the others, the ones who had never seen battle, they would know too, someday. Perhaps sooner than any of them would like.

"Your mother's riding party has been spotted near the village," Conrad said.

Garrick handed his sword to a squire and clasped his friend on the back. "Good," he said. "How long have you been standing there?"

Conrad had already changed for the midday meal. The largest meal of the day, it was his friend's favorite. "Long enough to know the pell did not deserve such treatment."

Garrick disagreed. Unwavering against his attacks, it had taunted him for as many years as he'd been training.

"What else have you heard?" Garrick asked, leaving the training yard. Once he did so, the other men began to disperse as well.

"Watch yourself," Conrad said. The ground beneath them was covered by a thin layer of ice, courtesy of an overnight storm that had brought more ice than snow.

"My mother's on the way, no need to take on her role," he said with a smirk. "Any tidings?"

Conrad always seemed to know everything. He wasn't sure

how, though perhaps it had something to do with the vast number of women who shared his bed or his affable nature. Either way, it had been that way since they were children. And he didn't disappoint.

"She must have brought some of Linkirk's men. There were more men attending her than you sent as escort."

"How many?"

"More than twenty."

His mother would be cautious after the attack. Rightly so.

"You've not changed your mind then?" Conrad asked.

Conrad still did not agree with his decision. Hell, Garrick would hardly have believed it himself a couple of months earlier, but the love he'd found with Emma was the sort that changed a man from the inside out.

Nay, he'd not lose her. Though this past week of waiting for his mother had nearly killed him—especially since he knew Graeme de Sowlis was with Emma—he was more determined than ever. He'd been furious, of course, that night. She'd run from him, turned her back on him. But on the cold ride back to Clave, he'd come to respect Emma's fortitude. It was one of the qualities he loved most about her. And it made sense that a strong woman who'd long felt controlled by her brother would encourage him not to let anyone influence his decision.

"Aye, Conrad. I've just this moment changed my mind," he jested. "Thanks to your wise counsel, I shall tell my mother the wedding is no longer delayed. Indeed, it can commence at once."

They climbed the stone stairs toward Clave's main keep. Its rear entrance, a door accessible only from the path they walked upon, which led directly to the training yard, was nevertheless guarded by two men. He was taking no chances after the attack. Garrick nodded to both guards before resuming his speech.

"I will, of course, need to send a messenger to Kenshire to inform Lady Emma of my decision. Pity the Scots chief is gone."

Conrad's sidelong gaze told Garrick he would attempt to

match wits with him. "And if he's not? Perhaps he is still there, an honored guest of the earl and his wife. He's not bound by the chivalric code as we are."

Garrick would not allow his friend to goad him. He attempted and failed to keep a straight face. "The only code you keep, Conrad, is to avoid the tip of an angry husband's sword."

Conrad, unapologetic, followed him through the dank corridor and up another set of stairs within the keep. "There was a time, my friend, I could rely on you to do the same. If I could have chosen any man least likely to fall in love . . ."

"You say the word as if it were poison."

"And indeed it may be, if I am forced to go to battle to defend you."

Garrick still hoped it would not come to that.

They arrived at an entrance to the great hall. "And this is where I leave you, amusing as you are, my friend," Conrad said. "You'll want time alone with your mother, no doubt."

It appeared word of his mother's arrival had reached the castle as well. Mable stood in the middle of the great hall, her hands expressive as she ordered the servants to and fro.

Despite his words, Conrad lingered. He looked at him, waiting for him to speak. "You know I disagree," Conrad finally said, "but I admire you as well."

Garrick would not have been more surprised if Conrad had announced he was finally going home. "Admiration from a skeptic such as yourself. A mighty fine compliment indeed."

Indeed, Conrad appeared to be quite serious. "I know you blame yourself for your father's death, but marrying the Scottish heiress will not bring him back. Though I do still believe you should marry her."

The conviction in his words gave Garrick pause. It was, perhaps, the first time the two men had been in complete disagreement on such an important decision.

Conrad's eyes widened at something behind him.

Garrick turned to see why his mother's appearance should so shock his friend, for the rush of cold air and raised voices had announced her arrival.

What he saw at the entrance made his blood run cold.

CHAPTER TWENTY-THREE

"*H*e's not coming."

Emma sat in Sara's chamber, staring at the flames in the hearth. When she first came to Kenshire, she had been shocked at the size of it. In most castles, it would be considered large for a great hall. Though she'd since become accustomed to many of the luxuries at Kenshire, she still appreciated them.

Even after a pleasant visit with Graeme, a man she'd come to like very much—though like a brother—she still could not bring herself to tell Geoffrey about Garrick. She promised Sara she'd do so, but it was as if he, and not her intended, were the final barrier between them.

"Mayhap because you told him not to come?"

If only she could deny it. "What could I have been thinking?"

Sara looked down at Hayden, who lay sleeping peacefully in her arms. She didn't answer right away.

Each night, Emma imagined Garrick's lips on hers. She thought of his warm, capable hands touching and exploring her body. She woke in the morning with the memory of visions still quite clear, her body craving his touch as much as it did food and drink. Her ears craving the sound of his voice. Her mind craving his conversation.

Other times, she was quite proud that she'd pushed him away, encouraged him to take his time and be sure of his decision. He would give up too much to be with her. Risk too many lives.

"I believe"—Sara looked up finally—"you were thinking like a leader."

A leader. No one had ever used such a word to describe her before.

"Once," Sara said, "when I was maybe ten and three, I wanted to accompany my father to London. He explained that there had been a rash of recent attacks and it would be safer for me to stay at Kenshire. It was a common enough refrain, so I should have been used to the disappointment. But I wasn't."

Emma adjusted herself on the chair, one of only two in the room. There was also an array of stools, but she was grateful for the cushion below her. "I saw the cart as a sign. My father rarely traveled with one, but he was bringing a gift of Scottish wool to the king."

"You didn't."

"I thought it was quite a clever plan."

"Until?"

"Until my father caught me, but not until nearly dusk. They'd planned to make camp for the night, but my presence changed their plans. Instead, he was forced to ask Lord Stanton for shelter."

Emma didn't understand.

"Lord Stanton had asked more than once for my hand in marriage. Each time my father refused. This time he was forced to do so in person. Though very few liked the old man, most respected his influence with the court. A powerful enemy, my father had called him."

"So what happened?"

"My father sent me home with an escort the following morning, but not before he gave me a blistering for forcing him to keep company with someone who could, and did, cause problems for Kenshire for years to come. Although my father never chastised me after that. He didn't need to. I understood, and learned from my mistake."

"The lesson?" She thought she knew but wanted to be sure. In truth, she had done something rather similar when she was a child. Every year, when her father and brothers refused to take her to the tournament, she would spend the day sulking, angry. Though her mother had tried to convince her father to bring her with the lads, on this he'd proved stubborn. On the last Tournament of the North before the attack on Bristol, word got around that King's Crown, the prized Arabian, would be coming, and Emma decided she could not accept her father's decree.

But, unlike Sara, her father discovered her trailing behind them almost immediately, and even now she could hear his admonishment.

"Girl, back to Bristol immediately or you'll earn the honor of being the first Waryn child to receive a lashing."

The thought of her father actually carrying out such a threat, even if she didn't believe he would, had made her turn around at once. When it came to her safety, the man was ruthless.

Not unlike her brothers.

Was it any wonder she had wished for an easygoing husband?

"I thought only of my own desire to go to London," Sara continued, jarring her from her thoughts. "Before I hid in that cart, I did not consider that my presence would require extra men, an altered route, or an increased risk to those around me. Over time I came to learn how my father's decisions impacted other people, but it was a new lesson at the time."

"So why did you support Garrick's decision to break the betrothal?"

Hayden made a soft cooing noise, and Emma stood to get a

closer look. She was anxious for him to wake so she could hold him. But the sweet boy fell right back to sleep.

She sat back down and waited for Sara's answer.

"His decision, your decision . . . they are not mine to make."

"So you would not have broken the betrothal?" The pinch at her heart told Emma she already knew the answer.

"I didn't say that, precisely. You know my own circumstances, between your brother and I." Sara frowned. "I simply trust you, and Garrick, to make good decisions. And I would support you, no matter the cost."

Emma froze. "The cost?"

Sara rocked Hayden, likely without realizing she was doing it. "You asked me what I've been thinking, and the incident with Stanton and the wool cart came back to me."

Sara didn't need to elaborate.

Emma's cheeks tingled, tears springing unwittingly to her eyes.

"I cannot live without him. I can't." When tears spilled onto her cheeks, she wiped them away and tried to make them stop. "But perhaps I must."

She hardly noticed Sara standing, but suddenly she was crouched next to her. Sara put one arm around her and pulled her close. After looking at dear, sweet Hayden's sleeping face, Emma sobbed into her sister-in-law's shoulder, only stopping when she felt the wetness of her own tears.

Emma pushed away and then looked into another set of eyes as blue as her own. Hayden was awake. She reached for him, and Sara handed her nephew to her. She held him against her, soaking in his sweet smell, a combination of his mother's and his own.

"Perhaps," Sara said. She didn't elaborate.

"Emma?"

Both women looked toward the oak door, which had swung open. Geoffrey.

"Something is wrong?"

"I—" She couldn't deny it.

"She will be fine," Sara said with such finality that her brother, rather than questioning her, simply walked toward his wife and thanked her with a kiss. He then came toward her, taking Hayden before she realized what he had been about.

"But I just got him," Emma said.

"Then perhaps you should have been quicker, sister." He winked, unapologetic.

Emma wiped away the last of her tears, well aware that her brother was still watching her.

She gestured toward a chair, but Geoffrey shook his head, pacing the room with his son instead. Emma sat, watching him. The look on her brother's face nearly brought her to tears again. It was one of pure joy. And love. She understood it. Emma loved that baby with every fiber of her being.

"Did you come for Hayden?" Sara asked, sitting back down herself.

"Nay." He looked at her, and Emma knew she wouldn't like whatever he'd come to say.

"Graeme de Sowlis. He's offered for you."

An uncomfortable silence settled into the room. Sara stood, took Hayden from Geoffrey, and began to leave.

"Sara, why do you—" Emma started.

"'Tis time for you to talk."

Though talking to Geoffrey was the last thing she had a mind to do—she knew what he'd say—it was time her brother knew the truth.

Geoffrey sat just as she started to stand, but he wouldn't let her. "Sit, please. When you circle me like a buzzard eyeing his next meal, I find myself . . ."

A loud crackle from the fireplace stopped him. Or perhaps he was not prepared to continue. Either way, Emma had to prompt him to continue. "Aye?"

"I find myself thinking of Mother."

Emma welcomed the vision that rose in her mind. Once, she would have shut out the memory of her mother. But no longer. Aye, it made her chest constrict, but the fear of not remembering, of her beloved parents fading over time, was too terrifying to contemplate. So she welcomed the smiling face in her thoughts.

"You know, you have much of her in you."

"Geoffrey—"

He leaned forward, hands on his knees. "You cannot marry Lord Clave."

"What are you—"

"There are matters at play you do not understand. For the first time in thirty years, there is serious instability at the border. This is not about stolen cattle or sheep. Nor is it about protection payments, which have become more and more common since we lost Bristol. Reivers grow bolder. Clave's uncle paid a group of Scottish mercenaries to attack him. Emma, listen to me."

"Have I any choice?"

"Further disruptions, like an English earl breaking a betrothal with a powerful Scottish border chief, will not stand. Blood will be shed, either by Magnus or Inverglen. Or perhaps at this point, both. In this, I must disagree with my wife."

She'd told him?

"Sara would never—"

"Break your confidence. Nay, she would not, but I know my wife. She believes in love. Hell, I do too, though I'd never imagined saying as much. But she's also mighty stubborn, a trait that sometimes guides her to the wrong decision."

"Don't you dare speak ill of that woman—"

"Speak ill?" He looked genuinely confused. "I would never do such a thing. We all have faults. Mine nearly cost me the love of my life, the security of my family, and my very soul. Accepting imperfections makes you stronger, not weaker."

He truly believed his words.

"So I suppose I should slow down, use my head, consider the

consequences."

Though she'd said the words glibly, her brother didn't take them as such. "Aye. And think about it more carefully."

She did stand then. "Well, I did. I told Garrick that I couldn't let him break off his betrothal without further consideration. I probably sent him back to Clave thinking I didn't want him any longer. And I may have lost him forever. So are you quite happy?"

He didn't flinch. "Happy? To see my sister so upset? To know she fell in love with an honorable man she can't marry? It keeps me awake at night, Emma. How could you ever imagine any of that would make me happy?"

Emma was taken aback by his sincerity, and by the evident grief in his face. Indeed, it seemed he might even be . . . but no, it couldn't be. Did she see a . . .

Emma walked closer to where her brother sat and knelt down in front of him.

Holy St. Mary, it was. Emma reached up, and he let her wipe away the single tear that traced a path of wetness down his cheek.

Emma could not remember seeing her brother cry before. Ever. Not even after their parents were killed. Knights were equipped with the same feelings as mere mortals, of course, but the tales would lead one to believe they did not cry.

She covered his hands with her own. "I'm sorry. 'Tis frustration talking, not your sister. How long have you known?"

The side of his mouth quirked upward. "Nearly the same time as my wife," he said, as if guessing her emotions were a sport. "And well before you," he boasted.

The heaviness of the moment began to lift. "Is that so?"

"When we were in the courtyard, the day you left for Scotland."

"You may know many things, brother, but on this you are—"

"I thought the look he gave you was one of desire."

Emma jerked her hands away from him. To hear him speak thusly . . .

"But then you spoke to each other, and I knew for certain."

She rolled her eyes and stood.

"Not that you were in love, of course, but that you would be. He could have mentioned his purpose for traveling to Scotland. But he did not."

"He had already told you, I take it?"

"Aye. He'd mentioned it the evening before. And kept it from you. Not to be deceptive, I believe, but . . ." He shrugged. "It matters not. You and Garrick Clave simply cannot be."

She could hear herself breathing.

"But Graeme—"

"Not now, Geoffrey, please. Not now."

Geoffrey pulled her toward him. His happy life at Kenshire had softened him, and embraces came more freely to him these days.

She didn't want to think of Garrick or Graeme. Or of Geoffrey's revelation that he'd known all along. In fact, Emma didn't want to think of anything.

Eventually, she pulled away. "I'm going to the stables."

He let her go, but not without a softly uttered reminder. "The chief will be wanting an answer. And given your aversion to well-titled Englishmen—"

"A Scots clan chief is no better."

"I believe he would serve you well."

Emma groaned. "I need time to think. I will speak to him myself and tell him to go home, that I do not have an answer," she said, giving Geoffrey a quick squeeze. "Thank you for not being upset about Garrick."

"I never said I wasn't upset."

And with those ominous words following her from the room, Emma tore through the castle and discarded any sense of decorum.

Graeme expected an answer from her. Unfortunately, she had none to give him.

CHAPTER TWENTY-FOUR

He straddled her, and Emma couldn't resist running her hands along the ridges of his stomach. Desire pooled in her core, the aching for his touch unbearable.

"Make me yours, Garrick."

Where were her clothes? Though she couldn't recall removing them, when he reached up and cupped both breasts in his hands, there was nothing to inhibit his caress.

"Not yet," he said.

It was an order that she didn't mind obeying. His thumbs rubbed her nipples, forcing them to peak under his expert touch.

And then his hand moved lower, the light touch along her waist a promise of more to come. Then lower still until it rested there.

"Please." Was that what he wanted? For her to beg? "Please," she whispered again, arching, finally getting his hands to move.

Her eyes snapped open.

Garrick was not in her bed, and the hand lying at the precipice of pleasure . . . was her own. She pulled it back and looked around the chamber.

Of course he was not there. It had been nothing more than a dream. A wonderful, beautiful—

Emma could wait no longer.

She'd told him to make his own decision. She'd made a mature decision.

Yet she'd never been more miserable in her life.

The last few days following her conversation with Geoffrey had been especially torturous. She'd nearly gotten herself killed on a reckless ride that could have ended badly if not for Eddard's companionship. She hardly slept, and when the blissful blackness finally settled upon her, it was always invaded by thoughts of him.

Garrick protecting her against the mounted Scottish warriors. Cherishing her body at the inn. Tossing snowballs at her. Touching her. After every single dream, she woke breathless and disappointed.

She would know her future.

Today.

Emma briefly considered finding Edith to tell her, but she didn't want her maid to be forced to lie for her. She also did not want Geoffrey riding to Clave to haul her back to Kenshire before she could even speak to Garrick.

What to do? It was perhaps a bit foolish to go alone. But she could not trust anyone to keep from telling her brother.

If she left without word, they would all worry. Though she could easily make it to Clave Castle and back within the day, she'd not return at least until the sun began to set.

Emma jumped from the bed and grabbed a small wooden box that contained parchment and quills. She was about to open it when her eye caught the carving etched into the box. She ran her finger over it and took it to her bed.

This box was the only thing she'd requested from Bristol. It had been her mother's, and when Geoffrey had brought it home to her, her hands had shaken so violently upon taking it she'd feared she would drop it.

What would Mother think of Garrick?

Everyone, from her brothers to her aunt and uncle to Faye and the servants—everyone reminded her of her similarities to her mother, not just in looks but in manner. The fact that she had died attempting to fight off a Scottish warrior likely twice her size had surprised no one.

Would her mother encourage her to preserve the agreement Garrick had made? Encourage her to allow what she'd told Garrick to stand? To do what he thought was right? Or would she urge her to follow her heart?

Emma flipped open the box and took out the quill.

After writing the message, folding it, and placing it on the bed where Edith would be sure to find it, Emma dressed in a practical navy-blue riding gown, a tunic, and a sideless surcoat. There was no time for anything but a quick brush of her hair. Grabbing a mint leaf, she popped it into her mouth and set off.

Avoiding the hall, and unfortunately the kitchens too, she made her way to the stables. She saw only a few servants, all of whom let her pass with a "good morn" and no questions.

With the sun just barely risen, it was quite cold. This time she remembered her cloak before stepping outside, and when Eddard himself appeared at the door of the stables, she stopped short.

"Lady Emma?"

She was not typically one to be up and about so early.

"Good morn, Eddard," Emma said. She ignored his look of surprise and strode purposefully toward Nella. "How is my girl doing this fine morning?"

She kept her eyes on Nella for fear Eddard would be able to guess at her purpose if he saw her face.

"You wish to ride so early?"

"Please."

One thing she'd learned from Bryce—the less explanation the situation required, the less one should offer. She walked back outside, hoping to avoid further questions. When Eddard led Nella to her, she thanked him and, without further comment, pulled her hood more tightly about her face and made off toward Clave.

Geoffrey would be furious to learn she'd ridden so far without an escort. Or that she'd traveled to Clave at all. But most of the journey would be on Caiser land, and she planned to ride along the coast for the remainder of the trip. Depending on the timing of her arrival, she may have to wait for the tide to allow her access, but Emma was not concerned about her safety.

What would happen when she found Garrick?

That was a different sort of worry entirely.

Garrick needed to get out. Since the party's arrival yesterday, he'd not had a moment to himself, and before he spoke to his mother, Garrick needed time to himself. Time to think through what could be the most foolish decision of his life. After first informing Mable of his intentions and his whereabouts, he hurried away from the castle. The previous day had been disastrous, and today would undoubtedly prove to be much worse. If it was rude to be absent from the midday meal, then let him be guilty of neglecting his unwanted guests.

Leaving the keep in Mable's capable care, Garrick strode down the path that led to the stables. He'd considered taking a ride to clear his head but had dismissed the idea. Though it was still low tide, the waters would soon rise, and he couldn't be away for very long. So instead, he took the path that led beyond the stables toward the training yard. It would be empty, of course, but it was the place he felt most at peace.

Garrick was about to turn a corner when he heard voices behind him, at the entrance to the stables. It wasn't the groom's voice that gave him pause, but the woman's. Clearly he was hearing things. It couldn't be *her*.

"There's no need for escort," she said. "But I thank you for your offer."

Nay, it was not possible.

"But the guards—"

"Knew well that Caiser is a friend to Clave. Do lead the way."

Emma.

They turned the corner and froze.

"Leave us," he said to the groom, who seemed all too eager to do just that. With a quick nod of his head, he hurried off.

Emma's expression matched Garrick's own feelings at seeing her.

"Caiser may be a friend to Clave, but he'd never let a stranger approach without escort. Even a lone woman." He reached her in three strides. "Most especially a woman."

He took her arm and guided her in the direction he'd been headed.

"Am I a threat then?"

He couldn't stop looking at her. "You are."

More than she realized. He'd best concentrate on getting them to the training yard. It wasn't far, and since he'd given his men the day off, a rare boon in honor of their guests, the armory should be abandoned.

Garrick couldn't reach the building fast enough, though he did wish he had somewhere more fitting to bring her. The small stone structure would be dark and cold, hardly a place for a heartfelt reunion.

"I've never been considered a threat before," she said.

He pushed open the door.

Empty.

Garrick closed it with one hand and pulled her toward him with the other. "Very dangerous indeed."

He kissed her passionately, wanting to devour her, wanting to make her his in every way. He'd done just that in his dream the night before, and the memories rose up. When he grasped both sides of her face, her hood fell back, exposing the mass of black waves.

"I need you, Emma," he murmured against her lips.

Their heavy cloaks made it impossible to get close, but Garrick needed more. She opened for him and their tongues danced together. His cock strained, hard and willing, desperate to be inside her. Her full lips slanted across his own as the pressure grew. It was like the rising tide washing away every remnant of the shore, consuming every last grain of sand.

Something snapped in him, and reality intruded on their unexpected reunion. "Are you alone?" How had he not thought of that earlier? "Did you really come here without escort?"

She pulled back, startled. "You're angry?"

"Nay, love. Never. Surprised. Worried. But not angry."

"I had to come."

"You could have gotten—"

"Nay, I can't bear to hear such talk from you too. Just kiss me, please."

He didn't need another invitation. Garrick did kiss her then and guided her toward an empty patch of wall. The clang of an errant sword rang out against the silence.

He kicked it aside and opened her cloak, remembering the dream clearly. Her bright blue eyes watched him. Part of the dream was off-limits to them, of course, until he settled the situation, but he could enact the rest of it with her. He'd shock her, likely, but the memory would be branded in her mind.

Garrick tore off his glove. He wanted to move slowly, give her time to adjust, but as his fingers brushed the soft white fur of her cloak, he thought of how she would feel and taste beneath his lips. Garrick knelt beneath her.

"What in God's teeth are you doing?"

He looked up to a bewildered Emma, whose face had looked much more confused in his dream. "I dreamed of you last night." Every night, in fact.

Garrick lifted both her gown and the shift beneath it.

"I've dreamed of you too," Emma said, "but that doesn't explain—"

Pushing both garments aside and pinning them with his hand, he used the other hand to guide her legs apart. He deftly untied the garter that held up the thick woolen hose that protected her from the cold.

"Trust me," he said. *Dear God, was she real?*

She allowed him to guide her, moving one leg away from the other. When he moved his head toward her, Emma pressed herself back against the wall.

"Are you nervous?" he asked, looking up.

"Aye."

He ran his hand gently up her calf, trying to ignore the effect her smooth curves had on him. "I'm simply going to kiss you, Emma."

He would have laughed at the look on her face if he'd not thought it might offend her.

"I did this in my dream last night," he said.

"Did I enjoy it?"

"Very, very much."

He paused just a moment longer, watching as her expression turned from confusion to resolve, and then leaned forward toward the dark curls. With only one hand free, he did his best to part the folds beneath his fingers, and then he kissed her there. Gently at first and then, encouraged by her response, more ardently. Her sweet wetness, combined with a soft moan, reassured him Emma had overcome her shyness.

When her legs began to shake and her hands moved to the back of his head, Garrick knew she was close. He brought her to the height of pleasure, her cries coinciding with the evidence of her orgasm against his lips.

He opened his eyes, her hands still clasping his hair, and groaned at the sight of her sweet, slick sex.

When he remembered what had happened next in the dream, Garrick forced himself to drop her gown and stand. He pulled her gaping cloak back together, his heart thudding against his chest.

If this was how it felt to be in love, Garrick should have considered doing it much sooner.

"How do you feel?" he asked.

She blinked, her mouth parting to speak, but no words came out.

"Good," he said.

He wanted to adjust himself but couldn't. Bringing attention to his own need would be useless. He would have to wait.

"I'm not quite sure I . . . that is . . . I don't, in fact, know what I was going to say. What are you laughing at?"

"You." He couldn't help it. "I love that you're unable to form a coherent thought because of how much I pleasured you." He traced her cheek with his finger. "I love that you came here, though I hate that you put yourself in danger." He moved his finger to her lower lip. "I love your passion. Your willingness to face the world with your eyes wide open." Garrick replaced his finger with his lips. "I love *you*," he said, claiming her with his mouth, kissing her with all of the pent-up worry and desire that had weighed down his gut these last days.

Reality began to intrude when she shivered beneath him.

Garrick stood back just slightly, giving her room. "You're cold?"

"Nay," she lied. "But why are we out here?"

"Why did you come?"

"Why have you not?"

Garrick took a step back, knowing their perfect liaison was about to be ruined. "She's here."

He could tell she didn't know of whom he spoke. "Your mother?"

Garrick shook his head. "Nay . . . well, aye, my mother is here.

She arrived just yesterday, which is why I haven't come back to you yet."

He couldn't take solace in the look of relief on her face, not when she did not yet know the worst, so he just blurted it out. "Lady Alison."

Emma looked as if he'd just slapped her. "Is here? At Clave?"

He nodded. "And her father too."

"What are you saying?"

He couldn't watch her face. Turning, he began to explain. "I didn't know they were coming. I sent word to delay the wedding. Asked my mother to return to England. But yesterday—"

"How could you not have told me sooner?"

He went to her, eager to explain. The need for Emma compelled him to touch her, taste her. All else fell away. Lady Alison was an attractive young woman, but he'd felt absolutely nothing for her. When the shock of seeing Emma faded, he understood fully. The course he'd set in motion was the right one.

"Nay, do not." She pushed him away. "You let me . . . you did that . . . with your betrothed just up there?"

"She's not my betrothed. Not for much longer anyway."

Her blue eyes turned to ice. "So you've told them?"

It was as if she already knew the answer.

"Nay, not yet. I—"

"Garrick? How could you? How could—"

"I need to speak to my mother first and haven't had the opportunity to—"

"The opportunity? They've been here for more than a day. How could you not have had the *opportunity*?"

"I was as surprised as anyone," he began. "And I will speak to her at once."

Emma was far from mollified.

"So what do you plan to do with me?" she said, her words tumbling out. "That's why we're here and not in the keep, I take it? I can understand why you've said nothing. If Magnus was likely to be angry about the canceled betrothal before, what will he do now that he's brought his daughter all the way to Clave?"

Garrick couldn't bear the pain in her eyes. "Emma, I'm going to tell my mother today. I—"

"No." Her lips pressed into a line so tight they were almost white. "I made the right decision, telling you to do what you felt was right. Coming here—" She shook her head. "This was foolish and wrong."

"Emma, no—"

"Marry her," she said. "'Tis the right decision, and obviously you know it to be true. Marry her, and forget about me."

Before he could stop her, Emma ran from the building.

Nay, he could not let her run away from him again. Garrick went after her and was nearly upon her when a voice stopped him.

"Let her go."

He stopped and turned. Conrad, of course, his self-appointed guard.

"Think of the consequences, Garrick," Conrad said. "Especially before you've spoken to anyone first. If you have a mind to break the agreement, you must at least do it the right way."

Garrick spun back and watched as Emma ran into the stables. "Conrad, I can't let her leave like this." And then he remembered. "The tide!"

He glanced out, and sure enough, wetness had begun to return to the sand around them.

"I have to get her."

"Garrick, stop," Conrad said.

She emerged with the groom and Nella.

"If she doesn't leave now, she'll not get to Kenshire before dusk."

"She's not going anywhere alone," Garrick bellowed.

"Let me escort her back."

Nay, he needed to do it. If he let her go now, she would think—

"You are needed here," Conrad said. "Unless you'd like to start a war this very day. She'll be safe with me. Go back, speak to your guests. Mollify them. Do whatever you must, but do *not* abandon them. Not like this."

Garrick watched her mount and looked back up to the castle. Though part of him hated Conrad for being right, he knew there was no denying that he was in fact correct.

"Go," he finally said, watching the wetness become water.

His friend didn't waste a moment. Garrick watched as Conrad ran to the stables and emerged on horseback a moment later, following Emma.

Hurry.

He knew the tide well, and if they were to make it across safely, there wasn't a moment to lose. But he should not have worried. Garrick had momentarily forgotten about Emma's skills. Conrad, an expert horseman himself, had difficulty catching her. He would eventually, but she wouldn't make it easy. And Conrad would have to wait for the next low tide to return unless he took a boat and left his horse behind on the mainland.

As they became smaller and smaller, Emma's words came back to him.

They've been here for more than a day.

She was right. So why had he not spoken to his mother yet? He'd told himself last eve that they were tired from travel. But he hadn't sought her out first thing this morning either.

Why?

Because he was about to devastate her. And he didn't wish to be responsible for breaking his mother's heart.

Again.

CHAPTER TWENTY-FIVE

*H*e was no longer following her.

Emma looked back to be sure. He was indeed gone.

Emma's heart had leapt at the sight of the man trailing her on horseback. At first glance, she'd thought it was Garrick, and irrational hope had filled her up. Only upon reaching the shore had she realized it was Sir Conrad, and not Garrick, following her.

Not wanting to speak to him, or anyone, she'd ridden on as fast as she could, relenting only for a short respite once she reached Caiser land. But Brookhurst had hung back, thankfully, and now he was gone.

Finally, after what had seemed like days, Kenshire Castle came into view.

"Lady Emma," said Reginald, who had been speaking to a groom.

She stopped Nella in front of the stables. Worry was etched on Reginald's face, but he did not comment on her excursion. If only she could be so lucky with her brother.

"Good day," she said. Though it was no longer daytime. Without the sun, the frigid January air turned uncomfortable, especially after a long day's journey. She hadn't been warm all day, and she could not wait to feel the heat of a fire on her hands.

And her backside.

She smiled, remembering a day from her childhood. After spending too much time in the saddle, she'd returned to Aunt Lettie and Uncle Simon's manor, promptly made her way to the fireplace, and turned around, sticking her backside nearly into the flames. Bryce had caught her like that and still teased her about it.

"You look happy, my lady."

Her smile dropped. Trying not to think of Garrick, Emma concentrated instead on Reginald, who, she suddenly realized, looked as miserable as she felt. "Is all well, Reginald?"

Where were the stablehands?

Reginald extended his hand, so Emma gave him the reins. "Nay, my lady."

And this was just one of the many reasons she liked the lad so much. Good manners dictated that he should respond in the affirmative, but Reginald always spoke his mind. Geoffrey encouraged him to do so, and she was glad for it.

"Your brother is none too pleased with me." Reginald reached up to calm Nella, who was pawing the ground anxiously. She knew food and rest were just moments away.

"Why?"

Reginald looked down at his feet and shrugged.

"Reginald?"

Nella let her frustration be known.

"I had best be getting her inside," he said.

Emma stared after him in confusion, vowing to speak to her brother about it later.

The courtyard was nearly empty, and by the time Emma stood at the front door, darkness had fallen in truth. Pushing the door open, a guard greeted her.

Should she flee to her bedchamber?

Nay, there was no escaping him for long, so she entered the

great hall, stopping at its entrance to watch the frantic preparations for dinner. Weaving her way through the maze of servants
and trestle tables, she sought out the warmth of the fire in the far
corner of the room.

"You must be freezing." Sara's voice lacked any anger or
recrimination.

Emma looked up and couldn't help but stare. "You look
beautiful."

Indeed, her sister-in-law had begun to wear some of her old
gowns; the wardrobe made for her while she carried Hayden had
been packed away for now. Dressed in a perse blue gown with no
adornments save a gold belt, she looked quite different than when
Emma had last seen her, in her boys' breeches.

"Thank you." Her response was always the same. While Emma
tried to explain why she looked a certain way, Sara never did so.
She accepted compliments the same way she did criticism. With
poise and grace.

"My hands are most especially cold." She glanced over Sara's
shoulder and peered around the hall.

"He's preparing for dinner."

"Is he angry?"

"Worried," Sara corrected.

Emma rubbed her hands together, resisting the urge to turn
around. If she truly did stick her bum in the fire, it would have the
servants' tongues wagging for weeks.

"You said in your note that you 'had to know.'"

"'Twas a successful trip then," she responded, trying to keep
the bitterness from her voice.

Sara stuck out her hands as well. As they warmed themselves
by the fire together, a flurry of activity behind them, she and Sara
remained silent.

Emma refused to think about what he'd done to her before
their fight. As many times as the image of him kneeling below her
came into her mind, she shoved it away. He'd given her pleasure

without asking for any in return. She knew enough from Edith to understand the selflessness of his actions. She'd just begun to summon the courage to ask how she could please him in return when—

"What happened?"

She looked up, grateful to see Geoffrey walking toward them. She would tell the tale once and be done with it. "I know it was not the wisest of ideas to ride to Clave—"

"Alone. Unescorted. Emma, do you have any idea—"

She would not be waylaid. "But as I wrote, I simply had to know. And most of the journey was on Caiser land. I—"

"Could have gotten killed."

Sara leveled a sharp glance at Geoffrey, trying to silence him, but this was not her fight.

"Geoffrey," Emma said, trying not to raise her voice. "Not now."

"Go ahead, Emma," Sara encouraged her.

She couldn't do this. Couldn't say the words aloud. It was over. Had Garrick truly intended to fight for her, he would already have done so. He'd waited for a reason. And for those same reasons, she had to let him go.

"I'm not hungry," she said, turning away. They called her name, but she didn't care. She walked briskly, heading out of the hall and through the corridors. She just couldn't make herself tell them all. She'd been so stupid. To think he would forsake everything . . . for her? Who was she to ask such a thing of him?

"Emma, wait!"

She wanted to keep running, but Geoffrey would only follow her anyway. So she stopped and turned. But he didn't censure her or continue to lecture her.

Instead, her brother opened his arms and she went to him. Her eyes filled with tears as he wrapped his strong arms around her and patted her back. "The pain will go away."

She didn't believe him but didn't wish to argue the point either.

"Shh," he said. Emma allowed the tears to flow then.

For Garrick. For her parents. For everything.

"I know, Emma. I know."

She shook her head against his chest.

"Aye, I do. When I thought I'd lost Sara for good . . ."

Emma sniffled.

"Love can be as harsh as it is beautiful."

Despite herself, Emma giggled.

"What is so amusing?"

She pulled back to look at the face that was so similar to her own. Well, at least his eyes. And hair. She wouldn't want to look like the rest of him, big brute that he was.

"The Geoffrey I was raised with would never have uttered such a thing," she said.

He didn't appear overly concerned. "Maybe I'm not that same man."

Most certainly he was not, and thank goodness for it.

"But neither are you the same girl who amused herself by bringing roosters into the hall or hiding frogs in her brother's bedchamber."

Oh, Neill had been so mad.

"I'm sorry, Emma."

"Sorry? Whatever for?" And why was he not lecturing her?

"You're a grown woman, capable of falling in love. Marrying. Having children. And yet, when I look at you, I still see a girl. I can hear Father admonishing me to keep you safe."

"He was a mite overprotective."

"Perhaps. But he—and I—care only for your safety and happiness."

Her shoulders sank. "'Tis too late for that." She refused to say any more.

"Whatever happened today, I think you would do well to

consider Graeme's offer. You know I will support any decision you make, but—"

"I accept."

She was not meant to be with Garrick Clave. And if she was going to marry a man she didn't love, why not choose a handsome, honorable one who could be an ally to Kenshire across the border? One who lived close to Clara and a good distance from Clave Castle. She could not continue to live here at Kenshire, knowing that Garrick was close.

"I won't allow you to make that decision now. Think on it—"

"Allow? Did you not just tell me I am a woman capable of deciding my own fate?"

He didn't look convinced. "Wait until—"

"I accept his proposal," she said with as much finality as she could muster. "But if you do not mind, I'd like to be alone."

She pushed around him and ran—aye, ran—toward her chamber.

So she'd be marrying a Scottish noble after all. Just not the one she loved.

CHAPTER TWENTY-SIX

*G*arrick nodded to the maid who scurried past him, away from the lord and lady's chamber, where his mother prepared for the evening meal. It was not the first time Garrick had the chance to speak to her alone. But the events of the previous day and this afternoon had deeply affected him. Emma had affected him.

When they were together, everything was perfect. He knew what to do, knew the only path forward. But then doubt crept in like the stealthiest of enemies, lying in wait to strike him down.

He'd chided himself for a fool as soon as Conrad had ridden off behind Emma. His friend's admonishment to stay at Clave, though logical, had torn at his very core. He hated himself for letting her go.

And hated himself equally as much for what he was about to do.

He knocked on the door and walked in as soon as she bid him to enter. "Mother?"

She turned, her hand resting on the material that draped from the top of a decorative wooden pole at the corner of the bed. Silk hung from each of its four corners, the bed an elaborate example of the luxuries they enjoyed at Clave.

He'd give them all up, every one, not to have this conversation.

"Your father always hated these," she said, running her hand up and down the bright green material. "I never asked him why, precisely, but I can imagine him shoving them away as if they were horseflies."

"I'm sorry," he said.

"As am I."

He let her misunderstand.

She looked up as if seeing him for the first time. "Is something wrong?"

"Aye."

She cocked her head to the side, a frown marring her normally affable expression.

"We need to talk."

She motioned to a stool across from the bed, and they sat at the same time—she on the bed, he on the stool.

"It's about Magnus. And his daughter."

She still did not appear concerned. Yet.

He took a deep breath. "I cannot marry her."

"You cannot . . ."

Garrick had steeled himself for battle many, many times. Disappointing her again was far more difficult. "I am in love with Lady Emma Waryn, the younger sister to the new Earl of Kenshire. I escorted her to Dunmure—"

"I remember you mentioned that when you visited."

"And we formed an attachment. This is why I delayed the wedding. I never thought—"

She shook her head. "Garrick, you cannot break this betrothal."

Gentle but firm. His mother's way.

"I understand the repercussions and am prepared to face the consequences. But I cannot, will not, marry a woman I will resent for the rest of my days." Garrick forged ahead. "I've learned that Uncle Bernard was behind the attack. I also understand that if I do not marry Lady Alison, his pursuit of the title will be relentless. Magnus will likely—"

"Declare Linkirk an enemy."

"Aye."

"Garrick, think about your actions. You—"

"Have made my decision."

He hadn't made it this morning after Emma's visit to Clave. Or the day before when Magnus and his betrothed had surprised him in his great hall. Or even when he'd snuck into Kenshire, no easy task, after learning Graeme had traveled there from Scotland.

He'd made his decision that night in Kenshire, in the cold, misty minutes between sleep and awake, with the taste of Emma still on his lips. The feel of her against him, the contentment that came from knowing, or thinking, she lay next to him. In those moments, he'd realized something: the thought of waking fully and not having her next to him, for the rest of his life, was unacceptable.

As he looked into the eyes of the woman who'd brought him into this world, an unbearable memory reared its head—King Edward, bringing him to his father's dead body on the battlefield.

"I know I've disappointed you again," Garrick said, gritting his teeth against the pain, "and I am sorry—"

"Disappointed me?" Her confusion appeared genuine. "Son, you've not disappointed me. Ever."

That steely tone nearly convinced him of her words. But not quite. While his mother may be willing to absolve him, he knew the truth.

Yet he wouldn't be the one to say the words aloud, to shed light on his deepest shame.

"Look at me."

He'd been doing so, though she somehow knew his mind had been elsewhere.

"When do you believe you've disappointed me?"

"Can we discuss—"

"Garrick. When?"

He felt his muscles tense as if in preparation for battle. Well, this was a battle of a different sort. "When I killed Father."

Neither of them spoke. Of course, when she did recover, his mother would tell him he was wrong. Like Emma, she would attempt to convince him that his father had made the decision to leave on his own. That he was no more responsible for his death than he was for a summer storm.

"So you killed your father." Her tone caught him by surprise. Rather than deny the truth, she stated it factually. "Let me see . . . you talked him into joining you on one last adventure. To use the skills he'd trained his whole life to gain. And because of it, I no longer have a husband, Clave and Linkirk have a new earl, and your father can no longer offer the advice you so crave from him."

"Aye," he gritted out through clenched teeth.

"Then you knew the man not at all."

What was she saying?

"I was his wife for many more years than he was your sire. And I loved him. Nay, not at first, for our marriage was arranged, but those first months were nothing compared to the years of love we shared. And do you know how he felt about me? About you?"

Of course he did. "Father loved us both."

"Aye, Garrick, he loved us both. Very much. Just slightly more than he loved his men and the defenses he built, though perhaps we were on equal footing with the victory of battle. He craved battle. Needed it as much as he needed to eat or breathe. Your father, like you, was a knight. A trained warrior devoted to his God, his family, his people, and when it suited him, his country. My efforts to keep him here were futile. He'd never accept my terms. To wait at Clave knowing he could have been fighting side by side with the boy who had become a man in his image?"

Her shoulders slumped, but she looked at him with flashing

eyes. "To consider it for even a moment desecrates the memory of one of the greatest knights—earls—in all of England. Certainly the greatest border lord, who was proud to have spent so many years of his life devoted to securing the border."

Garrick didn't know what to say. He'd assumed—

"You're wrong, son. So very, very wrong. You did not kill your father any more than I did." She shook her head. "Disappointed in you? A man who puts the needs of his men above his own. Who has more discipline in his right arm than Conrad has in—"

"Mother."

She enjoyed teasing Conrad nearly as much as he did. Though sometimes Garrick suspected she was not teasing.

"Very well." She stood and walked toward him. "I have never been disappointed in you. And never will be." She took his hands.

"Are you saying—"

"This is a terrible idea. You said you understand the repercussions, but they will be far and wide. Bernard will be infuriated, and if he was indeed behind the attack, he'll clearly not rest until my claim has been overthrown unless we can prove it was him. Magnus will declare Linkirk an enemy. He'll expect recompense, and there is a very real chance he'll join Bernard in a war against us."

"Then why are you so calm?"

His mother dropped his hands and looked up to the ceiling. "We will need to offer him something valuable. The man is richer than his king. I'd give him my share of Linkirk if I could."

"Mother, Linkirk is your ancestral home. The title is—"

"Nothing more than that. A title. You are my son. My living, breathing son who means more to me than a thousand titles and castles." She looked him straight in the eyes. "You love her?"

"Very much."

"And she loves you?"

"She does."

"What is your plan? To speak with Magnus after the meal?"

He reached for his mother and pulled her into his embrace. Emma had tried to tell him, to make him see reason, but he'd not been ready to listen.

"I love you, Mother," he said, a catch in his voice.

"I love you too, son." She pulled back and smiled, but the smile didn't reach her eyes. She was already thinking, plotting. Planning.

He was ready.

"Emma?"

She'd been dreaming of Garrick. Part of her wanted to get up, knowing his touch was simply her mind's cruel trick. But most of her wanted to go back to sleep and forget that the Earl of Magnus and his daughter currently resided at Clave and that she'd forsaken her claim to Garrick.

Sara's voice penetrated the fog of sleep. Opening her eyes, she was surprised to see her chamber fully lit. The sun had risen.

"I missed mass," she said.

"And the meal," Sara replied. "When Edith told me you wouldn't stir, I began to worry."

Emma pulled her covers closer, not making any attempt to get up. The bed sagged where Sara sat beside her.

"No gown this morn?" Emma asked.

Sara looked down at her loose shirt and modified breeches. "Would you like to join me for a ride?"

Normally, she would do so without hesitation. Today, she simply wanted to go back to sleep. "No, thank you."

She turned from Sara's look of pity and stared at a tapestry on the wall, looking at the blues, reds, and yellows. The vibrant colors did not match her mood.

"I did the right thing," Emma murmured.

"Perhaps."

"You even said you might have done the same."

"Emma, I don't know what I'd have done for certain. But I do know you should follow your own path. Not mine. Or your brother's. Yours."

"I tried to do just that. Going to Clave . . ."

"What happened there?"

Emma sighed. She sat up, knowing she couldn't stay abed all day. "Garrick found me in the stables. We . . ."

A flush crept up her neck to her cheeks. "I am a virgin still," she managed.

"I'd not tell your brother." Sara smiled. "Though, as you know, he'd have no cause to censure you."

Emma knew better than to respond to that particular statement. She continued, "But then he told me *she* was there."

"She?"

"His betrothed. She and her father, Magnus, came with Garrick's mother from Scotland. Presumably to protest the proposed delay, although I never actually asked him."

As much as she hated to say the words aloud, Emma wanted Sara to know everything. "He had not yet spoken to his mother, and I could sense he was hesitant to do so. That's why I left."

"I see."

"I ran. Well, I told him to marry her . . . and then I ran." What were they doing right now? Had they already set a wedding date? Was Garrick thinking of her?

"Geoffrey told me about Graeme."

Graeme. How could she have forgotten about that? "He's a good man," Emma said, her voice flat.

"Emma, perhaps you should take some time to think about the offer. After what happened with Garrick—"

"Nay," she said. Too quickly, she added, "I'm ready to marry."

"You say it as if you're being sent to the gallows. No one is forcing you. I just think—"

She shook her head. "I'm ready," she repeated. "Graeme is honorable and loyal."

She sighed. "'Twill be as good a match as any. Better than most."

"But he's only just offered. You have time."

"Geoffrey is sending word, or has done so already. 'Tis done." She tried to smile, hoping to ease the lines of worry on her sister-in-law's face. Regret was a needless emotion for either of them. It no longer mattered what she wanted. She'd made a decision, come what may. "'Tis done."

Emma jumped from the bed, prepared to start the day. "It seems we've much to do," she said, trying to summon some enthusiasm. She'd face this day, and all the ones after it, with the same strength and grace as Sara. "I'll need a gown, I suppose. Do you think a tailor could be found this time of year? And these trunks —" She pointed to the two large wooden chests at the foot of her bed. "Shall I take—"

"Emma, wait."

"I've not been married before. Will you help me prepare?"

"Of course, but—"

She pulled Sara from the bed with both hands and tried to smile. It felt more like a grimace. "Then come. We've a wedding to prepare for."

Though her feet felt as if they were made of iron, she forced them to move.

I will not think of Garrick. I will not think of Garrick.

Sara looked as if she wanted to say something but changed her mind. Emma held back hot, stinging tears, trying to put thoughts of the earl out of her head.

CHAPTER TWENTY-SEVEN

"Garrick!"

He heard the shout behind him, but Garrick would not slow down. He urged Bayard and his gift forward, ignoring Conrad . . . or at least attempting to.

"Garrick."

When he shifted to look back, Bayard instinctively slowed just enough to allow Conrad to reach him.

"If you plan to marry the Waryn girl, getting yourself killed en route will not help your cause."

He relented, if only to cease Conrad's incessant admonishments for him to slow down.

Now on Caiser land, Garrick couldn't get to his love quickly enough. He would have made the trip the previous night if not for the rising tide, which turned Clave into an island twice a day.

"I'm anxious to get to know the woman you'd have started a war to wed."

"And nearly did," Garrick replied.

He'd expected Magnus to fly into a rage when he approached him the previous evening, and indeed, the Scotsman would have attempted to cleave off his head had he not been armed. Magnus had charged at Garrick, bellowing as only a warrior going into battle could do. His roar had echoed off the stone walls of his solar, servants from as far away as the great hall likely overhearing the exchange, and if Conrad had not been present to intervene, it would have gone very badly for him. And then a miracle had happened.

"What do you suppose Magnus would have done had his daughter not declared her pregnancy?"

"I don't know," he said, angling Bayard around a brood of hens that had wandered onto the road. The dry, hard earth beneath Bayard's hooves allowed for a faster pace for which Garrick was grateful.

"You've the luck of the devil, my friend."

Garrick didn't believe in luck, but given Conrad's superstitious nature, he'd not argue.

Just when it seemed certain Magnus would attempt to end his life, Alison, who'd stood quietly to the side up until that point, burst into tears. Garrick had asked for her to be there, a decision that would prove fateful. Her father's face practically turned purple when she blurted out that she'd no wish to marry Garrick either. She was in love with another, although she refused to give her father his name. Of course, Magnus did not care what she thought and said so.

But when she burst out, "I am with child," she had her father's attention.

"Do you suppose Magnus will forgive her?"

"I'd like to believe so," he said, grateful for Conrad's attempt to distract him. Garrick had spent a sleepless night preparing his speech to Waryn. For the first time since he'd met Emma, he allowed himself to imagine their future. Making love to her, waking up to a woman who would bring life back to Clave.

"I'm sorry I've not supported you in this."

He glanced over at the man he'd known for most of his life.

Conrad, rarely serious, looked back at him, his lips set and expression grim.

"You were right not to," he said.

"I won't pretend to understand it. To risk so much for a woman."

He'd have said the same before meeting Emma. Someday, perhaps Conrad would be fortunate enough to learn just how far a man would go to be with the woman he loved.

They fell silent until Kenshire Castle came into view. The air changed as they skirted the village and approached the coast. Garrick had always preferred to travel during the winter months. Some shied away from the bitter cold, but the roads were safer with fewer travelers.

"I've never become accustomed to this view," Conrad said.

They'd come here often as boys, but Garrick agreed. He'd seen much during his travels, but Kenshire was still one of the finest castles in England.

"Have you thought of how her brother might respond to your offer?"

Garrick had thought of little else since realizing he was free to wed Emma. Once Magnus had stormed from Clave, taking his disgraced daughter with him, Garrick had sought out his mother. Though she agreed that a match with Emma Waryn may present further problems for Linkirk, especially if his uncle wasn't brought to justice, she was joyful that he'd found love. Garrick and his mother decided to leave his uncle's fate in the hands of the wardens. He'd "trust in the process," as Emma had said.

Garrick also realized he'd be asking for the earl's only sister's hand in marriage. Emma may want him, but if her brother did not, he would have a tough go of it.

"I'm grateful Edward trusted me to negotiate with his enemies. Compared to that, surely one former reiver will not be a problem." As soon as the words left his mouth, Garrick wanted to take them back. For Kenshire Castle loomed large in front of them, and very soon, he'd find out just how much of a problem the earl would present.

"What of Lady Sara? At least she knows you well."

Garrick picked up speed, wanting to be there *now*. "Aye," he yelled back to Conrad as he passed him. "Which is precisely why I am worried."

CHAPTER TWENTY-EIGHT

*E*mma had avoided everyone since her talk with Sara the evening before. She'd skipped the evening meal, much to Edith's and Sara's dismay.

No one truly believed she had a headache.

Emma had tossed and turned all night, only to wake still thinking of the masked man on horseback from her dream. He'd ridden toward her with no markings on himself or his horse, but Emma had refused to retreat. Instead, she'd charged directly toward him, unsure of how she would defeat an armed knight. Then he'd pulled off his mask, revealing himself as a messenger from Kenshire.

Realizing it had been but a dream, Emma rose from her bed, added a log to the fire, washed her face and hands, and promptly crawled back into bed.

Ultimately, it was not prodding from Sara or Edith that finally forced her to rise, but her own mother. After her father had caught her in her attempt to attend the Tournament of the North and sent her home with a severe scolding, Emma had expected her mother would also want to have a strict word with her. And though she'd managed to avoid her for a spell, her mother had eventually found her at Bristol Sprout, a waterfall not far from the manor. But rather than berate her as her father had done, she simply told her to "keep fighting like a knight cornered in battle. As a woman, you'll be forced to do so until the day of your death."

Of course, she'd not known at the time her mother would be forced to fight *to* her death.

What would she say to me now? Likely that hiding in my bed is no way to get what I want.

Fight like a knight cornered in battle.

How did a knight cornered in battle fight? He would strike harder, but she'd already done so. Hadn't she risked everything to ride to Clave? She couldn't very well go back to the man who'd made it clear he would not fight for her. Who hadn't even tried to go after her.

But perhaps she'd been a tad rash to tell Geoffrey she would marry Graeme. It certainly would be difficult to live in Kenshire if Garrick was to be wed at Clave, but perhaps all was not lost? Even if it were, why rush into marriage with someone she did not love? The chief would be a perfect match for some lucky woman . . . just not for her. And didn't he deserve a chance at love too?

Emma jumped from the bed. She had to stop this wedding. She changed quickly, donning a simple undertunic and sideless surcoat, but jumped at the sudden knock on her door.

"Emma?"

Geoffrey's voice.

Emma pulled the brush through her hair a few times more and called him inside.

"Oh," he said, startled. "I was told you were still abed."

"Sulking like a young girl," she finished.

Geoffrey's eyebrows pulled together. "You don't sulk, Emma."

"Mayhap I did when you and Father trotted off to see the finest horseflesh in all of England without—"

"This again?" He sat on her bed and stretched his legs out in front of him.

"Aye, this again. Every single year—"

"Emma, I'm not here to talk about the tournament."

Of course not. In fact, this was as good a time as any to inform him of her change in plans. "I can't marry him."

She waited until his hearing caught up with her words.

Aye, now he understood. His bright blue eyes darkened as they tended to do when he became angry.

"Emma, I asked if you were sure. You cannot—I knew I should not have listened to you." When he raised his voice, Emma crossed her arms. "Why did you not wait? I told you—"

"Aye, you asked if I was sure. I was. But now I am not. Have you never made a mistake before?"

"This is not some simple mistake. This is a man's life we're discussing."

"You think I don't understand that? 'Tis his life, and mine. But I was upset, and—"

"Emma—"

"Stop saying my name like that!"

"Like what?" His hands balled into fists, and something about his posture—angry yet restrained—reminded her of her father. She missed him so very, very much. She'd even be happy to be rebuked by him. Her eyes welled with tears.

"You look exactly like Father just now, all blustery and—"

"I do not bluster."

They both knew quite well that he did, in fact, bluster.

"I am sorry that you're in pain," her brother said more softly, getting to his feet. "I'd take it from you if I could."

And she knew he meant it. Always.

Panic tickled at her. Could it truly be too late? Had she doomed herself with her own impetuousness? She wanted Geoffrey to offer another idea, but his only answer was to reach out and smooth down her hair.

"I'm sorry," she said, standing. "I need to think."

He must have assumed she planned to stay in her chamber, for when they both attempted to walk to the door, she collided with the stone wall that was her brother.

They walked from the room together, Emma heading to the only place that she truly felt at peace.

Emma opened the door to the stables and was greeted by nearly every groom at Kenshire, or so it seemed. They stood in a circle, a horse at the center of their gathering. As she walked toward them, she attempted to get a better look.

"What's happening?" she asked.

They all turned toward her at once.

"Is it Nella?" She rushed forward. "Is she . . . Oh my!"

They parted for her to get a better look, and Emma gasped. The magnificent pure white horse was not one of theirs. It had a long, broad neck that tapered down to a strong, massive chest. She stared at its thick mane and moved closer. Docile, despite being completely surrounded, she didn't flinch when Emma ran her hand down her sleek flank. She looked down to the horse's completely unblemished legs.

"Whose is it?" she asked no one in particular.

Eddard answered.

"Yours," he said.

She straightened. "Mine?" she asked in bafflement, tearing her gaze away from the beautiful creature.

"Back to work," Eddard said to the others.

"I don't understand."

"She arrived just moments ago. The messenger only said 'twas a gift for Lady Emma Waryn."

"Where is this messenger?" She looked around but saw no one unfamiliar.

"I sent Reginald to escort him to your brother. I also sent word to you, but—"

"Who would do such a thing?" She knew enough about horses to know this one was worth a fortune. "Pure Spanish?" she asked.

Eddard nodded. "Aye."

Emma's hand froze. Graeme? Could it be a wedding gift?

Nay, of course not. He would not have even received the message yet. At the moment, she was still unattached.

"I thought perhaps you might know, my lady. There was no message, just 'a gift for Lady Emma.' He did also say, 'Since she could not go to them, I brought one to her.'"

She did not wait for the rest—if, indeed, there was more. She ran to the door of the stable, looking out, hoping to see him, needing to know she was right.

Garrick had sent the horse to her. He'd gifted her with the finest horse Emma had ever seen in her life.

Why? Did he feel poorly about the way things had ended? Was it his way of apologizing? Or was it possible he'd spoken to his mother after all?

Emma turned back to catch a glimpse of white as Eddard led her new horse into the back of the stables. She needed to find the messenger, who could verify the gift was indeed from the Earl of Clave. She ran all the way back to the keep and into the great hall. No one.

Until she spied Faye emerging from the back of the castle, near the kitchens.

"Faye," she called. "Have you seen my brother?"

When the older woman looked up toward the balcony, Emma immediately knew. She didn't wait for a reply but ran up the winding stone stairs into the solar. Opening the door without knocking, she gasped.

Her brother, and Sara, were indeed inside. But it was the room's third occupant who caused her heart to skip a beat.

CHAPTER TWENTY-NINE

"*H*ow did you . . ."

They all turned to look at her, but Emma stared straight at Garrick. Her heart was beating so rapidly, she feared it would fly out of her chest.

"When did you arrive?" That was certainly not the question she wanted to ask. But it would do, for now.

"Within the hour," he said, getting to his feet. Garrick was not happy. "Your brother," he said, his words slow and measured, "was just explaining why he is unable to accept my offer of marriage yet."

Marriage?

"That you—" He cleared his throat. "Are to be wed to Graeme de Sowlis."

Geoffrey's eyes narrowed. He was no more pleased than Garrick.

"Wed?"

"I'd have spoken to you first, Emma. But I thought you'd readily agree. It seemed prudent to speak to your brother before seeking you out."

Emma couldn't seem to straighten out her thoughts. The room suddenly seemed too warm to bear.

"But when I left Clave, you . . ."

"Told my mother, and Magnus, I couldn't possibly marry Lady Alison."

Her eyes widened. "You did?"

"Of course I did," he ground out.

"But what happened? What did they say?" She was so sure he would not fight for her. How could she have mistaken his intentions so badly?

"Does it matter?" Garrick turned to Geoffrey and spoke to him, ignoring her completely. "It seems we are done here. My apologies for having caused your family any distress."

Then, without another word, he made for the door.

"Wait," Sara called.

But he did not stop. Garrick moved past her without a glance, whisking so close she could almost feel his warmth, and walked away. It took her a moment to recover.

Emma looked around the room and then turned toward the door.

"Excuse me," she mumbled. When a hand grabbed her from behind, she tried to shrug it off. "Nay, Sara. I must go to him."

"Wait," Sara repeated. The urgency in her voice stopped Emma from attempting to leave. "You may not be pledged to Graeme," she said.

That got her attention.

"What?" both she and her brother asked at the same time.

Sara's tiny shrug of her shoulders and tight-lipped grin could only mean one thing. She had done something she feared would displease Geoffrey.

Her brother folded his arms and waited.

"The messenger you sent," she said to her husband. And then, more forcefully, "I stopped him."

"What do you mean, you stopped him?" Emma asked, a spark of hope blooming in her chest.

"Just that," Sara said. "I knew you"—she jutted her chin out to indicate Geoffrey—"were anxious to see the whole matter finished." She turned to Emma. "Only because he loves you and despises seeing you in pain. But Sowlis was not the answer. At least, not so soon. When Geoffrey said he sent a message to the chief, I sent another to retrieve the messenger and am still waiting on word of his arrival."

The look on her brother's face should be one of shock. But it wasn't. Instead, he appeared—

"Geoffrey?"

"You haven't received word because your man will not be able to intercept the messenger."

Emma was not the only one confused by her brother's statement.

"I've already brought him back," he continued.

She and Sara simply stared.

"I should not have pushed the match. But I hated seeing you like that, Emma," he said. "I should have told you earlier today, but I wanted you to sort it out first before giving any definitive orders either way. But for now, the message to Graeme is safely within these walls."

"Then why did you tell Garrick—"

"I said I couldn't approve the match *yet*. I wanted to speak to you first. And," her cheeky brother finished, "I thought he should know about Graeme."

"You just wanted to see his reaction," Sara accused.

"Perhaps." He shrugged unapologetically. "This is my baby sister's happiness at stake. I wanted to be sure he truly loves her."

She couldn't believe it. Geoffrey had stopped the messenger.

"I have to go!" she shouted, feeling so light she could float up to the ceiling.

She threw her arms around Geoffrey and squeezed, and then

did the same to Sara. Perhaps a hug would help soften his mood. Then she ran as fast as her legs would carry her, down the stairs and through the hall. Garrick was just being handed his cloak when she called out to him.

"Stop! Garrick, wait."

The hall was beginning to fill with servants preparing for the evening meal. Almost all of them turned to look at her, but she couldn't bring herself to care.

"Garrick." She stopped directly in front of him. "We need to talk."

He took the cloak and turned from her. "I don't believe—"

"I am not getting married," she blurted.

He froze.

"Please, just please stay. Listen to me."

He didn't look at her, but he didn't leave either. It was something.

"I didn't think—"

He spun around then, and the warrior, not the man, stared back at her. "Nay, you did not think."

She'd planned to tell him that Geoffrey, and Sara, had stopped the messenger from reaching Graeme. To ask if he truly was here to ask for her hand in marriage. To find out what had happened at Clave.

But his words—actually, his tone—stilled her stubborn tongue. Though she wanted all to be well, too much had happened in the last two days for that to happen so easily. They would need to talk, really talk, and that could not be done in the crowded hall. But she wasn't letting him leave without explaining.

Apparently Sara agreed with her, for her sister-in-law had followed her into the great hall. "We would very much like you to stay for the evening meal," Sara said. "And perhaps for the night, as you'd planned?"

They had obviously spoken before she arrived in the solar, and now Emma wondered exactly what had been said. She looked at him hopefully. Would he accept?

"I'd never refuse such an offer from the Countess of Kenshire," he said. Spoken so formally, without a hint of wanting to stay for her. Only for Sara.

At least he was staying.

"Faye, will you have the earl shown to a private chamber to prepare for the meal?" Sara said.

The maid appeared from nowhere, as she so often did, and curtsied. Without another glance, Garrick walked away.

"He's here to marry you, Emma."

That much she understood. "Then perhaps he could stop glaring at me as if I was one of the unmarked men who attacked him." And then she remembered what Sara had done. "You both really stopped the messenger?"

Sara grabbed her hand, and they walked back toward the stairs.

"I did," she said. "Just in case. But had no idea your brother had already done so."

"Garrick is furious, and I don't blame him. I don't even under-stand myself what I possibly could have been thinking."

"I don't believe you were thinking at all." It wasn't an insult, but a pure fact. Emma's heart had felt as if it had been torn from her chest. Nay, she'd not been thinking. Only feeling. And she never wanted to experience such heartbreak again.

"What did he say? Tell me everything."

"He only arrived a few moments before you did. He asked to speak with Geoffrey and me privately, and I must say, I was quite surprised to see him after everything you'd told me."

"And?"

"And he said he was no longer promised to the Earl of Magnus's daughter, and he'd be honored to have you as a bride. After the shock wore off, Geoffrey began to explain that Graeme de Sowlis had offered for you, and before I could stop him, he added that you'd accepted the suit. And then you found us."

Emma stopped, remembering the horse. "He brought a gift for me."

They'd reached the stairs, but rather than climb them, the two women remained at the bottom, their heads tipped together as if they shared an important secret.

"He did?"

Emma pictured the horse's perfect white coat and sighed. "The most beautiful pure Spanish you've ever seen."

"A wedding gift?"

That and so much more. "I suppose," she said, not wanting to explain just now. "But I wonder what the earl said to Magnus? Is his army marching on Clave now?"

"I don't believe Garrick would be here preparing for dinner if that were so." Sara pulled on her hand, and Emma followed her sister-in-law up the stairs.

"I need to tell him about the messenger."

"Aye," Sara answered. "You do."

"I should go to him now—"

"Nay. It won't do well for you to be alone with him."

"Uh, no. Of course not."

"Under the watchful eye of your brother," Sara finished.

Was Sara really suggesting she should go to him later?

Aye, she would. They needed time alone, away from prying eyes, to settle all the questions that remained between them. But before the night was through, there would be no doubt.

The man she loved would be hers.

Tonight . . . and forever.

CHAPTER THIRTY

*W*hy was he still here?

He owed as much to Lady Sara after listening to his offer—nay, his plea—for Emma's hand in marriage. For her friendship and their shared history.

Who am I fooling?

He was still here because of *her*. Could there truly be hope? Geoffrey had made it fairly clear there wasn't any, and yet he couldn't bear to accept that he was too late.

"Lord Clave." Geoffrey Waryn strode through the hall to where he stood waiting by the mantel. "Come, sit with me."

Garrick followed Geoffrey to the raised dais. His host indicated for him to sit next to him, and so he did.

"The ladies should arrive shortly," Geoffrey said, then thanked the cupbearer for filling his goblet with wine, and Garrick did the same.

"I assume a toast will be in order?" his host said.

Though Garrick didn't understand his meaning, he lifted his goblet anyway.

Which was when Geoffrey burst into laughter. "I can see they didn't tell you yet."

As they watched the hall continue to fill, a flash of green and blue peeked out from the crowd. Sara and Emma appeared on the opposite side of the hall.

The men stood.

Bloody hell.

It was her smile that he noticed first. She beamed as if she had not a care in the world. Her mood, coupled with Geoffrey's odd comment, was Garrick's first indication the situation was not quite as he'd thought.

"Tell me what?"

The ladies were halfway to the dais when a pleasant but indistinguishable scent announced the arrival of the first course. But Garrick didn't look at the servants waiting at the side of the hall for their lady to sit. He didn't look at Geoffrey for a response to his question.

He looked instead at Emma, who stared straight back as if she'd just been told a tantalizing secret. Her smile held both promise and desire, and his body instantly responded.

"That both my wife and I, independently, intercepted the message to Sowlis."

It took him a moment to grasp Geoffrey's words. "Intercepted?"

"Stopped him from delivering it. I wanted to speak to Emma first before I gave my approval. Which, of course, you have."

She is not marrying Graeme. I have her brother's approval.

Emma began to follow Sara around to Geoffrey's left, but the countess stopped her.

"I do believe you have a new seat this eve," she said. They both looked at the empty seat next to Garrick.

Emma simply smiled as she made her way to the chair. She stepped up, thanked the servant who held the ornate wooden chair for her, and sat.

When a trencher was placed between them, Garrick peered around Geoffrey to greet Sara. "Good eve, my lady."

"Lord Clave."

It seemed everyone other than him was smiling and in good cheer. Perhaps if he'd learned about their change in circumstances before sitting down to the meal, he'd feel the same.

When Sara leaned in to say something to her husband, Garrick took advantage of their distraction and turned back to Emma.

"Why did you not tell me?" he whispered.

Her smile faltered, likely at his harsh tone. "I had hoped for the chance to speak with you, alone."

"So it seems you are free to marry once again?"

Garrick hated that she'd accepted Graeme's proposal, even though they had parted under less than ideal circumstances. He was not happy with her decision, but neither did he pretend the outcome would be anything other than Emma belonging to him.

And he to her.

"Aye, my lord."

He ignored the herring and herbs that had been placed on their shared trencher.

"And you're sure you are not wanting to send that messenger back to Scotland?" he pressed.

Her eyes narrowed. "If you're sure you don't want to find another Scottish heiress to secure your claim to Linkirk."

The mood shifted. Despite the tone of their words, the very air around them seemed lighter, less oppressive than it had been just moments before.

"There is only one thing I want, Lady Emma. And I believe you know what it is," he whispered.

She held his gaze, boldly and with more promise than he deserved. "What, may I presume to ask, is that, my lord?"

"You shall find out soon enough." With that, he gave his attention to their hosts. "Lord—"

"Geoffrey," the man corrected.

Though he'd known Sara since childhood, he could not say the same for her husband. The earl's easy request for Garrick to use his given name confirmed the words he'd said before.

"Garrick Helmsley. Brother-in-law." Sara's broad smile was infectious enough for him to stop thinking, for the moment, of Graeme de Sowlis and Emma's ready acceptance of his offer.

"Pardon me," Emma interrupted.

He'd been deliberately indiscreet, and though this was hardly the proper place for it, Garrick did not wish to wait. "Aye, my lady?"

He tried not to smile, unsure of why he felt the urge to tease her when his mood had been so dark just moments before. She was simply too easily incensed, and the thought of doing this for years to come was one that filled him with happiness.

Her eyes widened. "Did you not wish to include me in this particular conversation?"

At least they would never be bored.

"I'm not sure I know what you mean?" He pretended to see the meal between them for the first time, and pulling out his knife, he cut a portion of the fish, the best portion, and slid it to Emma. He then took a bite for himself. "You know, my father attempted to steal Cook away from Kenshire many times. She—"

"I'm glad you're enjoying the meal," Emma said.

She was up to something.

Taking the portion he'd cut for her, she picked it up between her thumb and forefinger, popped it into her mouth, and then proceeded to lick both fingers just enough for his cock to respond —though not enough for others to take notice.

"Emma . . ."

She did the same with the second portion, this time licking her lips when she was through. It had been too long since he'd tasted those lips.

Of course, that thought led to another.

Outside of his dreams, he'd tried not to imagine taking Emma as his own. Every time his thoughts wandered that way in the past, he had stopped them.

But now he gave his mind free rein. Continuing to watch her deliberately entice him, he could think of nothing else. He had to remember where they were. Who sat next to them.

And though Sara and Geoffrey carried on a conversation between themselves, the four of them were on display in a room full of retainers. They were not yet alone.

But she'd won this battle.

"Stop," he insisted.

She looked at him questioningly.

"I want you," he said. "I need you."

Emma turned serious.

"Will you be my wife, Emma Waryn?"

She reached for his hand, only to pull it back. Her eyes shifted to the crowded hall before returning to him.

"'Tis so difficult not to touch you," she said.

Oh God, she had no idea.

"Aye, Garrick. I will be your wife, gladly."

When she reached for her goblet, he took advantage, placing his hand over hers and pretending to help her guide it to her lips.

Pulling his hand away, he made a promise he intended to keep. "I will love you, Emma Waryn, every day for the rest of our lives." And then lower, to ensure they were not overheard, "Starting this evening."

She blinked, understanding creeping into her expression.

And before he lost himself completely, Garrick turned and attempted to converse with his hosts.

It would be a long meal indeed.

Emma had not been nervous all evening.

She should have been before the meal, before knowing how

Garrick would react. Whether he would, indeed, forgive her. Or mayhap when she'd pulled Geoffrey aside after the scene in the solar and begged him to accept Garrick. Or the moment when she'd pledged herself to him, forever.

Nay, she'd not been nervous then, but she was very much so as she stood in her chamber with her lady's maid, preparing for the night ahead.

"Yer poor fingers," Edith said, standing back to look at her as if she were a prized horse. "If ye keep doin' that to 'em, you'll have old lady hands."

Edith despised Emma's penchant for squeezing her fists so tight the knuckles cracked. She'd done it so often as a young girl, for the simple pleasure of annoying her brothers, she no longer realized when she was doing it.

"You look lovely, despite that awful habit."

Edith had helped her prepare, knowing what was to come. She'd never been so thankful to be separated from Geoffrey and Sara, whose bedchambers were far away from her own. While she and her earl were now pledged to marry, her brother would hardly approve of what she was about to do. Of course, Sara had said—

"Now remember," Edith said. "Don't let him go too fast, or ye'll likely have a babe in your stomach before ye even wed."

As Edith lit yet another candle, Emma burst into laughter.

"How do you know so much since you've not done it yourself?" she teased.

Edith shrugged. "The maids talk," she said.

Garrick was coming to her. He'd made that very clear at dinner. And though they'd been intimate before, this would be different.

"Perhaps I should wear another shift," Emma said. "Mayhap the cream one, or any of the others with slightly more fabric."

Edith shook her head vigorously as she placed a final candle and stood back, presumably to view the effect of her efforts.

When Emma had shared the evening's events with her maid after the meal, Edith's high-pitched squealing had risked summoning the entire household. Once she'd recovered, however, Edith went to work immediately. Where she'd found the fresh lilacs, Emma couldn't guess. But the room smelled like a garden in the middle of spring and looked more like the hall during a great feast than it did her bedchamber.

A fire roared in the hearth, and wood for the entire evening was stacked next to it, courtesy, of course, of Edith.

"You are a wonder," she told her, and Edith knew it. She strutted around the chamber, turned down the coverlet on her bed, and with a final wink, moved to the door. Before she could leave, a knock at the door startled them both. Edith opened the door, revealing Faye in the doorway, and Emma's heart started racing for a different reason. What was she doing here?

"Good evening, my lady." If Faye noticed the altered state of the chamber, she didn't comment. Instead, she handed Edith a box. "My lady wishes for Lady Emma to open it at once," she said, already backing away. "A gift for her future husband. And she bids you both a good evening."

And just as quickly as she had come, Faye was gone.

Edith brought the box to her, and they both stared at it for a spell. Painted white with a decoration of small blue flowers, the box, no larger than her hand, was nearly too lovely to open.

"'Tis beautiful," Edith said, handing it to her.

Hesitating for just a moment, Emma finally opened the lid.

"What is it?" Edith asked.

She knew this ring.

Though simple and unadorned, other than a fine gold line that wound its way around the ring, its quality was obvious. She lifted it from its velvet bed to look inside. Sure enough, its inscription was still there.

"Look," she said to Edith.

As the maid peered inside, Emma read the script aloud for her.

"*Amor vincit omnia*," she said. Then, realizing Edith would not know the Latin, she translated, "Love conquers all."

"But whose ring is it?" she asked.

Emma placed it back inside its box. "'Twas Richard Caiser's ring."

The girl's eyes widened, with good reason.

Sara's father, the powerful earl she'd heard so much about but never met, was still revered by all at Kenshire. The day Sara had shown her this ring, she'd talked fondly about the father she'd lost just before meeting Geoffrey.

"What does it mean?"

Emma gripped the box so tightly her fingers ached. "Everything," she said.

With that, she set the box down on the table, and hugged Edith with all her might. After wishing her a good evening and thanking her for all that she'd done, she saw her out.

The door closed and Emma whispered aloud, "It means she knows. She knows . . . and approves."

The ring would welcome Garrick into their family just as surely as Emma was about to welcome him into her bedchamber and her life. And if the soft rapping on the door was any indication, she would be doing so now.

CHAPTER THIRTY-ONE

*G*arrick blinked when she opened the door. Could this woman truly be his?

A long, black braid fell over the front of her shoulder in stark contrast to the chemise beneath it. She blinked back, and not for the first time that night, Garrick reminded himself that Emma was a virgin still. His fierce need for her would need to be curbed.

"Good evening, my lady."

She stood to one side, allowing him entry. "Lord Clave."

Enveloped in the dark chamber, Garrick moved toward the soft glow of the fire in the corner of the room. Nay, not completely dark. Candle after candle spread soft light onto the bed and a table on the opposite corner of the hearth. He could sense Emma behind him.

Turning, he watched as she moved closer. Willing himself not to grab her, tear off the only barrier between them, and make love to her immediately, Garrick reached for the pewter tankard on the table instead. "Wine?"

She nodded, and he filled two goblets, handing her one. They drank in silence, the liquid running down his throat, sweet and smooth.

"Are you nervous?"

"Perhaps a bit," she said, taking a small sip.

"You should not be," he said. "You'll find only pleasure in this bedchamber tonight, Emma."

When she licked a drop of wine from her lip, Garrick looked away.

"Do you remember the first meal we shared at The Wild Boar?" he asked. The urge to reach for her, to touch her, was so strong Garrick's knuckles ached with it.

"Of course. 'Twas when I told you Edith could not continue—"

"And you accused me of having poor eyesight."

"Hmm. I remember."

"I had not kept my purpose for traveling to Scotland a secret intentionally." He glanced at her. "Until that night."

A loud crack, a log being broken in half, demanded their attention. Watching it fall, Garrick continued, "I nearly told you the truth then, but something stopped me."

"Something?"

"I wanted to be alone with you. Kissing you was the first thing I thought about when I learned Edith would not be continuing with us. Holding you in my arms and giving in to the temptation that had plagued me since the moment we met. And, God forgive me, I remained silent."

"When did you know you loved me?"

He drank deeply, wanting to give her an honest answer. A romantic part of him wished to tell her it was the first night they met in the stables, but that was not true. He'd wanted her, lusted for her, since that night. But he hadn't yet known he was capable of love. "The day of the attack."

She peeked over the rim of the jeweled goblet, and Garrick finished his wine.

Not yet.

He filled his own cup and poured Emma more wine as well.

"When you spoke of your desire to see the 'jewel of the crown.' You said you wanted to see it even more than you wanted a family of your own." He swallowed back the bitterness of the later part of the memory. "When I told you Graeme was a good man and would make a worthy husband . . ." What a fool he'd been. ". . . I knew then I did not want him, or any other man, to marry you. I imagined us riding side by side to the Tournament of the North, thought of your excitement and how I wanted to give you that more than I'd ever wanted anything."

He placed his wine on the table beside them.

"That's when I knew." Garrick took her goblet and placed it next to his own. "I loved you then." He took her hands in his. "And I've loved you every day since. I just didn't know how to make you mine."

He rubbed his thumbs along her palms. Slow, circular movements meant to help her relax.

"I never did properly thank you for the mare," she said. "Where did you get her?"

"From Edward."

Her eyes brightened. "King Edward?"

"Aye. A gift for my services. I brought the horse back from Acre. I knew she had to be yours." He continued the slow movement of his thumbs, increasing the pressure.

"But how . . . when . . ."

"When I returned to Clave, I had him prepared and would have sent him to you sooner, but Cacho became ill and needed to recover first."

"Cacho?"

"Edward gave him the name. 'Tis a castle in Kakoun, to celebrate our victory there. You're welcome to change it."

She shook her head. "I think I will keep him to . . . Oh!"

Garrick had dropped her hands and reached for her breasts instead. Through the thin fabric, he continued the same circular movements until he felt the tips of her nipples.

"You are most welcome," he said, this time moving one hand beneath the shift. With the other, he pulled her toward him.

"When did you know?" he asked as his hand slid up her thigh and found the treasure it sought.

Propping her hands on his shoulders for support, Emma attempted to answer. "The night—"

She stopped when he slipped his finger inside her.

"The night?" Garrick tried not to think about the fact that she was already wet and ready for him. He concentrated instead on her words.

"I . . . I can't—"

"Try."

She was close to climax already.

"You said . . ."

Emma closed her eyes as Garrick ignored the silent screams of his body. Knowing this time he wouldn't be forced to stop.

Nay, not yet.

"What did I say, love?"

She was so close.

"Open your eyes and tell me. What did I say?"

His cock strained as Emma's breathing became faster and she struggled to open her eyes.

When she did, he nearly lost himself. The passion there matched his own so completely. "You said neither you nor I would ever feel that way again in our lives."

He remembered it well. And at the time, he'd believed that.

Increasing the pressure, he vowed to prove himself wrong.

Now.

Emma throbbed beneath his fingers, but he would not relent.

"And was I right, my love?"

She clenched and squeezed, and he withdrew his hand, pulling her close enough to feel his need.

"Nay, you were not." Emma opened her eyes. "I felt it again, just now. Exactly the same."

Garrick stepped back and removed his tunic. Still watching her, he removed every piece of clothing, exposing himself to her completely.

Eyes round, Emma looked down. "Is it always—"

"When you're near me? Aye." He took a step toward her, reached down, and in one quick movement lifted the chemise above her head. Groaning, he couldn't decide where to start.

"Garrick?"

He glanced down at her breasts. He would start there. "Aye, love?"

He reached for her, but Emma backed away. He'd hoped to distract her enough for her to forget about being worried.

"I don't think—" She stopped, having reached the bed.

He stopped as well, and though he nearly exploded with the effort, Garrick didn't move. He didn't talk. He didn't advance.

Instead, he simply watched her, waiting for her to take the lead. Looked at her beautiful breasts that he ached to touch. Glanced down and imagined himself inside her. But still, he didn't move.

Someday, he'd think back on this night in amusement at the sheer physical pain of holding himself away from her.

Someday. But not tonight.

Oh God, Emma. I can't wait much longer.

"Take me," she said.

He'd never heard more beautiful words in his life.

When he lifted her onto the bed and laid her head against the long, soft bolster that she typically tossed on the floor each night, Emma forgot to worry. Well, mayhap a small part of her wondered how the long, hard length of him could possibly fit inside her. But more than anything, she just wanted to know what it felt like to truly be one with him.

She concentrated on the ridges of muscle on his stomach. Touching him there as he propped himself above her, Emma moved her hands to his shoulders, exploring. Every so often, a flicker of candlelight illuminated a different part of him that she hadn't seen closely before. If she could sit up, she'd kiss each and every place her fingertips traced.

Then she glanced down.

"Look up at me," he ordered.

"I don't enjoy being told—"

"Have you done this before?" His hands ran from her stomach upward, toward her breasts.

"Well . . ." she teased.

The flash of fire in his eyes attested that he didn't appreciate the jest.

When a strand of wavy brown hair fell on his forehead, she reached up to put it back in place. But before she could pull her hand away, he captured her finger in his mouth. She kept it there, moaning as he wrapped his lips around it. His tongue flicked against her finger before letting it go.

"You can question me, scold me," he said, resuming his ministrations, making her nipples peak once again, "advise me and tease me."

Garrick reached down between them.

"But here, in our bed, tonight, I am the tutor and you, my love . . ."

He guided himself toward her. She could feel the tip of him teasing her down there.

"Are the pupil."

For a moment, she thought he'd enter her. She braced herself for it.

"Emma?"

She looked up, away from the muscles of his stomach, and concentrated on his face.

"What do you think will happen?"

Though she knew, from Sara, it would be painful, she still wanted it and pushed against him to encourage it. "'Twill hurt, at first."

"Nay, it will not." He nudged her legs open with his knee.

"But I've been told—"

He entered her then, just slightly. "Does this hurt?"

She shook her head. "Nay."

When he pressed inside further, Emma didn't feel pain. Instead, she wanted more.

"And this?" he asked.

Still no pain. Just the opposite, in fact. As Garrick filled her, she wanted only to become his. Completely.

"Not at all," she said.

He stilled.

Emma felt no pain, only a need to press against him, which she did.

The muscles in his neck bulged, which was when she realized Garrick restrained himself.

"You wish to go further," she said. He swallowed, and Emma placed her hands on both of his arms.

"This is the part you were told about," he said. "The one that will hurt."

Garrick had reached the barrier that she'd been told would only be broken by her husband. Well, he would be her husband soon enough. For now, he was simply the man she loved. And it was enough. She urged him on by pressing her hips upward.

The question in his eyes now gone, Garrick thrust himself into her as she wrapped her arms around him. *That* was the pain she'd so erroneously anticipated?

"Does it hurt?"

"Not really," she said. "It feels . . ."

She couldn't describe it. Nor did she want to. And when he moved, just slightly, she encouraged Garrick by moving with him.

Groaning, a deep guttural sound, Garrick started to thrust into her, and she met every movement with her own. Wanting more, she pulled him atop her so they could be closer still. As his hips circled, hers moved with him. Slow at first, and then faster and faster.

When he kissed her, it was pure instinct that made her lips move under his, that brought her tongue into combat with his. Because she couldn't think—the sensations were too much all at once.

As the pressure built and his tongue mimicked the movements down below, she began to feel the same peaking sensation she'd experienced when he'd kissed her there. A tension that was at once pleasure and pain built and moved through her body, stronger than ever before.

It was too much at once.

She shattered into a thousand pieces as he ripped his mouth away from her and cried out her name. She gripped his back with her fingers, clutching as the throbbing continued. With a final thrust, he collapsed on top of her, the glorious weight of him a welcome feeling.

"Stay there," she said. Emma couldn't bear to think of being separated from him.

"Always," he replied as he lifted his head.

When Garrick bit the corner of his lip, she lifted her head up and kissed him there.

"I love when you do that," she said.

His eyes narrowed. "Do what?"

She touched her finger to his mouth. "Bite your lip."

Pulling out of her, he pretended to frown. "Ah. I thought you meant when I filled your sweet—"

"Garrick!"

He'd reached down to touch her, obviously referring to their lovemaking.

"So you don't love it when I touch you here?"

Surely he would not—

"Or when I do this?" He flipped them both around so that she lay atop him.

Pushing herself up, she laughed at his obvious attempt to waylay her. "Well, of course I do. I only meant—"

"Or this?"

The man was insatiable. He shifted down to take her breast in his mouth, and when he wrapped his lips around her nipple, she arched her back, allowing him greater access.

"I love that, and everything you do to me," she whispered.

Garrick paused his ministrations for just long enough to look up and wink at her.

"Good," he said. "Because this is just the beginning."

Emma closed her eyes and smiled in anticipation.

CHAPTER THIRTY-TWO

*H*e hated to wake her. But staying much longer would guarantee an awkward conversation with both Geoffrey and Sara. He would slip out and explain in the morning.

"Garrick?"

He'd put out the candles and stoked the fire earlier, and though he could sense sunrise was but a few hours away, the only light now came from the corner of the room. But he could still see her face clearly.

Emma's eyes fluttered open.

"I didn't want to wake you." Trying to remind his body that Emma had been a virgin just a few hours earlier, he attempted to distract himself from thoughts of taking her again. Lifting the coverlet over her, he kissed her on the nose.

Her lips were much too dangerous.

"Stay, for just a bit longer."

He'd stay, but he didn't dare moving any closer to her. "Not for too long, love. Unless you care to have an awkward breakfast conversation with your brother and sister-in-law about the order in which we've done things."

Fully awake, Emma sat up. When she tossed her legs over the side of the bed and stood, Garrick forced himself to turn away.

Moments later, the bed sank under her weight once again.

"Come under here," he said. Thankfully, she didn't question him. Had her beautiful body been fully exposed to him, he wouldn't have been able to resist.

Sitting up, Emma pulled a sheet over her bare breasts and held a box out to him.

He pointed to the sheet. "There's no need for shyness between us."

She shrugged and let it fall back down. Garrick grabbed it before it fell completely.

"But," he said, "you may cover yourself now."

"You speak in riddles."

Garrick nodded down at himself, at the evidence of his need for her. "You lost your maidenhood just hours ago. If we—"

Her eyes widened. "Four times is too many?"

"Nay!" he amended. "Nay, but not this morn. Are you not sore?"

She paused long enough for him to glean her answer.

"'Tis too soon," he said, his suspicions confirmed.

He took the box. "What is this?"

It would seem he wasn't the only one in need of a distraction.

"Oh, 'tis a box. Can you not tell?"

He held back a grin at her teasing remark. It was very obviously a box.

"Open it."

He sat up and did just that. The ring inside appeared to be old but valuable. He lifted it from the box.

"I do believe Sara knows you're here. She sent this to me just before you came. Look inside."

When he spied the inscription, Garrick knew immediately to whom it had belonged. "This was Richard's ring."

Her smile held a thousand promises. "Aye."

The full impact of what he held in his hand forced him to drop the ring back inside the box. "I could never—"

"Sara bid me give it to you," she said, pulling the box from him and taking the ring back out. "And I've just done so. You'd not be so churlish to refuse a gift from me, would you?"

Though she teased, her words held more than a question about a ring. She asked if her opinion meant something to him.

He didn't hesitate when she handed the ring to him once again.

"I'd not refuse anything from you," he said, turning it around in his fingers. "Why does Geoffrey not wear it?"

Emma frowned. "I wondered the same."

He handed it back to her, and Emma returned the ring to its box.

"Thank you," he said. "I shall wear it with great pride."

Emma put the box on the stand beside the bed and turned back to him. God, she was lovely.

"Did you know him well?" Emma asked.

"Aye, we sometimes wondered if he and my father were actually brothers. They looked similar, in build at least, and both spent their lives devoted to their people, to Northumbria, and to their families. He was a good man. One of the best."

He spoke of Richard, but of his own father too.

And he could tell Emma knew it. She reached for his hand and squeezed it as she laid her head on his shoulder. What would his father have thought of Emma?

"He'd have liked you," he said. "Immensely."

"Richard?"

"Nay. Well, aye, I'm sure he would have. But I meant my father. He deferred to my mother in many things, save one."

She shifted but did not look up.

"Everything about him was 'large.' Not just his stature, but his movements. His speech. When he walked into a room, you knew he was there."

"Is that a kind way of saying your father was not very dignified?"

"It is." Garrick couldn't see her face but forged ahead anyway. "My mother often chided him, but he never changed his ways. She eventually gave up on him and concentrated instead on 'civilizing' the sixth Earl of Clave."

"You?"

"Aye."

Emma looked up at him then. "And they respected him still?"

He cupped her face in his hands. "They did, my love. Those of us who knew him best respected him more for his willingness to defy convention. He would have been proud to call you his daughter."

Garrick swept his lips across hers, careful to keep the touch chaste lest he forget his vow to allow her to heal.

"As proud as I will be to call you my wife," he said when he pulled away. "And now, I fear, I really must leave. Perhaps then you can get some rest."

She yawned and shifted down, under the coverlet. Garrick kissed her forehead and dressed, glad at least one of them would sleep this night.

"Lady Emma!"

Emma sat up in her bed as the door burst open.

"'Tis so very exciting," Edith said, nearly running to the hearth. "Everyone is talking about it. I am so very happy for you."

She placed a log onto the fire and picked up Emma's discarded chemise, draping it across the trunk at the foot of her bed.

"I told 'em you do like to sleep in the morn, and your man just smiled. Lord, he is a handsome devil. I can see—"

"Edith." She sat up in the bed. "What precisely are we speaking of?"

"Why, your wedding, of course."

"My . . ."

"The banns were posted this morn. Lord Clave spent the entirety of the morning meal speaking with my lord and Lady Sara. They must be hungry, having missed—"

"Wedding?"

"Oh, aye. You've missed much, slumbering away as you will. Faye is nowhere to be seen." Edith smirked. "Sir Hugh arrived just as the announcement was read, and well, they're 'reuniting,' it seems. I can hardly stand to think of it. 'Tis like thinking of your grandparents—"

"Edith . . ."

"Oh, aye. Well, it seems Lord Clave has not waited for you to rise to make arrangements. Reginald heard from James, who heard from—"

"Edith!"

"Beggin' your pardon, my lady, for gossip'n, but I heard your future husband is most anxious to see the deed done." Edith wrinkled her nose. "Deed isn't the right word. Well, not for a weddin' anyway. Though mayhap 'tis for what happened in here last eve."

Emma peered under the covers, the evidence of their "deed" very much apparent. "Help me dress, if you please."

When she swung her legs around the side of the bed, Emma groaned. Edith's cackling did not help, and though she loved the maid dearly, this was one morning she would have preferred to have been left alone.

"And now I see why he's in such a hurry," Edith said.

After more comments like that one, and a bit of cleaning up courtesy of the fresh bowl of rosewater Edith had brought with her, Emma was finally ready for the day—and ready to find Garrick.

"Don't you worry, my lady. I'll clean this all up—"

"Edith." She spun around and took the maid's hands. "It just occurred to me. I'll live at Clave."

The look on Edith's face said she'd already thought that.

"You'll come with me?"

But rather than the excited agreement she'd expected, Edith hesitated.

"Edith?" Emma couldn't tell if her maid wanted to smile or weep. "What is it?"

She dropped the other girl's hands and waited. And then she remembered her affinity for Reginald.

"You'll be staying here at Kenshire."

When Edith looked down at her feet, Emma lifted her chin up. The maid was waiting on her answer. She'd miss her dearly, but Emma knew all too well the heart's pull. "You will visit Clave often?"

Edith's face brightened. "I would like that very much, my lady." And then she pushed her toward the door. "Go . . . 'Tis late already."

When she arrived in the hall, the meal had already ended. As Edith had said, Garrick was nowhere to be seen.

The hall was empty.

Not one servant was present. Aye, it was late, but not this late. Where had everyone gone?

Emma went to the kitchens, for that was the one place Cook and her maids could always be found. But that too was empty.

She ran to the lord and lady's chambers, and the solar, but everywhere she looked there was not a person to be found.

Finally, she made her way back to the hall, where Edith was calling frantically for her.

"Oh, my lady. I couldn't find you. I forgot to tell you something."

"Did you forget to tell me where everyone has gone, perhaps?"

Edith wrung her hands. "Of sorts," she said. "I was supposed to tell you to go to the chapel when you were ready."

The banns. Edith's extra care with her dress.

She smiled, remembering something that Garrick had said the evening before.

I'll not leave Kenshire again without you as my wife.

She had not thought him to be serious, but it seemed he was quite so. Emma hurried to the main door of the keep, threw it open, and ran to the chapel. And for the first time in as long as she could remember, no silent voice told her to walk instead.

EPILOGUE

"*A* missive for you, my lady."

Emma took the message from Mable. "Thank you."

The steward left her alone in the solar. She opened it, read the contents, and placed it atop the table. She heard Garrick enter but didn't look up until he was standing over her.

"What is it?" he asked.

She lifted her head, and Garrick moved to stand directly next to her. She handed the piece of parchment to him, its seal broken and unrecognizable. Not that she'd have known the Clan Scott crest by sight. Due to the warden's decision to imprison his uncle and subsequent tension between Linkirk and Inverglen, Garrick thought it best they wait to visit Scotland until things settled.

As his expression changed from concern to anger, Emma said, "'Tis a kind gesture, is it not?"

He tossed the missive on the table, crossed his arms, and looked at her as if she'd *asked* for Graeme de Sowlis to write her.

"If you scowl at me so every time Graeme—"

"There will not be an 'every time.'"

Emma rolled her eyes, pushed back the wooden chair, which

scraped against the stone floor, and imitated her husband by crossing her arms as well.

She didn't have to wait long.

He reached for her, pulling her arms apart, and hauled her up against his chest. "I do not like it."

Unlike his harsh tone, the kiss he placed on her lips was soft and most welcome.

"You said yourself the man is honorable. He wishes only to congratulate us and offer continued assistance with the matter of Linkirk."

This time, he kissed her neck, and Emma turned her head to allow for better access.

"He could have written me," he murmured, his tongue flicking across her flesh as he moved his mouth closer and closer toward her chest.

"I had to apologize for all that happened. Besides, I do believe there's a message for you as well." Though she nodded to the still-scrolled missive addressed to Garrick, her husband didn't look at it. Instead, he gave his full attention to his ministrations.

Knowing what was coming next, Emma reached behind Garrick and held on. Soon, she'd be unable to stand of her own volition. "You will need every ally you can get."

His hand whipped around and began to untie the laces at the front of her gown. "Hmm."

Her gown now completely untied, only her shift lay between Garrick and his destination. "Geoffrey says—"

"I don't want to talk about your brother right now." He moved lower still, pulling the fabric down to reveal the top of her breast.

"Then who," she teased, "shall we speak of? I know, just this morn Conrad—"

She gasped as he continued lower still.

"I don't wish to speak of anyone." He looked up. "Or anything."

She pretended to misunderstand. "Then what exactly do you wish to do?"

He groaned, lifted her up onto the table, and stood between her legs. "I wish, my lovely wife, to make love to you. And then, when the tide lowers, to take you on a ride and perhaps find another place to make love to you. Then tonight—"

"Let me guess. You wish to love me yet again?"

The corner of Garrick's mouth lifted, just slightly, but she knew that look. In this, she found his "earlishness" to be most welcome.

"I do," he said. "I will love every part of you, my sweet Emma."

"And I you," she said.

He was her earl.

Today and always.

ALSO BY CECELIA MECCA

The Ward's Bride: Prequel

Sir Adam Dayne, to keep peace along the border, must accept a betrothal to the Scottish Marcher warden's beautiful daughter. Lady Cora Maxwell hates everything English. When Adam proposes a unique challenge to Cora, she's forced to face her greatest fears and the burgeoning desire he has awakened.

The Thief's Countess: Book 1

Sir Geoffrey has been reduced to stealing the resources he needs to reclaim his family legacy. Lady Sara is distraction he resents. With her betrothed coming to claim her hand in marriage and a distant cousin intent on usurping her earldom, the countess feels beset by controlling, unwanted men including the reiver sent to protect her. As the threats continue to mount, Sara must decide what's more important—her duty or her heart.

The Lord's Captive: Book 2

After reclaiming his brother's inheritance, Sir Bryce is faced with an unwanted distraction—the sister of his greatest enemy. Divided loyalties pull the English knight and his Scottish captive, Lady Cora, apart even as passion ignites between the unlikely pair.

The Chief's Maiden: Book 3

The Scottish king gives Toren Kerr a dangerous but important mission—kill the English Warden. But when he travels to England to participate in the Tournament of the North, he's immediately drawn to Lady Juliette Hallington. The English noblewoman longs to escape her sheltered life, but learns the very thing she wants most might consume everything she holds dear.

The Scot's Secret: Book 4

When his brother foists an English squire upon him, Alex Kerr is disinterested in training the lad—until he discovers she is actually a beautiful Englishwoman in disguise. The Scots warrior makes Clara long to leave her disguise behind. . . except to do so is to risk the lives of everyone she cares about. Will her secret doom the unlikely pair before they have a chance at love?

BECOME AN INSIDER

The best part of writing is building a relationship with readers. The CM Insider is filled with new release information including exclusive cover reveals and giveaways. Insiders also receive 'Border Bonuses' with behind the scenes chapter upgrades, extended previews of all Border Series books and a copy of *Historical Heartbeats: A Collection of Historical Romance Excerpts* from various authors.

CeceliaMecca.com/Insider

ABOUT THE AUTHOR

Cecelia Mecca is the author of medieval romance, including the Border Series, and sometimes wishes she could be transported back in time to the days of knights and castles. Although the former English teacher's actual home is in Northeast Pennsylvania where she lives with her husband and two children, her online home can be found at CeceliaMecca.com. She would love to hear from you.

Stay in touch:
info@ceceliamecca.com

facebook.com/CeceliaMecca

twitter.com/CeceliaMecca

instagram.com/ceceliamecca

Made in United States
North Haven, CT
18 April 2023

35561784R00178